Praise for
CAPTIVE DR
by Diane White
Angela Knight

"Will leave you longing for more."   —*Romantic Time*s

"This book makes dreams come true . . . I highly recommend [it] to anyone who likes erotic stories written with skill and passion."   —*ParaNormal Romance*

"Sensual and luxurious . . . uninhibited . . . any reader of erotic romance should be sure to pick up [*Captive Dreams*]."
—*Sensual Romance Reviews*

"This book is so incredibly hot! It is eroticism at its best, and it is definitely not for the faint of heart . . . You will blush. I guarantee it!"   —*Romance Reader at Heart*

"Hot and out of this world."   —*Midwest Book Review*

Praise for
Diane Whiteside's
Texas Vampires Novels . . .

"Audacious . . . a shockingly heady brew."   —*Publishers Weekly*

"A vampire romance trilogy by the master of erotic prose . . . [An] incredible, sensuous story."   —*Booklist*

. . . and for
Diane Whiteside

"Deliciously sexy."   —Angela Knight

"Prose so steamy that it fogs one's reading glasses."   —*Booklist*

"Hot and sexy . . . Diane Whiteside writes steamy tales of sensual delight. Once I started reading . . . I couldn't stop until I reached the end."   —*In the Library Reviews*

Captive Desires

DIANE WHITESIDE

HEAT | NEW YORK

THE BERKLEY PUBLISHING GROUP
Published by the Penguin Group
Penguin Group (USA) Inc.
375 Hudson Street, New York, New York 10014, USA
Penguin Group (Canada), 90 Eglinton Avenue East, Suite 700, Toronto, Ontario M4P 2Y3, Canada
(a division of Pearson Penguin Canada Inc.)
Penguin Books Ltd., 80 Strand, London WC2R 0RL, England
Penguin Group Ireland, 25 St. Stephen's Green, Dublin 2, Ireland (a division of Penguin Books Ltd.)
Penguin Group (Australia), 250 Camberwell Road, Camberwell, Victoria 3124, Australia
(a division of Pearson Australia Group Pty. Ltd.)
Penguin Books India Pvt. Ltd., 11 Community Centre, Panchsheel Park, New Delhi—110 017, India
Penguin Group (NZ), 67 Apollo Drive, Rosedale, North Shore 0632, New Zealand
(a division of Pearson New Zealand Ltd.)
Penguin Books (South Africa) (Pty.) Ltd., 24 Sturdee Avenue, Rosebank, Johannesburg 2196, South Africa

Penguin Books Ltd., Registered Offices: 80 Strand, London WC2R 0RL, England

This book is an original publication of The Berkley Publishing Group.

This is a work of fiction. Names, characters, places, and incidents either are the product of the author's imagination or are used fictitiously, and any resemblance to actual persons, living or dead, business establishments, events, or locales is entirely coincidental. The publisher does not have any control over and does not assume any responsibility for author or third-party websites or their content.

PRINTING HISTORY
Heat trade paperback edition / November 2009

Library of Congress Cataloging-in-Publication Data

Whiteside, Diane.
  Captive desires / Diane Whiteside.—Heat trade pbk. ed.
      p. cm.
  ISBN 978-0-425-22998-9 (trade pbk.)
  I. Title.
  PS3623.H5848C37 2009
  813'.6—dc22
                                                    2009019531

PRINTED IN THE UNITED STATES OF AMERICA

10 9 8 7 6 5 4 3 2 1

Captive Desires

ONE

BOOM! The vortex ripped open and spat out Alekhsiy Iskandronovich like a dragon's discarded toy. Ghostly scythes tore
into his belly, carving smoky trails to feed the void's greedy maw.
He slammed into a brick wall and bounced off, the rough edges
tearing at his axe's leather scabbard.

"Thrice-damned masons!"

He instinctively tucked into a ball, only to land on the slop-
ing lid of a metal bin. A jagged, knife-edged patch of pitch-black
sky pulsed and reformed into a myriad of shapes too fast to
be watched. But it constantly spat out sparks along the silvery
braids binding it to him.

BAM! His sword and dagger thudded into him. His gear col-
lided with each other and the damn box. Echoes roared through the
alley's narrow confines like the Red God of War's angry hungers.

He fell, rattling over bumps and bars on the searingly hot
metal cover. He flung out his hand to stop himself, yelped at his
scorched fingers, and dropped onto the ground.

He landed on his ass, like a youngling knocked off his first boarding ladder. Demons ripped through his stomach again, eager to hurl its contents back to Torhtremer.

Alekhsiy gagged. His brother Mykhayl had warned him of this reaction to journeys across the void. He could master himself. He'd done his duty before after a night's carousing. Surely this couldn't be any worse.

But the next time I accept a quest to cross the void, hoping to see my little dancer, remind me what an idiot I am, Mother of All Life. No matter how great the temptation to just once catch a closer glimpse of she who's brought me so much joy and peace before unimaginable trials over the long years.

His stomach heaved another objection but he forced it back. An odd handle on the box's side offered him a grip and he pulled himself onto unsteady feet.

Large metal pots stood to his left, while the faceless wall protected his right and back. The paving beneath him was almost flat, unlike cobblestones, but its treacherous cracks caught at his boots.

The vortex snapped shut, booming like a gigantic thunderclap directly overhead, and chopped off the knives cutting into him. The sky disappeared into a few patches of clear, cloudless blue, in between the army of gray stone buildings eager to grasp it.

Alekhsiy dared to take a single breath, testing his lungs' limits.

Heavy metal crashed into more metal somewhere close by, crumpling like paper. No such noise had ever been heard in his father's forge.

Alekhsiy promptly dropped into a battle crouch, every nerve coming alert to face such a catastrophe's source.

More metal screeched and a foul burnt odor erupted nearby.

A cacophony of horns sounded, completely unlike the sweet music of huntsmen.

Somebody yelled, "Watch where you're going, idiot!"

A woman screamed back, proving Alekhsiy could understand even the foulest of language, thanks to his sister-in-law's spell. At least he didn't have to worry whether the speaker was alive and well. Her lungs were undoubtedly in fine fettle.

He swallowed hard and straightened up. He was a graduate of Torhtremer's finest military academy and a veteran of the Great Wars. He would walk, even though his legs were weaker than water-soaked straw. He had a quest to perform.

Thanks be to the Horned Goddess that he'd arrived safely. When he returned home, he'd sacrifice a hundred baskets of star lilies to the Lady. His amber amulet would blaze the way, thanks to its soaking in dragon's blood and spell bindings.

He patted it fondly, reminding himself of its protective warmth, even through his festival tunics and chain mail.

But the cloth was cold.

"By all the gods . . ."

Alekhsiy tore open his tunic and pulled out the carved pendant. An inert lump of rock lay in his hand, little more than brown streaked with gold, and cold to the touch. It should have been crystal clear, with flames leaping through its center, and hotter than a lantern's globe.

It held no magic and could not take him home.

A knife stabbed him hard and fast in the heart, more brutal than any endured during the wars. He gritted his teeth against the shout of denial rising in his throat. Never again to swim in the western rivers under the high waterfalls, dandle a niece or nephew on his knee, or wrestle with Mykhayl . . .

How many times had he been warned death would be an easier price to pay than what this quest might demand? His throat tightened. May the gods be gracious unto him and forgive his prior disbelief.

There were only two ways to recharge the precious wizard's amulet. The easiest would require a longer lifespan than both he and his son could offer. The other? He might as well beg Chaos's gray gods for a miracle.

But he could still do his duty—find the enemy and stop him on this side of the void. No matter where that left him personally.

He slowly turned around again. The dragon had promised he'd arrive at the closest place in space and time to the enemy and the key to the lock, which guarded the gate back to Torhtremer against their foe.

Where should he start?

Moisture filled the air, aching with the heaviness of heat unbroken by any rain for far too long. It beaded on the metal pipes edging the wall and lurked in the mold glistening along the bricks. It hunted every fold of his festival wear, slipping between his linen outer tunic and into his chain mail's links, pressing down on his lungs.

An angry river was moving quickly past in the distance, creating a loud, dull roar. A few horns sounded there, too, but not many.

How had his sensitive sister-in-law survived so many years here? No wonder she'd accepted Torhtremer so quickly. The High King's palace offered far more joys than this.

A shoulder-high ledge rose next to the large metal bin, cutting off the entire alley's rear. A single door shimmered in the darkness behind it.

Small wagons without horses or oxen—called cars, according to the spell—and larger wagons, known as trucks, were crawling through the street beyond the alley. Men and women walked past in an odd assortment of breeches and short skirts, most carrying heavy packages. A few pushed tall, wheeled ladders that were heavily laden. Many glanced at him, then looked away without speaking, despite the obvious differences in their attire.

He needed to move on quickly before somebody questioned him.

Torhtremer's great patrons had bestowed on him two guides for his quest. Khyber, the Imperial Dragon, had given him a golden serpent with a ruby head and a long, forked tongue looping around and around his finger to lead him to the enemy. Svetlhana, the Imperial Tigress, had granted him a silver tiger twisting over itself, as if playing with its paws and tail, to light the path to the key. But magical gifts, especially from that pair, always had their own goals, which rarely matched their wearer's.

Would this work? How much choice did he truly have? His mouth twisted wryly.

"Show me the fastest road to my prey." Alekhsiy cupped his hands and blew on the two rings, choosing the simplest method to summon their magic. Otherwise, they'd signal him when and how they chose.

Instantly, two narrow beams flashed into the darkness behind the ledge. They lingered on the door for an instant, then winked off.

Couldn't they have sent him into the city, where he could defend himself against enemies? Not a dark, cavernous fortress with no room to swing his axe or sword?

The silver tiger lit up again, returning the alley to noontime brightness.

"By the Red God of War, of course I will enter it!" He hastily covered the ring with his other hand.

It faded into a steadily pulsing glow and he shook his head. Gods willing, no one would notice anything was amiss.

Alekhsiy braced both hands on the ledge and heaved himself up. An instant later, having heard no noise coming from behind the door, he turned the knob and walked in, his hand on his dagger.

Danae Livingston yanked open her hotel room's curtains. "What the hell was that—a sonic boom?"

"In downtown Atlanta? Don't be silly." Larissa never glanced up from the pins she was rapidly shoving into a cobalt silk tunic. "Probably a thunderstorm."

"No clouds." Danae pressed her nose to the glass. The outside view was better from her bedroom than from the sitting room, since its corporate logos provided an even better guarantee of anonymity for the coming weekend. It was damned unlikely those blue-collar neighbors had ever heard of her.

Larissa snorted in disbelief. "How can you tell . . . ?"

Danae turned back to face her, the familiar bubble of laughter rising once again inside her.

"When you can't see anything!" she finished simultaneously with her best friend. They'd known each other so long, they knew which jokes had been laughed at before. Worse yet, they still found them funny.

She leaned against the wall and howled. Larissa joined in from the floor, shaking her head.

"Thirty years they've held GriffinCon at this hotel and you still can't see much of the sky. Only other high-rises." Larissa pointed out finally, when they'd subsided into giggles. "Seeing you do that like a two-year-old is as weird as catching you in a tabloid, just for wearing a pretty dress."

"Hey, ballerinas do sometimes know clothes, and looking out the windows here lets me at least guess at the weather." Danae handed her a fruit juice from the immense room service platter to divert Larissa from the media's ongoing fascination with her. "And confirm that the loading docks' traffic jam is even larger than usual."

"It's a sellout crowd this year. They had to double the Dealers' Room." Larissa juggled the drink but managed to indicate another pile of fabric.

"Why?" Danae obediently handed it to her, raising an eyebrow at the truly minuscule amount of spandex involved. Who was going to wear this little item? Larissa didn't usually put her husbandly hunk on display. "Didn't the ConComm swear not to do that again, no matter how they had to arrange things?"

She bent over into a stretch, automatically keeping herself limber for next fall's dance season.

"Hadn't you heard? They needed someplace to put all the day-pass people."

"Day-pass people?" Danae looked over at Larissa from between her legs, her arms braced on the floor. She still had on her camisole top and thong, more clothes than she would have worn in New York for fitting costumes. But they made it easy for slipping in and out of the fine silks her friend preferred. "Are there a lot this year?"

"For the movie trailer!" Larissa rolled her eyes, curved and comfortable in an oversized Jarred Varrain T-shirt and blue jeans.

"For the Torhtremer saga?" Danae started to lower herself farther, considered the space available and the carpet's roughness on her forearms, then came slowly upright again. "Why are so many people coming for one day? Surely they can see the trailer at one of the other big fan conventions."

"You honestly haven't heard?"

Larissa was genuinely gaping at her. Maybe she needed to take this seriously.

Danae shoved the pile of costumes aside and sat down on the floor. "Hey, you know I've been on the road for the past six months. I didn't even have time to read all of my e-mail for the past month. So give—what's going on here?"

"They're showing a special extended trailer of *The Raven and The Rose* on Saturday night."

"Extended?" Danae swallowed before she squeaked again. "Just how long is extended?"

"At least thirty minutes. Some people say an hour."

"Ohmygawd!" Danae hugged her friend. "The sixth movie! We'll be the first to see what the final movie looks like!"

"Not the *final* movie," cautioned her friend. "Remember Corinne Carson never wrote the seventh book before she died. So we don't know what happened to the Imperial Terrapin or who Mykhayl fell for."

"Nobody else completed the saga either." Danae shrugged and sat down in the lotus position, settling and resettling her feet on her knees for amusement. "There are only fanfic authors now."

"Working within the Torhtremer universe, according to the rules Corinne Carson laid down."

"Mm-hmm," she said noncommittally. That was true of everybody except her, and she'd only broken one of the laws very recently. She'd certainly never written a story about Alekhsiy, her sole interest in Torhtremer, for money. And, of course, no wise fan would ever advertise any deviation from Corinne Carson's Great Laws of Torhtremer Fanfic.

"All your costumes are from Torhtremer." Larissa waved a hand at the piles of cloth.

"All of them?" Danae stared at the unrevealing stacks on the bed. "Don't you want to do something from Celeste Carson's Varrain universe? After all, whose handsome face is splashed across your chest, honey?"

Larissa blushed. Celeste Carson's book covers were notoriously popular among female fans for advertising the hero's attributes.

"Or *Star Wars* or *The Lord of the Rings* or . . ."

"Nope." Larissa's jaw set hard. "We're doing a special tribute to Corinne Carson, in honor of the sixth movie's opening this year. Although I am doing half of my big masquerade entry from Varrain, just for contrast," she added hastily.

"And because she and her sister Celeste died here, after that book signing."

"Who can forget that fire with all the smoke and flames going up from the condo's penthouse?" Larissa shuddered, her face turning pale under her freckles.

"Yeah." Danae stroked her father's class ring instinctively. She stood up and poured herself a large glass of sweet tea, that sovereign Southern remedy for all disasters.

"Do you have one of *the* posters?"

Danae stiffened. Damn, she hadn't sidetracked Larissa.

"You know, the one where the smoke looks like a dragon landing on the high-rise's rooftop in the middle of the fire?"

"Nope." She didn't need it because she'd been there that night—and there really had been a dragon. He'd stalked her dreams for months.

"It's a great photo. I'll get you a copy of it."

Danae's stomach somersaulted.

"No, thank you, Larissa, it wouldn't fit into my suitcase."

"But your New York apartment . . ."

"Is tiny. It's in Manhattan, remember?" *Besides, it was already stuffed with pictures of Alekhsiy. Movie stuff, not the way she saw him, but it was better than empty walls.*

"That's right. I keep thinking you still live in a nice, suburban house with three bedrooms, just the way you used to.

Your two older brothers leading the way and you running after them, while your mom insisted you do an hour of ballet for every one of kung fu. And your big brother Mike was so cute, too."

"Nah, you just picture that because you haven't spent as much time at any other home I've ever had." Danae shook her head, her smile grown a bit too sharp.

"Now I've put my foot in it. Sasha would shoot me." Larissa cocked her head, her mouth twisting ruefully. "Forgive me?"

"Always." She held out her hands and they hugged again, lingering a little longer this time. They separated slowly, eyes not quite tearing.

"Sorry," Larissa apologized again.

"Stop apologizing, Lara." They had to move on; all these years hadn't made it any easier to deal with reminders of the past. "Hey, we've been together since our moms wrapped Star Trek blankets around us and our dads taught us how to fetch supplies at Cons. If you can't bring up the past, who can?"

"You're being nice and I'm just really twitchy. It's my first time away from the baby." *Oh, God, don't let her start bringing up babies, too.* "And I really want to make master costumer this time around, instead of staying journeyman forever."

"Which you will, I know you will!" Danae leaped on the new topic. "Your stuff is awesome."

"Well, you've definitely helped by sending me all that fabric and supplies from New York and Europe."

"I like shopping." Danae shrugged. "And you have a bigger place than I do," she added slyly, "for working on it."

"But you have the better figure for wowing the judges—plus all those dance moves! Whoooo!"

Danae flushed but rallied. "Bet you saved the gigantically accurate costume, with tons of documentation, for yourself."

Larissa's mouth fell open. Her eyes darted from side to side, seeking an escape.

"You did, didn't you?" Danae hooted. "So even after I dropped out of those special kung fu workshops, just so I could strut your costumes, you're going to wear the best one of all. Isn't that right?"

"Yes." Larissa folded her arms across her ample chest. "And I'm going to enjoy every minute of it." She started to grin.

"Hmm, because Sasha will be there to celebrate with you afterward?"

Larissa's smirk spread across her face.

Lucky girl to have a man she could trust, and who would keep her warm at night, not somebody looking for celebrity eye candy.

Oh well, she could always work on another story about Alekhsiy. Even with all the reenactors here for GriffinCon's famous tournaments, it was unlikely any of them would be hotter than a dream of him.

Wait a minute—was she becoming too fussy, valuing a fictional creation more than a living, breathing man in her life? But she wouldn't—no, *couldn't*—settle down, given her dancing schedule. So there was every reason to enjoy herself in the meantime, right?

And maybe at least one of the guys here would even have some real muscles, enough that she could close her eyes and pretend he was Alekhsiy for a minute or two. Stupid, stupid thought! As if she'd ever meet him in the flesh.

"In that case, we'd better do the final fittings for the rest of these outfits. I want to steal a kiss from Sasha before you take up all his time."

Larissa threw a pile of green and gold silk at her.

Danae ducked, laughing.

*   *   *

Alekhsiy followed the older woman, carefully towing her heavy cart behind him. A myriad of boxes were lashed down onto it, ever urging it to proceed in an alternate direction. Two of them had dodged her rope just inside the entrance; he'd caught them for her, and she'd immediately accepted him as her esquire. She wore a short black tunic tucked into her trews, emblazoned with a snarling lion and the words *McKinnon's Smithy*. Surely the gods were watching over him, to send such aid for a smith's son. He'd never have entered here so easily without her.

People pressed around them, bounced into them, and raced past, all carrying or pushing or pulling their own burdens. Younglings dodged between legs and carts trundled past emitting unearthly squeals. Both men and women wore a similar garb to his guide's: a short tunic and sturdy trews. Only his height enabled him to keep track of his far shorter lady. She had only a few years on him but she forced her way through the throng with a queen's assurance.

They burst out of the crush into a more spacious area, marked by neatly taped lines on the carpeted floor. Here and there, men and women pushed tables into place or screwed rods together to form small booths. Ranks of whistles and drums swung merrily together in one completed stall, while a heavily shaded one offered a vast array of candles. A man was carefully hanging up tunics and brocaded coats, while a woman pinned rainbows of skirts to the walls of another. In the distance, he could see enough books to make a temple librarian jealous.

A bazaar. Thanks be to all the gods, he'd found his way to the local market, the best possible place to hear gossip. Surely here he could find the information he needed.

Its ceiling was low and ugly and the walls were stone, painted in an unsightly brown color. The air here was too still and dry, as if he walked through a mine in a land tainted by machines.

Alekhsiy's stomach twitched again but he forced it back into reluctant obedience.

His guide took them directly to one of the larger booths, marked with heavier than usual rods. One side held painted images of long swords, from every possible angle and shining like jewels. A tall banner rippled along the ridgepole—MCKINNON'S SMITHY, LAKE CHAMPLAIN, NEW YORK.

The big man assembling it, aided by a youngling and a stripling, glanced over, assessing him with a warrior's lightning speed. His gaze sharpened.

Alekhsiy nodded courteously to his guide's tribe.

"I found the last swordsman for your fighting troupe, Kyle," his lady announced.

Fighting troupe? Only under the direst circumstances would he ever break the peace at a festival.

The two boys gaped at him. Poles started to plummet toward the floor but a father's rapid elbow jab reminded his sons how to maintain their hold. The family resemblance was remarkable—carved features most notable for a beaked nose, blue eyes, close-cropped light brown hair, stocky frames without a trace of softness. All three carried small knives, half-concealed at their waists, which he'd not seen elsewhere in this fortress. An elderly lady was setting out finely cut jewelry in the booth next to them with the rapid dexterity of long practice.

Alekhsiy set the heavy rolling ladder upright with its heavy load, freeing himself for anything that might transpire.

"He was on the loading dock, looking a bit under the weather, poor baby."

Alekhsiy blinked at the many translations the wizards' language spell offered him for her last phrase.

"So I brought him here, knowing you could use him." She beckoned. "Hand him a ginger beer, will you, honey?"

Without ever taking his eyes away from Alekhsiy, the man produced a slender brown bottle from a hidden chest. A quick twist of his hand wrenched the cork out and he handed it over.

Alekhsiy accepted the drink cautiously, startled to find it ice-cold. Yet Corinne had warned him there'd be strange magics in this far place.

"Many thanks, sir." He bowed slightly.

"He's even got the Torhtremer manners right," the younger lad muttered.

"Hush!" his brother hissed.

Torhtremer? Of course he did—but how did they know what those customs were?

"Don't worry about drinking it. We're a licensed micro-brewery."

Alekhsiy hoped he looked as if her assurances meant something to him.

"Ginger beer will do wonders for your stomach. I always bring plenty of it along when we come to a Con."

Alekhsiy sipped. Bubbles exploded in his mouth and dived down his throat. Spicy, tart, then sweet—his abused innards sighed in relief and began to relax.

"That's right," she urged, "just drink it slowly. And next time, don't try to save money by eating the regular hot dogs."

Hot—dogs? He drank more of the glorious brew, without waiting for the spell to supply translations for trivialities.

"Always buy kosher. It's better to pay a little more than take your chances with crap."

Well, "crap" translated easily enough, at least.

"I will heed your advice, my lady." He bowed slightly.

"Wow . . ." breathed both boys.

What were they agog about this time?

"Name's Kyle McKinnon and this is my wife, Nora." Their

father took charge of the conversation. "Our sons, Colin and Evan."

The swordsmith extended his hand and Alekhsiy shook it properly, sliding his hand forward so he gripped the other's elbow. After all, they'd shown him hospitality.

"Alek Alekseiovich." Best to use a simplified version of his own name, so he'd remember it.

Kyle's eyes widened before a grin split his face. "My god, how do you manage to LARP all the time?"

"LARP?" Alekhsiy raised an eyebrow.

"Still saying in character, are you? Wow, just wow."

"I said he was perfect, didn't I?" his lady chortled.

Why did admitting ignorance elevate his status?

"LARP is Live Action Role-Play—and you're the best damn reenactor I've ever seen. You're wearing flawless Torhtremer costume and you've got the mannerisms down pat. Doesn't he, boys?"

"As good as any of the movies," enthused Colin, the elder son.

"And all those weapons are cool! Are you carrying an axe, too?" blurted out Evan.

"Quiet, dammit, or you'll bring the marshals down on us," snarled Nora.

Marshals? He couldn't afford to encounter the authorities.

Kyle and Colin scanned the room warily but Evan tried to brazen it out.

"Oh, they won't be around yet, Mom. It's only Thursday, and GriffinCon doesn't officially start until tomorrow."

"You know damn well they're crawling through Dealers' Hall like locusts, making sure all the weapons are checked in. Keep your voice low or there'll be no time for you at the comics dealers, young man."

Evan's mouth fell into a horrified gawp.

Comics?

"Now, go dig up some peace bonds for his sword, in case Alek doesn't want to join our troupe."

"He'd rather fight," Evan announced, bouncing back quickly from the deadly threat, and stepped back inside the stall.

Alekhsiy hid his admiration for the lad and looked questioningly at his host.

"This fan conference specializes in fighting—reenactments, workshops, costumes, tournaments of various sports like archery and martial arts." Kyle rubbed his chin, laughter fading from his eyes. "There will be at least fifty thousand people here this year, more because the Fourth of July falls on Monday."

Fifty thousand? Only the Seven Kingdoms' capitals were that large. How could he find the enemy amid so many people? Or the sorcerer who held the key to the lock?

"And Saturday's the big Torhtremer movie premiere," added Colin.

"Trailer," corrected Nora.

"Whatever," said Kyle.

Alekhsiy agreed with him. Two festivals, one of them to celebrate his home? He cared not what they were called, only that the event was enormous.

"There will be lots of weapons here. Different types, too, and the marshals will be very twitchy."

"As would I."

Kyle nodded a warrior's agreement. "So they stick to easy, obvious rules. The biggest one is that only members of fighting troupes can carry edged weapons. Otherwise, it's either peace-bonded . . ."

Evan held up two strips of leather, clearly designed to tie Alekhsiy's sword into the scabbard.

Alekhsiy's eyes narrowed. They wouldn't slow him for an instant, should the need arise—but every instinct revolted against any such hindrance.

"Or the would-be fighter has to leave GriffinCon. Immediately." Kyle's voice held all the softness of an executioner's axe being sharpened.

"Indeed." Alekhsiy had spent too many years leading his brother's armies to let his thoughts show.

"You're wearing the best Dragon's Scales uniform I've ever seen, as good as the movies or maybe better," Nora commented. "General's rig, right?"

Alekhsiy bowed, not deeming it wise to either confirm or deny her guess.

She whistled. "Risky to go for somebody that high ranking, but you've pulled it off very, very well. Cloth is easy enough to do, but the weapons and armor can trip you up any time."

"And he's even got the little details right, like the wear on his sword's hanger." Colin pointed at Alekhsiy's belt.

Alekhsiy stiffened lest he bend over and study his gear like a new recruit.

"Relax, my clumsy son is congratulating you," Kyle soothed. "Usually leather either looks brand-new or is evenly distressed across its length so it appears old. But yours—hell, yours is worn down in very specific places. Just as if you'd walked for hundreds of miles wearing exactly that belt and sword. How'd you pull it off?"

"I hiked through some mountains with friends," Alekhsiy murmured. *In snow and ice for far longer than I prefer to remember, and in terror that we'd arrive too late . . .*

"Look, I've got a troupe." Kyle turned serious. "But we need one more swordsman to compete in the big tournament. You do have experience with that, right?"

"Years," Alekhsiy said flatly. *Of fighting for my country and my family's and friends' lives.*

His tone stilled even the restless youngest son for an instant before Kyle nodded acknowledgment. "We won't use your axe in the fighting, except maybe in an opening demonstration."

"Show off, talk some smack." Evan was demonstrating with all of his previous bounce.

Smack? His spell did not provide him with a suitable translation. He briefly wished confusion on all loving women who believed their menfolk would never need to know terms more recent than those uttered in a drawing room.

"Frighten our opponents?"

"Oh yeah." Colin mimed whirling a two-handed axe through figure eights.

"We've got the two archers for the projectile division." Kyle brought them back to business. "Plus, two guys with karate black belts for the unarmed division."

Unarmed? Alekhsiy frowned.

"Hand-to-hand combat."

"There are lots of really cool bouts," Colin added. "Judo, tae kwon do, karate, kung fu, wrestling, you name it!" His blue eyes shone with commendable excitement.

His mother rolled her eyes. "Most of us are geeks so the rules get rather complex. For example, a fighter can substitute in the other disciplines. Most don't because it's too exhausting."

"We need two swordsmen for the blades division. Will you help us?" Kyle's blue eyes were intent on Alekhsiy. "You'll need a shield, of course, and you'd have to prove to the marshals you can fight safely and politely. You only have to show up three, maybe four times, depending on the number of troupes. I can give you the schedule once it's posted."

Alekhsiy hesitated. He could produce a shield readily

enough—his mouth twitched at how easily—but dare he spend time on this? He could not afford to be distracted from his quest.

"Finals will be held Sunday night in the big stadium by Centennial Park. Big scoreboard, instant replay." Evan's eyes were enormous.

And see pictures of the combat shown again and again, far larger than life-size?

"Very cool," breathed Colin.

The rings on Alekhsiy's fingers both heated. A trap—or the culmination of his quest. The enemy and the sorcerer would both be there. He had no choice.

"I would be honored." He touched his fist to his shoulder, warrior to war leader.

Traffic was starting to increase. McKinnon's Smithy was situated on a corner close to a great stairway. Passersby would have to walk past them or their neighbor, the goldsmith, to reach any of the cavern's exits.

"Awesome! We're called Yevgheniy's Spears and here's your badge." Kyle handed over a small brooch, painted with a snarling, silver tiger.

"A tiger?" Alekhsiy's head snapped up and he stared at Kyle. This was the symbol of the Imperial Tiger, who'd been unseen in Torhtremer for centuries until a few years ago.

"Yeah, I designed it." Nora smiled at it from beside him, bouncing on her toes until she could see over his shoulder. "Feng shui tigers are usually feminine, right? I thought it'd be neat to have something of our own that was really Torhtremer."

"Better than ugly old Turner's badge," muttered Evan.

"Maybe, but he had Madison Avenue design everything for his troupe." Nora lifted her shoulder, her mouth flattening.

Kyle gave her a quick hug.

"Plus, he had those master Japanese swordsmiths make his men's swords." Colin sniffed. "Even the rattan ones used during tournaments."

Nora gulped. "Oh shit, those blades will bruise like fire and ashes. And can break anybody else's."

Not mine, even after it shifts for the match.

"And he's paying the troupe's members full-time salaries to train for this."

"Where did you hear that?" Kyle asked sharply.

"The official unofficial gamers' board where I learned the tips to get me through the ice fortress."

"Are you sure?" Nora demanded.

"The post was gone the next day. Would they have deleted it, and the cached copy, if the third richest guy in the world hadn't found it and forced them?"

Reluctant belief sank into Kyle and Nora's expressions.

"He'll have the best in the world then, at all positions," Kyle growled.

"He won't want to look too good," Nora cautioned, "or everybody would know what he was up to. Turner always wants to play the underdog."

"There's also that Japanese-American team out of California, who've won four of the past five years." Kyle drummed his fingers on his booth's corner pole, his gaze absent as he counted up opponents.

"The Texans are great, too." Evan's eyes were wide with enthusiasm. "They get so many points in archery and hand-to-hand fighting that they can afford to take the penalties for illegal swords."

Alekhsiy would enjoy learning what that meant—and probably sacrifice a few crocks of mead to the Red God of War for granting him this suit of armor.

"Evan, you'll scare him off," growled his mother.

"It's the truth, Mom."

Nora rolled her eyes but didn't argue.

"Maybe we won't win, but we have a good chance of making the final round," Kyle insisted.

Of course we do. Alekhsiy smiled privately. *Who in this world has more years of battlefield experience than I do with cold iron?*

Still, he needed to be wary. He had yet to learn either the ways of this tournament or how this world fought.

"When is the first bout?" Alekhsiy pinned the brooch onto the leather straps crossing his shoulder.

"Tomorrow. Are you sure you want to join us?"

"It will be my honor, sir." He bowed again.

The jeweler in the booth next to them stepped back into the aisle to study her completed arrangement of glass-fronted boxes and delicate metal trees. Mirrors backed them, while other mirrors offered buyers the chance to admire their beauty. Tomorrow they'd be draped with glittering delights to tempt anyone who cast a glance in their direction. An easy task indeed, judging by the samples adorning the delicate proprietress.

The air stirred, marking the arrival of a larger party. A man strode down the stairs, moving faster and smoother than his own footwork could account for. A wizard?

No. The stairs themselves were moving. The serpent's tongue flicked Alekhsiy's finger. Could this be the enemy he was sent to find?

The newcomer was swarthy and bald, standing a little less than average height. Unlike everyone else here, he wore a fine linen coat and trousers over an even more elegant shirt. A single colorful strip of silk was knotted around his neck, left to dangle across his deep chest.

He was accompanied by another man, adorned with a sash of office entitled "Con Staff." He cradled a small tablet in his palm and wore the black tunic and trews so common in this room.

The pair were followed by a half dozen men who attempted to hide their multitude of weapons behind linen coats and trousers similar to their leader.

Evan and Colin dived inside their booth. Their parents stood up straight in its entrance.

Alekhsiy came to full attention.

"I do not see why *I* have to wait," the first man said impatiently. He turned sharply at the stairs' foot and headed for the great portal, his head cocked expectantly toward the Con official.

"Turner," breathed Colin.

The other man fell back, eyeing the goldsmith who was standing in the middle of the aisle. He glanced from side to side, clearly measuring alternate routes. "Sir," he began.

"What are you hesitating for?" Turner spun around but kept going, moving rapidly backward. "I haven't got all day to waste."

He slammed into the elderly jeweler, knocking her over and onto the floor. She yelped, a screech more of alarm than pain.

"Dammit, what the hell were you doing getting in my way?" Turner roared, barely keeping his balance.

Kyle and Nora raced to help her, closely followed by other artisans. The goldsmith's eyeglasses had been knocked awry and her clothing disarranged. But she was already starting to sit up.

"What madness claimed your thoughts, Turner, when you knocked down an elderly gentlewoman who had done you no harm?" Alekhsiy demanded.

The entire room fell completely silent.

Turner spun to stare at him. "Who are you, to call me to account?"

Alekhsiy didn't place his hands on his weapons. He didn't need to. He knew where they were and how fast he could reach them. He could also reckon exactly where every one of Turner's so-called bodyguards were and how quickly they could snatch up their arms. They didn't matter, not when he could kill Turner long before they moved.

But he couldn't do that yet, even though the serpent ring was fiery hot against his finger. He still didn't know where the sorcerer was who held the key to the lock in the gate to Torhtremer. Both dangers had to be stamped out if Torhtremer was to be safe for generations yet unborn.

"A concerned gentleman, who believes in honoring all ladies." Alekhsiy tilted his head slightly, indicating their audience.

Would vanity cause Turner to back down? If so, he'd be all the more dangerous on the tournament field. If not—well, perhaps this strange world permitted hand-to-hand combat to settle disputes of honor.

Turner glanced around and saw the rapt crowd. He snarled, a harsh flush mounting his cheeks. His fists clenched.

"I'm sorry I didn't see you, ma'am." He managed to stretch his lips into a fanged semblance of a smile for his victim, who had reached her feet.

She nodded jerkily and sidled a little closer to her booth.

"I hope you're not injured."

"Not at all." She shook her head desperately.

"Good, good. But I'll have my secretary contact you tomorrow, just to make sure."

Her thanks were barely audible. Turner must be a brutal merchant, indeed, to inspire such caution.

The crowd relaxed and turned away, raising its own conversations once again.

"You're in one of the mixed troupes, aren't you?" Turner glared at Alekhsiy.

"I have the great honor to have been accepted into Yevgheniy's Spears, sir."

"Then I'll see you again at the tournament."

The Con official squeaked softly and closed his eyes briefly. His skin turned a vapid shade of green.

"It will be entirely my pleasure, I'm sure." Alekhsiy bowed formally.

Turner snorted and brushed past, followed by his men. The official brought up the rear, drumming anxiously on his tablet with his thumbs. He shook his head at Alekhsiy for a moment, then raced to catch up with his unpleasant guest.

"Are you all right, Pam?" Nora asked the jeweler, her arm firmly around the other's waist.

"Yes, yes, I'm fine. Only my pride was bruised." She produced a shaky laugh. "I can't believe I didn't hear him coming, not when he and his entourage always create such a ruckus."

"Well, I, for one, need a good drink, and you'll just have to help me find it. The boys can watch your stall while we're gone."

"Oh, but I . . ."

"Excellent." Nora bore her vaguely protesting neighbor off to the great stairway, briefly opening a gap in the crowd.

Starflower scent swirled through the aisle, erasing the machines' taint.

Alekhsiy whirled, searching for its source.

Green-gold eyes met his, luminous as the sun dancing on a southern sea. His little dancer? He'd only ever glimpsed her before from high above, while he was trapped at the void's edge, unable to do aught but watch her dance. He'd never touched, never spoken, never heard her voice . . .

Sable hair spilled over her creamy shoulders, begging to be gathered into his hands. She was slender, yet stronger and more richly curved than he'd expected from his distant sightings. Her head reached only to where she might hear his heartbeat begin to drum. Her features were made to set a man dreaming and inspire him to his greatest deeds—conquer a kingdom that she might rule it, carve a statue for the world to remember her by, build a farm to content her for a lifetime . . .

Her delicate scent deepened, tugging at his heartbeat.

Her mobile mouth rounded into a question. By the Mother of All Life, those lips should be wrapped around his rod.

"Alekhsiy?" she whispered. It was as though he'd stepped directly out of her imagination and into real life.

How could she know his true name?

TWO

"Danae!" Colin, the smooth talker, was suddenly brushing dust from his clothes. Alekhsiy could hardly blame him.

"How long have you been here?" Evan demanded, unhindered by any such lovelorn qualms. "Did you bring me anything?"

"The latest anime from Tokyo, my friend. Less than three days old." She tossed him a translucent pouch and he surged up on his toes to catch it like a starving wolf cub.

"Plus the best bets in anime and manga from the Far East, courtesy of Dance Explosions' stage ninjas."

Colin whooped and snatched the much larger cloth bag out of the air.

Her gaze slid back to Alekhsiy for a moment, washing over him like a caress.

"And, of course," her voice was huskier, "there are the final episodes of . . ." She paused dramatically.

"You didn't!" Kyle gasped. He vaulted over the counter and hugged her.

Alekhsiy considered, and discarded, a dozen ways to throttle him.

"Nora will be so thrilled to finally have them. How can we thank you?"

"Win the damn tournament?" Danae shrugged, still sneaking glances at Alekhsiy.

He preened privately like a strutting fool. But her clothes could have distracted one of Torhtremer's few celibate monks. A soft tunic painted with brilliant images of flowers and birds clung to her body down to her hips and slender trousers—or were they stockings?—enveloped her legs. Her clothes concealed everything, and yet they sent his imagination racing into worlds where delectable parts of her would be uncovered and she'd be begging him to touch her again.

He clasped his hands behind his back, lest he run a fingertip along her jaw now.

"Seriously, it just felt good to have an excuse to get out and about while I was over there," she assured Kyle. "And thank you for providing those cool knives to go with Larissa's costumes."

"Piece of cake." Kyle waved off her thanks, his packages securely tucked into his arms. "We sell tons of Torhtremer reproductions, since we're the only movie licensee. It was easy giving her a couple."

"Always said you were the best bladesmiths." She flicked another glance at Alekhsiy, this time at his shoulders. "Did you find your swordsman, Kyle?"

"Oh yeah." Their host shook himself and turned toward Alekhsiy. "Danae, this is Alek Alekseiovich. He's here on a Torhtremer LARP but he's agreed to be our other bladesman."

Her eyes narrowed for a moment.

"Alek." She rolled the name over on her tongue, then held out her hand. He was ridiculously relieved. Surely a dancer's approval meant little to his quest.

"My lady." He bowed low over her hand and kissed it.

She caught her breath and her slender fingers trembled in his. He turned her hand over and pressed another kiss into her palm, and another onto the delicate blue veins tracing her wrist.

"Alekhsiy," she sighed, so softly surely only he could hear her.

Heat dripped down his spine with the need to hear her say that again, louder, in his bed.

"Alek, this is Danae Livingston. She first introduced me to Nora here at GriffinCon."

Alekhsiy nodded, understanding the warning. He wasn't being ordered to back off, only to treat her very well indeed.

"Well, the boys and I had better finish setting up here. The tournaments start tomorrow and we need to get some sleep tonight."

"I'll be cheering for you."

Alekhsiy shifted his grip so he was holding hands with Danae. She shot him a startled glance but said nothing.

"We'll be cheering for you, and Larissa's unbelievable costumes."

"Wait till you see this year's batch." Danae giggled softly.

"Really something, are they?" Kyle whistled before looking at Alekhsiy. "I'll text you, Alek, with the time and place for the tournament's welcome session. What's your addy?"

Addy? He used *text* as a *verb?* The wizards' spell offered no help. Alekhsiy gaped at him.

"Or e-mail," Kyle added more impatiently. "Come on, just a little crack in your character won't hurt. The session's the standard overview on what's going to happen during the tournament. Every participant needs to attend at least once during their career."

"Send it to me, Kyle, and I'll give it to him," Danae cut in. "We're going to dinner now."

She glanced up at Alekhsiy, who quickly nodded.

"Oh, sure, that'll be fine," Kyle agreed, far too heartily.

Alekhsiy kissed her hand again and wondered about the customs of this strange land.

Danae blushed.

Thursday night before the Fourth of July was quiet in the barbecue joint across the street from the hotel, at least in a corner booth away from the bar. The food was good and the servings were unlimited, evidenced by their remains scattered across the red-and-white checkered tablecloth. The latest country tunes blared out of the loudspeakers. Normally that would be her favorite sign that she'd returned home. Now she just wanted to focus on her companion.

The college kid waiting on them had quickly figured out he'd make more money running drinks to the Happy Hour crowd than he would hovering over a nearly deserted restaurant section.

So she was alone with Alek, watching him eat ribs as if they were the most delicious thing in the world.

Alek—or Alekhsiy? He looked exactly the way Alekhsiy Iskandronovich, younger brother of Mykhayl, High King of Torhtremer, did in all her stories.

He did not resemble the Alekhsiy of Hollywood's blockbuster movies. Or rather, how Peter Calhoun, rising movie star, played him. Calhoun was too short and skinny for a character who did all that marching and fighting in chain mail, if you asked her. But, of course, nobody ever did ask a fanfic author. They had only talked to Corinne Carson, author extraordinaire of the original six Torhtremer novels—and she'd only had script approval, not casting.

Danae was just another fanfic author—albeit one whose following snatched up everything she posted within hours, thank you very much—who was working to explore Torhtremer a little bit more. But just with stories about Alekhsiy Iskandronovich.

And this man was, God help her, perfect fuel for her dreams.

He stood well over six feet tall, broad shouldered, deep-chested, yet incredibly graceful under all that chain mail. His thick blond hair fell past his shoulders, yet he was clean-shaven, brazenly displaying his strong jaw.

His face held the hawkish beauty, utterly self-contained yet ready at a moment's notice to erupt into passion, that looked out from so many Viking bodyguards on gilded mosaics. Even his nose—oh, Lord, even his nose had just the right dent in it where somebody might have nicked it with a sword.

And his mouth—firmly disciplined, of course. She'd given him so many adventures where he got laid—and in damn exotic fashion, too!—all written from his happy partner's perspective. She had no ambitions to write great literature—she was a dancer, dammit. But she'd never been entirely sure whether she'd captured the experience of being his lover or simply written down her own fantasy, however engaging.

He finished his last bite and pushed his plate away. Despite his care in using his napkin, telltale traces of his meal still lingered, as they did for everyone who ate here.

"May I?" A crooked smile curved her lips.

He frowned but nodded after a moment.

She reached up and lightly touched her fingertip to a drop of barbecue sauce at the corner of his mouth, then started to settle back into the seat beside him. But he caught her wrist and kissed her finger, licking the sauce off.

A warm, deep tug surged between his mouth and her heart. She gulped, shaking a little. How could her heartbeat speed up from such a simple caress?

He slowly dragged his teeth over her finger. The harsher caress set a deeper pulse throbbing inside her, all the way down between her legs.

"Alek," she breathed.

"Do you want to stay here?" He nuzzled her palm.

She snuggled closer. "Don't be silly." That was an easy answer.

She laid her head against his shoulder, tilting it back to see his face. Good God, it had been too long since she'd been laid if she was getting starbursts under her skin from something so simple as having her hand kissed. Or maybe it was this guy and his definite expertise.

"We need to pay the barkeep." Alek sounded a bit uncertain for the first time.

"I already tipped him a bundle not to bother us, far more than the cost of our meal." She stroked Alek's jaw, exploring the contrast between strong bone, soft skin, and emerging beard.

His blue eyes flashed, sending a jolt of heat through her core.

The practicalities learned during the past fifteen years spent living on the road raised their head.

"Do you have a private room with a king-size bed?" she asked, a little unsteadily. After all, GriffinCon did take up every hotel room in downtown Atlanta for the entire weekend. Who knew what Alek's arrangements were? And he was sure to need a damn big bed.

He shook his head, his beautiful mouth a little twisted.

"My room it is then." And he'd better not say anything about its condition. At least she'd sent the laundry out to be done.

"You honor me, my lady."

She stared at him blankly. *Honor?*

He tilted her chin up with one finger. "Honor," he repeated

firmly. He kissed her hair, his lips traveling forward until they brushed her forehead.

Danae shivered and slid her arms around his waist. He wasn't behaving like any other lover she'd ever had.

He scattered more kisses over her all the way back to the big hotel. Her hands, her hair, her cheeks—never too frequent or lingering too long. But always making her aware of his every move, his heat, his scent, his eyes intensely fixed on her alone despite the crowd around them.

Her heartbeat skittered and raced like an out of control Russian ballet. She couldn't breathe for wanting to drag his mouth down to hers.

He stood behind her in the elevator, his fingers resting lightly on her waist. How could that mean so much? Why were her knees so weak?

She desperately counted off the floors, thankful her room offered the concierge level's privacy. But that meant surviving the sweet torture of close contact longer and longer. Until at the end, she had her eyes shut and her head thrown back against his shoulder.

The chime sounded once again.

"May we disembark here?" Alek asked hoarsely.

The doors started to hiss shut.

"What?" She opened her eyes. Her nipples rubbed eagerly against her tank top, desperate to seek him.

Alek bowed formally, his hand indicating her path forward— and keeping the door open. He was still doing the role-playing of being a Torhtremer warrior, as he had since she met him. How unusual—and how delightful, given that it played directly into her fantasy.

"You're amazing." She turned around just outside and ran her hands up his shoulders.

"Where's your room?" he whispered against her ear.

"That way." She tilted her head and pressed herself more firmly against him. Wow, his chain mail was really supple. She could definitely feel his chest and his thighs and . . .

He half-swept her off her feet, half-tugged her down the hall.

She blinked but blushed when they passed the concierge's lounge, spilling its loud bursts of current news and social chit-chat into the hall. On another day, she might have hunted a partner there, but not tonight. Not with Alek at her side.

The room numbers spun past, anonymous and boring. His strong muscles rubbed against her legs, driving her forward more harshly than any partner she'd ever had onstage.

Her hand was shaking so hard, especially with his hot breath in her ear, that it took her three tries to successfully insert her cardkey into the lock's tiny slot.

He reached around her and slapped down the latch, then shoved the portal open. She staggered inside, too crazed with lust to care what anyone thought.

Light blazed into the large room from the evening sky outside. Alek kicked the barricade shut and pulled her up against him. Danae leaped at him, heat throbbing through every vein.

His head came down to meet hers and they finally melded together. Mouth to mouth, lip to lip, hunger blazing through them both. He tasted spicy, rich, uncannily smoky and complex.

She moaned and rubbed herself against him. Damn his dedication to accuracy! He was covered from head to foot in layers of silk, chain mail, and linen. All she could feel was strength and solidity over the harsh outlines of a man.

But his mouth—oh, dear God in heaven, his incredibly skillful mouth!—traveled over her face and down her throat, kissing and inciting her to madness. Her ears, the pulse at the base of her throat, even her collarbone . . .

"More, please, Alek, more!" She whimpered, unzipped her favorite hoodie, and tossed it onto the pile of assorted clothing and paraphernalia in the room's corner.

He rumbled his approval and nuzzled the swell of her breasts, his big hands shaping and kneading her ass to pull her closer.

She fondled him eagerly in return but found her hands blocked by an array of pouches, belts, and weapons. She sniffed, considerably disgruntled. As a theater professional, there were certain standards to maintain, such as both partners being equally easy to undress.

He chuckled a little roughly and kissed the corner of her mouth. "Give me but a moment, sweeting."

She crossed her arms over her chest and tapped her foot.

He proceeded to undress with amazing speed and rapidity. His axe, sword, and dagger, the belts that crisscrossed his shoulders or hung at his waist, and the pouches that loaded them were soon neatly draped over her big armchair. He stripped off his brilliant scarlet silk surcoat, then his chain mail hauberk as if it weighed no more than the silk. The indigo linen tunic underneath hid another thin, quilted tunic. He neatly folded them all and set them down on the sleek, modernist desk.

She didn't give a damn about his jewelry—his earrings, cuffs, rings, even the pendant around his neck. She wanted man.

Finally he stood in a sheer white shirt and drawers, which stretched from neck to wrist to ankle. They clung to his body, thanks to his sweat and the pre-come seeping out of his rearing, crimson cock, only lightly veiled by the lucky cloth.

"Dear God, you're beautiful," Danae whispered. She could finally see his muscles' hard curves, his nipples' small dark circles, the fast rise and fall of his chest.

She needed more.

"Party box," she muttered and looked around.

"Party?"

"Condoms, honey, condoms." No matter what her room looked like, she could always quickly put a handful of those on the nightstand.

"Excellent," he growled.

Errand done, she kicked off her shoes, letting them land wherever they wanted, and ran toward Alek.

He caught her up and spun her around. "Adored one."

Adored? Ooh, delicious nickname!

She wrapped her arms around his neck enthusiastically and tried to kiss him more slowly this time. But it was so difficult when his body pressed and flowed against hers, making her so aware of his different textures and shapes, the planes of his pecs, the hard ripples of his abs, the columns of his thighs, the jut of his cock against her mound . . .

"Lovely Danae." He tilted her back onto the bed and knelt between her legs. His hand slipped under her tank top and spanned her belly, warmly inciting more heat to fan through her bones and into her core. She rocked against him, moaning, and he rubbed her, fondling her breasts underneath the thin knit.

What a wonderful way to go insane.

He explored underneath her jeans waistband the same way, unbuttoning it but not unzipping it. He had some wicked, wicked ways to tease her without ever putting his hand inside her, until she was thrashing wildly, her jeans' inseam teasing her clit, and fire raging through every cell. Cream rippled and flowed until she was mindlessly, achingly wet.

"Alek, please, oh please . . ." She clawed at his shoulders, desperate for him, only for him.

He fumbled at her zipper and yanked it down. Cool air—or was it hot?—surged onto her belly, ripping her toward fulfillment. Her hips surged toward him impatiently.

He tugged again and pulled her jeans off with more haste than style. Perfect, just perfect. He wasn't a polished, twenty-first-century gentleman.

Now, surely now.

She rolled onto her side, ripped open a condom, and caught his hip.

"Danae!" He stilled for a moment and she rolled it onto him, showing the same frantic urgency he'd used on her trousers. His cock swelled into her grasp and she palmed it in welcome.

"Great gods, woman, you know how to rouse a man," he growled.

She glanced up at him, his belly rapidly rising and falling against her other hand, and deliberately licked her lips. Tasting more of him, feeling all of him, couldn't come too soon for her drumming senses.

Alek pushed her back and she held out her arms in welcome. He poised for a moment over her, his blue eyes intent. She wrapped one leg around his hip, opening herself up to him.

He groaned and found her entrance as smoothly as she'd somehow known he would. She hummed her pleasure and pulled him closer, begging for more.

His thrusts filled her, hot and strong. Every inch of her, inside and out, gripped him, fought to keep him. He snarled and hunger surged through him, blatant on his gritted face—and then ripped into his eager drive for fulfillment and blasted away the last links to his consideration for her.

Nothing existed for Danae but this moment, this man. Everything in her spiraled into a whirlpool of magma, centered on him. Pulsing shockwaves beat through her bones and her blood, tearing her loose from her foundations.

And when he shouted his climax, and spilled his seed, the hot flood pulsed into her, setting off a cataclysm of pleasure from the inside out. She shattered, tendrils of fire spinning around and through her, behind her eyelids and through her nerves.

Afterward, all she could do was lie half across him, her fingers tucked inside his shirt tracing the lines of his muscles. She dreamily tapped out his heartbeat on his arm with her finger as if it would teach hers how to beat steadily again. She yawned and tucked herself a little closer.

He stroked her hip possessively. "Sleep your fill, sweeting." His voice was a little unsteady, she noted smugly, and she fought back another jaw-breaking yawn. It had been too long since she'd had a good fuck or slept really well.

The only logic for why she trusted him was his resemblance to Alekhsiy. Even the wry smile at the back of his eyes was similar.

But her instincts had never led her wrong yet.

"Rest." He kissed the top of her head. "The night is young yet."

"Mmm, yummy." Her eyelids drifted farther down.

The last thing she remembered was him wrapping her close.

Several hours later, Alekhsiy pulled the curtains shut against the gaudily lit buildings outside and the velvety black sky. Fireworks displays had more colors but they evaporated in moments, unlike these fortresses of light. He should sleep and gather strength for tomorrow's trials, like his oblivious darling. But he could not, not when the gods offered him the chance to fill his senses with his little dancer.

Danae. His lady who'd given him hope and pleasure so many times during the long war against the Imperial Terrapin and his great ally. Now she slept exactly where he'd left her, while he'd made his way to the window to avoid eyeing her temptations—

or the horrific mess her clothing and equipment had made of everything else in the room. Not that such a mare's nest meant anything next to the joy of spending time with her.

He stretched his back one last time and turned off the table lamp. Corinne, his sister-in-law, had given him a spell explaining much of daily life here. (She hadn't included how to dispose of a used condom. He'd deciphered that mystery for himself.)

A delicate warmth rippled across his chest and pooled under his collarbone.

Alekhsiy stilled for a moment. Then he spun to face himself in the big mirror.

A very small spark flickered inside his amulet, only visible because of the room's darkness.

"Praise be to all the gods!" Making love to his little dancer, she who'd given him so much, so many times before, had rebuilt his chi enough to relight his amulet.

Alekhsiy leaped, joy racing through his veins like dragon fire, and clasped his hands together over his head. He would sacrifice a dozen baskets of red roses to the Horned Goddess!

Now he had hope he could one day return to Torhtremer, if he exchanged pleasure with Danae often enough. And who would consider such pastimes a hardship?

Dare he wake his darling? She'd abandoned herself to slumber as passionately as she did everything else. The single golden light from the ceiling picked out little details of her to tempt him—her thick lashes waiting to reveal her green eyes, her dark hair displaying itself to tease his fingers, and her sweet breasts still hiding under far too much cloth.

She hadn't moved since she'd fallen asleep in his arms. She was a professional dancer, blessed with an athlete's strong, supple body. Surely she couldn't be too exhausted for another bout of delightful exploration. This one would come far more slowly, of course, than the ravenous plundering of their last round.

He smirked and blew a kiss toward her alluring mouth. Those few minutes had been far more than anything he'd ever hoped for. Who could blame him for wanting hours more?

His bruised body, battered by his arrival this afternoon, had forced him to take a short nap.

His heart and loins ached for another taste of his sweeting. The salty bite of her sweat, the heat of her breath on his skin, the spicy musk of her excitement spiraling from between her legs . . . By the Horned Goddess, he hadn't tasted her there yet. Surely she would forgive him if he coaxed her back into rapture by drinking her carnal liquors, the finest wine a man could ever hope to taste. The drug that could bind a mortal into serving a sorceress for the rest of his life, with only a single taste.

Pour one mouthful of a sorceress's sweetest, most hidden delights over a man's tongue and he'd hunger for her all the rest of his days. That honeyed cream would be an irresistible temptation to him.

His little dancer twisted slightly, sending the sheet sliding down her arm.

Alekhsiy's mouth dried. How often had he watched her shoulder roll the very same way from high atop that cloud?

Could she be a sorceress? Probably, to have successfully meddled in his life so often. Perchance that was why the amulet had taken fire so quickly: Her chi was strong enough that finding pleasure with her once was enough to relight it, praise the Maiden.

Surely she was nobody to fear, unlike the sorceresses he'd fought during the Great War. She'd always only done good for him. It didn't mean she was the one who could open the gate back to Torhtremer. Corinne, his sister-in-law, was also a sorceress but she couldn't travel between worlds unassisted.

By the red roses of Bhaikhal, he had every reason to frequent her bed and enjoy it, too, if it meant setting his amulet ablaze and returning home that much faster. And giving him memories to burn in his heart through the long cold nights ahead.

He quickly shrugged off the thought, his jaw tightening. He was the High King's brother and duty-bound to serve, whether that meant patrolling the cold northern wastes or making sterile conversation in foreign courts. He could take these few hours for himself, before he returned to his quest.

He turned back to his oblivious darling, still slumbering peacefully under the lamp's golden glow. She stirred and flung out a slender arm, a rosy nipple peeking out from her breast band.

She was perfection indeed. Why should he resist anymore?

He picked his way back toward her, every step as carefully chosen as his heart's focus. He sat down on the bed and slid her long hair off her shoulder, baring so many delightful opportunities for savoring her. He cupped her cheek in his hand, his fingers fanning out into her hair.

"Danae."

He nuzzled her skin, inhaling her scent to hold as a priceless memory. He dipped lower, finding and tasting the tangy salt pooled at the base of her throat. He lapped, taking little licks, running the tips of his teeth over her delicate collarbone . . .

Thrice-damned academy instructors, they were insane to teach that a dancer couldn't be strong and delicate at the same time! When he returned, he would force them to recant the error of their ways. But not, of course, with Danae.

His pulse drummed harder and his fingers trembled. Ridiculous, that. A woman's heartbeat under his fingertips shouldn't shake him, nor should her breath stirring his hair.

He'd seen as much fighting as his elder brother, now High King of Torhtremer. When the Cadet Corps was dissolved at the start of the civil wars in order to provide officers for the raw levies, he'd gained his commission as a stripling under the old king, before Mykhayl came to the throne. The sights he'd seen and the blood he'd shed for so many years had hardened him. And he knew his way around women—or he'd thought he did. He'd been well-trained and he'd had many pleasure loves, each for a night or two.

Danae's breast rose to meet his palm under the sheet.

His breath stopped. He was an educated man; surely this time he could decipher how to remove her breast band. It appeared to be tightly knitted of a very stretchy fabric, with narrow straps and no apparent fastenings. Much as he'd longed to, he hadn't dared rip it open before—and he loathed shoving it into her armpits now. Surely that wouldn't gain him any tender feelings.

What else?

He pushed it down a little farther and nuzzled the delicious upper curves of her breasts. They were perfectly shaped, too—round, sweet, rising eagerly to meet his mouth. Her adorable nipples were a trifle larger than usual for dancers, hardening rapidly under his fingers' focused attentions.

Encouragement spilled forth in his own language. Too much needed to be said to wait for translation.

"Ohmygawd, Alekhsiy." She sighed and rolled to bring herself more fully under him, kicking off the covers. Her fingers sank into his hair, caressing him, and her chest rose and fell faster. "You do know how to wake a girl up nicely."

He chuckled a little roughly, his heartbeat thudding faster. His rod swelled and he cursed privately. Idiotic telltale pawn of Chaos, he'd planned to take his time pleasing her, not rush to satisfy his own foolish flesh. By all the gods, there were excellent reasons the temple priestesses made their male students adorn their rods with rings before class. Sometimes discipline was best attained with steel, not mental games.

He teased the little sensitive areas under her ribs where her chi dwelt, allowed himself to briefly cup her flank—he'd approach her from behind another time—and feathered his fingers over her belly. Warming her, awakening her chi to his touch.

She moaned and arched, opening herself up to him, supple as a cat.

Goddess, help him to think for a little longer!

He nuzzled her waist, breathing in her musky scent, and played with her breast band. It was definitely very pliable.

He took a chance.

Propping himself on his elbow, he guided Danae into the crook of his arm. Then he slipped his hand under the fabric loop and tried to peel it off her, in the same motion he'd use to strip hoops off a barrel. It flexed, rippled, and flowed off her, aided immeasurably when she luxuriously flung her arms over her head.

"Danae."

He brushed his hair over her beautiful belly and she bucked against him. "Alek! What the hell!"

He teased her again. She twisted and fought to catch his head. But he tumbled her onto the bed and caught her hands. "Danae."

He kissed her belly, licked lower, swirled his tongue over her hip bones. She was strong, very strong, with muscle there—and very wet, too. He smiled privately and slid one hand between her thighs to stop her from rubbing them together.

"Alek, please." She thrashed under him, her hips driving against his hands. Musk filled the air and his pulse drummed in his ears. His skin was hot and tight over his chest.

"Dearling . . ." He purred. Cream coated his fingers, her sweet drugging wine.

"Alek." She bucked again, falling into a ragged rhythm. She was close, very close to fulfillment—but only he could take her over.

He fanned his fingers wide and forced her legs to spread. "Please, soon," she moaned.

He slowly licked his fingers. Starbursts of delight leaped into his blood and his bones, richer and deeper with every taste.

He swirled his tongue through her most intimate folds. He found her pearl and brought it to stand even more proudly erect. He found her woman's portal and drummed it with his fingers, stretching her—and rejoicing in the cream she granted him. More effervescent than the finest champagne, more fiery than the most superb whiskey, more complex than the most famous brandy. There was not enough cream in this world to satisfy him—yet he was always guided by the delight pouring through his Danae's veins.

She tumbled into ecstasy, sobbing her rapture. His rod ached for fulfillment yet he drove her onward again. She was beautiful, so beautiful, and far sweeter than honey.

Did she take her pleasure three or four times before he slowed? His breath was coming hard and fast, heat spiking through his veins and into his balls. He had to regain command of himself.

He rolled over after a moment and fought to stop his lungs from rising and falling like demon-possessed bellows.

"Alek," she whispered hoarsely.

"What?"

The drawer slammed shut and the bed creaked. He hastily pulled his arm away from his eyes.

"You foolish, foolish man." She cautiously crawled down the bed to kneel over him. By the Mother of All Life, her portal looked even more delectable now than it had before.

He fought to remember his manners.

"You must be exhausted," he growled.

"You're stubborn and stupid," she shot back and ripped open one of those small metal packets holding a condom.

His rod promptly surged higher into life, pleading its eagerness with drops of hot liquor.

She squeezed him hard. A jolt of lust rocked through him, from the soles of his feet to the top of his head. He hissed and clenched his hands in the bedcovers. His rod faded slightly.

She dipped her head and captured it in her mouth, pressing a long, loving kiss down its entire length.

Alekhsiy gaped at her, beyond words. She'd rolled the condom onto him with her mouth?

"Two can play at this game, Alekhsiy, and it's called sixty-nine." She came up onto her knees and looked back at him, smiling slightly, her lips lightly bruised and her green eyes dark with lust.

He caught her hips, controlling their tempting little dance.

"Now I'm tired as hell of seeing you play the gentleman and be frustrated. Will you just have a good time?"

"My timing," he warned her, wondering how he could form a thought, let alone speak it.

"If you insist." She shrugged and ran her tongue over her lips. Her slender fingers tickled his balls.

His eyes almost crossed. An instant later, his tongue was savoring her hot cream once again. Her mouth clasped his rod and he privately cursed his greater height, then twisted and squirmed until somehow they reached an accommodation. Her happy sigh and the swift spike of fire through his balls rewarded him.

By the Goddess's Dance, could there be any pleasure greater than this?

He encouraged Danae's rapture more fiercely than before, shocked when her attentions to his rod soon matched his rhythm. What temple priestess had the strength to do so when he was this deep in rut?

Lust pounded in their heartbeats and hunger echoed in their breath. His pulse drummed through his bones and in his ears like the waterfall of life until he could hear nothing else. Two made one in an endless loop of chi, spiraling ever higher and higher.

It was time, beyond time, to go further.

Alekhsiy pressed down on her woman's pearl and Danae took her pleasure yet again, rapturously granting him her cream.

He started to catch his breath—and she lashed his rod with her tongue directly under the tip in that most sensitive spot of all.

He gasped.

She gathered him in her hands and took him down her throat, embracing him intimately, warmly, moistly.

Ecstasy flashed through him, from her mouth over his rod to his lips still kissing her yoni. He yowled like a tiger—and spilled his seed without mortal thought or wisdom, only sinew and nerves knowing the time was now. Fire poured through his bones and balls, lifting him into a realm where neither flesh nor blood existed, only ecstasy. Stars spun like dragonflight at the Goddess's Dance and he died the little death.

He cradled her afterward in a sweaty tumble of sticky skin and tangled hair, grateful Danae preferred to sleep rather than talk. Words weren't something he would have enjoyed finding, even to share solely with himself.

THREE

Danae wriggled her fingers through the thick pelt on Alek's chest and felt, more than saw, him look down on her.

"I thought dancers preferred men with clean-shaven bodies," he remarked lazily.

"Some might, especially if they're gay." Which was true both on Torhtremer and on Earth. On the other hand, she'd seen so many pretty boys while dancing, their looks had blurred together.

She puffed a breath and chortled when his treasure trail's little hairs lifted, exposing his gorgeous six-pack abs. "This girl likes furry men."

"Do you ever become tired of playing?" Alek ruffled the far longer strands on her scalp.

"Are you objecting?" They'd already had multiple naps and shared a shower. That had turned into a truly delicious romp, before ending up back here in bed. Thank God for hotel house-keeping, who changed sheets regularly. They'd have quite a job cleaning up in the morning

"Not at all." His big hand continued to idly rub her shoulders, the rough calluses sending shivers through her bones. His textures were nothing like the guys she usually wound up with, the money men who funded ballet troupes. They could be strong—heck, she preferred that—but their muscles had been built in a gym and their fingers were always smoothly manicured.

She slithered farther down the bed, happily nuzzling Alek's belly. His cock rose lazily in welcome, too sated to surge.

She smiled fondly, agreeing with its inclination for slow morning loving. For just a quick fling at a con, her body's instincts and Alek's matched remarkably well. And even if he didn't resemble Hollywood's idea of Alekhsiy Iskandronovich of Torhtremer, he definitely fit hers.

She'd opened the blackout curtains earlier but left the gauze ones underneath closed. The early morning light allowed her to look at him in a glowing golden haze, softer than anything the stage easily produced.

He was handsome—almost beautiful—roped with muscle yet not an ounce of fat, as if he could burst into action at any moment. Golden fur accented his lines in a thick pelt across his chest, slimming to the tempting treasure trail running down to his superb cock, and thickening to the darker nest near his balls. Brighter gold dusted his legs and arms, allowing her to see his belly's creamy skin.

She stroked his hip and he agreeably let one leg fall to the side, opening himself to any exploration she cared to make. Had there ever been a more generous lover?

She gave his cock a quick thank-you kiss and he chuckled, a bit huskily.

But that wasn't what she wanted to look at.

The branching blue lines of his veins and the clean sweeps

of his sinews ran swiftly across his torso and legs, sweeping his arms as elegantly as any Greek vase painting. But while in the shower, she'd thought there might be some nicks marring those graceful sweeps. Any money man would have quickly removed such imperfections.

Danae stroked Alek's hip. She shuddered slightly when her fingertips sank into the warm hollow leading to his ass; it so perfectly reflected the leashed strength of his entire body.

"Danae?" he queried.

"I'm fine, just looking."

"As you wish." He relaxed again.

She'd better shift so she was doing something more innocuous, like looking at his leg. She could always return to the direct approach.

His legs had big slabs of muscle, making the kneecap seem the finely tuned joint it was between thigh and calf, rather than an equal partner in the long line. Just another mark of the difference between working man and pretty boy.

She gently kneaded his thigh from the knee up, using both hands, and he purred like a great lion. "You've been well-taught, my lady."

"All dancers learn how to look after their legs and to help others'." She smiled, enjoying his slit-eyed pleasure.

"I still say you're very good."

"I've been lucky enough never to have been severely injured," she admitted, pleased with him. "But I work hard to protect myself."

A small knot made her frown and she pushed the sheet aside so she could place her hands completely on the offending spot. It was a nasty one, too, very old and quite deep. She had to close her eyes to truly focus on it.

Stroke, stroke, glide, glide, always carefully, carefully—and the lump yielded. She crooned softly and delicately petted him, urging his muscle to relax and completely heal.

His muscle heated lightly, exactly where she'd been working. Good, now he should heal.

She settled back on her heels and thoroughly scrutinized his thigh for the first time. Was there more to the old injury than this? Muscles, tendons, bones, up the leg toward his hip. Front of his leg or on the side . . .

Her breath choked to a stop.

A great, puckered scar leered just below his hip. Dark red and multi-fanged, it clawed at his healthy flesh like a ravenous beast. Only the golden circle around it seemed to stop it from spreading throughout his body.

Alekhsiy had taken a wound just like this—high up in his left leg—from one of the Imperial Terrapin's ice demons at the ice fortress, just before the Amazons broke the siege and rescued the few remaining fragments of that beleaguered garrison. He'd very nearly died.

For the first time, she felt cold, very cold.

She'd seen it before many times, in exactly the same shape, down to the obscenely deep pit at its center. She'd written about it, too—odes to the delight of celebrating survival and life, while being fucked by the strong man who had survived such a blow.

A scar which she'd always said could be covered by her hand.

But she was a fanfic author. All she'd done was take the original author's few words and imagine their image, right? Right.

That wasn't the same as seeing exactly that vision, here and now, in the flesh. The only person who'd know for sure was Corinne Carson, author of the Torhtremer Saga.

"What is it, Danae?"

She waved him to silence, unable to find words.

She reached out slowly, agonizingly slowly—and the scar disappeared under her palm. She covered her mouth.

"Danae, it's just a scar." He rolled to face her, his wonderful blue eyes concerned.

But ice demon poison was foul, worse than anything except an ice serpent!

What was she thinking—to speak of ice demons as if they were real? And yet—and yet, the scar's shape was so distinctive. It was more complicated than a finely etched Japanese maple leaf. The colors were also very significant, with the dark red and purple of ancient infection. And how else could he have gotten the golden circle around it unless Khyber, the Imperial Dragon, had cauterized it with his breath to stop the poison from spreading? He was Torhtremer's patron, but he'd been known to show a sneaking fondness for Mykhayl's younger brother.

Only one person would know and she might just be able to tell her, too.

"Tell me what's wrong, Danae." Alek's hand locked around her wrist.

"Let me go!" She wrenched herself free and his hand fell away immediately. He sat up, his face closing into an icy mask in the mirror.

Danae barely glanced at him, racing instead for her scrapbook.

Corinne Carson had died, along with her sister, Celeste, in a great fire seven years earlier. But her last project had been to work on the movie adaptation of the Torhtremer Saga—or at least the first six books, since she'd never written the seventh. She'd scrutinized everything—sets, costumes, makeup, language—as attested to by behind-the-scenes interviews and crew notes.

Most Torhtremer movie memorabilia was pricey, but Danae

used her damned inheritance to collect what she chose. Even so, the piece she wanted now had been a gift from one of the few theatrical friends who knew of her obsession.

Every movie actor's makeup was controlled by continuity charts, which ensured it would remain the same from scene to scene. This was especially critical for details like tattoos and scars. Those charts weren't glamorous enough to be collectible items for fans. The Torhtremer Saga's makeup and F/X designers were always willing to talk about how much Corinne Carson had been involved in their area.

Danae skidded to a stop on her knees and tossed aside her favorite rock star hoodie, with its Chinese phoenix. She'd shown Larissa her latest clippings yesterday so the scrapbook had to be somewhere on the floor, underneath something.

"Don't you ever get tired of the mess?" Alek's tone cut like a knife.

"I've never lost anything important yet." And she wasn't about to start now.

Ah, there was its leather corner! She lunged for it and started flipping pages.

Even after six movies, Alekhsiy's body makeup continuity chart was still exactly the way Corinne Carson had approved it. However, he'd never appeared in a movie with bare legs, on or off the cutting room floor. The movies were so popular, even the deleted scenes had made it into the public's hands somehow.

But Danae's buddy, a theatrical makeup artist who'd seen Danae's extensive collection of all things Alekhsiy, had acquired Alekhsiy's chart from a coworker and given it to Danae.

The book fell open to the desired page.

She smacked her palm down to hold it open and looked up.

Alekhsiy Iskandronovich stared down at her, ice demon scar on his thigh, imperial cadet brand on his shoulder—*Why hadn't*

*she noticed that before? Did it truly fade into insignificance for
enemies and reemerge for friends?*—and knife scar nicking his
jaw.

She squeaked and prostrated herself in the finest Dragon
Hoard style, as she'd learned to perform one of the Torhtremer
ballets.

Alekhsiy dragged the scrapbook out from underneath her
hand and stared at it. "Where in the Seven Hells did you obtain
this?"

"Corinne Carson left it behind when she died and a friend
gave it to me." *That axe had to be Fire Wind, didn't it? Oh shit.
Maybe she should add something obsequious.* "Uh, my lord."

"Don't start calling me 'my lord' now; it doesn't become
you."

"Thank you, sir."

"And don't bow."

She sat back on her heels with a relieved sigh and tried not to
stare. Wow, Corinne had definitely left a lot of things out, starting with how gorgeous he was.

"They're not perfect." He spun the scrapbook on the desk.

"But fairly close—Alekhsiy?" She dared to come to her feet.

"Too damn accurate." He shoved his hand through his hair
and considered her. The amber pendant at his throat glowed
softly on its gold chain. "What the hell do we do now?"

"How can I help?" She instinctively wrapped her arms around
him, her ring nestling comfortably against his amber jewelry.

He choked, spluttered, and hugged her. "Is that all you have
to say?"

"You're behaving exactly like Alekhsiy Iskandronovich,
younger half brother of Mykhayl Rhodyonovich, High King of
Torhtremer." She rolled the names over on her tongue, startled
at how solid they sounded when spoken out loud. That was

always her test for a truly good sentence. She gulped and took another step along the path of true belief.

"I sure don't want to believe that, but nothing else fits all the facts. You have the manners and the clothes. Your armor is extraordinarily lightweight and flexible, for example, judging by how easily it adapted when I rubbed myself over you last night."

"But I didn't feel you nearly as well." A big hand fondled her ass.

Men! They needed to talk first, dammit.

"Well, I didn't bruise myself like an idiot. I'd learned by the time I was eighteen not to cuddle a dude in chain mail. Why did it work with you?"

"Bron'a," he explained simply.

She gaped at him. Another chunk of the wall of disbelief shattered at his matter-of-fact tone.

"The enchanted armor that feels like silk but is stronger than steel?" She gulped, cold air suddenly wracking her bones.

He picked her up and sat down in the big armchair, casually wrapping a blanket around her.

"Are you carrying any other magic?" she asked faintly. *Magic.* She was talking about magic with somebody who sounded like he knew how to live with the stuff. "That you can tell me about?"

"I can obtain fresh garments easily or hide the ones I'm wearing. These offered protection, in case I met enemies upon arrival."

"Instead you're bruised and battered, as if you were rolled around in a cement mixer." He couldn't be hurting too badly, judging by how they'd enjoyed each other last night. But the tournament would be a nastier test.

"I know not what a cement mixer is. But the void deposited me here with little ceremony."

"How did you come? Can you return safely? Corinne mentioned that Khyber can travel between worlds but . . ." Danae stopped cold, afraid she was prying.

"My wizard's amulet has been soaked in dragon's blood and spellbound. When it is full of chi, it will take me or anyone else back to Torhtremer."

"Full of chi?" She blinked at the stone. It had been a dark brown lump last night, when she'd first assessed his jewelry.

"Coming here drained it, until it had no spark inside. Now, thanks to you and our pleasure making, its fire is growing once again."

"Are you saying . . . ?" The amber was still brown but held stripes of light gold running through it, like invisible flames. She tried again.

"Are you telling me that you need to make love to power that thing up so you can return to Torhtremer?"

"Yes."

"I've never heard of anything so ridiculous in my life! That sounds like an excuse to get into my pants."

He raised a very superior, very masculine eyebrow.

"Okay, so you've already accomplished that."

She fumed and racked her brain for another comeback. Surely somebody had to have used an amulet for traveling during the Torhtremer Saga.

"*The Wizard and The Wisteria*," she announced suddenly.

"What?"

"Your sister needed to reach the Amazons." She poked him in the chest. "So she stole a travel amulet from that ancient cache. But it was so old, it had gone totally dormant and she needed help to revive it." Some very hot chapters of the book surged back into her memory. "Oh shit."

"Which my future brother-in-law provided very well, correct?"

Danae nodded, blushing. Those scenes still ranked among fan favorites for all-time sexiest love scenes.

"Can you manage?" Alekhsiy gently rubbed her back.

Cocooned in his arms, with a blanket around them, in an aerie too high to hear any sounds from below, they could have been anywhere. The world fell away until there was only the man cradling her. She had so many more questions she wanted to ask about why he was here, but could sense he wasn't quite ready to answer them.

She sighed and lightly kissed his chest. "Oh yes, if you can."

"That will not be a problem, sweeting."

"But we both have meetings and so on."

He harrumphed.

"You're in Kyle's fighting troupe and I have to strut Larissa's costumes."

His hand insinuated itself under the blanket.

"Plus, there are my morning exercises, and I'm sure you'll need to work out—Alekhsiy!"

Alekhsiy held Danae's chair in the hotel's restaurant and glared at the latest male daring to ogle her.

The fellow jumped back, his eyes wide behind round black spectacles, and tripped himself on his cheap woolen cloak's hem. He tumbled into three others, dressed in colorful knitted—stockings, perchance?—and sent them all to the ground.

Alekhsiy sniffed, somewhat mollified. If it had been his choice, he'd still be in the hotel room, helping Danae don her black leather *impression* of a Torhtremer mercenary's attire.

Long leather trousers, high leather boots, sleeveless leather vest, and long dagger were all common enough. Even her cuffs and jewelry were very familiar, as was the small pouch holding the old ring.

But the black *bustier*, which lifted her breasts to be admired? He'd never dreamed of such an enticement before. Veins he'd thought too sated to flicker had promptly rushed into life and his lungs gasped for air. His hands had reached to grab her.

Goddess knows how he'd barely managed to restrain himself long enough to help her dress. Now he'd never permit any mere passerby to do more than glance at her politely.

She patted his wrist briefly and he sat down beside her, careful to once again mind his manners. The restaurant was crowded and the noise high, with the seats very close. A series of golden terraces towered above the lobby, while golden cages crawled up and down its sides. Great panels hung from the lowest balcony, displaying notices or images regarding GriffinCon. Corinne's spell described them as the *audiovisual system*, naming them this world's equal of the town crier.

Hordes of people streamed past in a bizarre variety of clothes, from sturdy canvas to fragile feathers to stiff, unusable armor. They came from all ages and all races, in a bewildering array of shapes and sizes. Their colors—whether skin, eye, or hair—frequently owed little to nature. Some stalked, others raced, and a few strutted.

All in all, a man could scarcely breathe for the magic workers assembling here.

"Larissa! Nora! I'm so sorry we're late," Danae cooed, holding out her hands to the other two ladies. "It took us longer to get dressed than we expected."

Alekhsiy concealed his smirk.

They tore their gaze away from him to greet her.

"Larissa, this is Alek Alekseiovich, who's come on a quest from a far country." Danae waved her hands and Alekhsiy bowed formally. "Alek, this is Countess Ramona von Havelland of the Northern Horde."

Larissa's eyes lit up and she extended her hand to be kissed. He saluted it with all the care he'd offer to the greatest of court ladies.

She sighed happily and Nora clapped.

"Mistress Nora." He lifted her hand to his lips and she twinkled.

"Kyle and the boys said to say hello if I saw you. They'll see you at the tournament intro this afternoon, of course."

"Of course," he echoed. He took a sip of water, watching for the waiter. He'd had coffee the night before at that restaurant but he'd prefer tea.

"You are so lucky to have found him, Danae," Larissa enthused, examining him as if he were a new horse. He raised his eyebrow but said nothing, relieved he'd followed Danae's advice. He'd shifted to his field uniform, relying on its simple dark green tunic to conceal his chain mail. His beloved axe now rested in a pouch at his waist, a disposition that had fascinated his lady. He still blatantly wore his sword and dagger, plus the silver badge of Yevgheniy's Spears as token of his right to bear arms.

"What's underneath all of that? What about his underwear? Is he wearing any?" Larissa reached toward his sleeve.

Underwear? Alekhsiy choked on his water. What kind of world would permit new acquaintances to demand details of his most intimate garments?

Totally unruffled, Danae handed him her napkin and batted Larissa's hand down toward the tablecloth. "Yes, he's wearing undergarments, and no, you can't see them."

"You're cruel." Larissa narrowed her eyes at the other woman and Danae sniffed, unimpressed.

"You told me that when I was five, remember? When I wouldn't give up my favorite Barbie costume because you were three inches taller."

Alekhsiy relaxed slightly, relieved by the conversation's more sedate turn.

The panels' images shifted again, with words crawling over some, while others flashed images of oddly garbed individuals or beasts. No two panels displayed the same pictures at the same time.

Nora hooted and Larissa tossed a rude gesture at her, then laughed. "Okay, okay, I give in. We've got too many years between the three of us to blow it all now for a *man*. Besides, your mom was always my inspiration as a costumer."

Danae's smile twisted a little. Alekhsiy shot a sideways glance at her, unable to study her more closely and still remain polite.

"Look, I'll tell you what everything looks like." Danae leaned forward.

"Oh yeah?" Larissa tilted her head, her eyes' close-held caution at odds with her mouth's hopeful quirk. "What's in it for you?"

"I get to point all questions to you."

"You'll get a million of 'em." Larissa goggled at her. "This is a huge event for costumers, even if we are limited to fight-related styles. Everybody will think I made his outfit."

"So? How much can you say, since you have to honor a LARP?" Danae sat back and crossed her arms over her chest. "His stuff is very traditional, anyway. As good as or better than anything up there on the silver screen." She waved a hand at the panels, some of which were now showing scenes from what looked like the Torhtremer throne room.

Nora whistled softly.

"Just answer the questions," Larissa mused. "If they ask too much, like if I actually made them, then back off and start sounding like an accessory to his LARP." Her gaze rotated between the three of them. "Yes, I can do that. I wouldn't be lying, and I'm doing your costume."

"Cool."

Tension Alekhsiy hadn't known existed eased out of his shoulders.

Danae had found a plausible explanation for his clothes, as Kyle had arranged for his weapons. Now he could walk openly through this strange place without fear of being challenged as a stranger before he so much as spoke.

He squeezed her hand under the table and she flicked a smile at him.

The table behind him signaled urgently and a harassed waiter poured coffee into a cup only a few hand spans from him. The bitter stench filled his nostrils and he fought not to jerk away.

Faugh! Even the most overburdened mess hall would never produce such poison lest the troops revolt and brew the cooks in it. Danae had warned him but he hadn't believed her. He would pay more attention to her cautions the next time.

"Here's your room key." Larissa slid the small, shiny rectangle onto the table. "I finished fitting all your clothes so I shouldn't need to use the connecting door anymore."

"No, you keep it." Danae frowned. "Won't you want to come back and forth between our rooms as usual, in case you want to tweak the costumes? I'd planned to hang on to my key, in case you wanted me to drop anything off for mods."

A long, considering silence fell, broken only by the high-pitched whine from the great panels overhead. Was that a common practice among their kind?

"Gotcha." The wee bit of plastic disappeared back into the side of Larissa's purse.

Danae waggled her fingers at them in thanks at the same instant the waiter arrived with their drinks.

"What do you mean by *fight-related* styles?" Alekhsiy asked to give himself time to learn a new style of tea. Thrice-damned barbarian mess hall, tea should be brewed carefully and with ceremony. He grimly accepted the small pot of boiling hot water and tried not to smell any of Larissa's vanilla latte. If there was anything worse than the local coffee, it was the stench of its sweetened form.

"You know GriffinCon specializes in fighting," Nora began.

He nodded and ripped open the tea bags Danae had given him. *Bags.* He shuddered again, dipped them carefully into the water, and started to count. They were, as she'd so acidly re-marked, better than nothing.

"Everything here is supposed to relate to fighting, especially costuming. There are no prizes for anything just because it's pretty, inspired by something historical or science fiction-y. Oh no. It's got to be for a fighter or somebody accompanying one." Larissa sounded a trifle bitter. "Of course, that doesn't stop or-dinary fans from dressing as anybody they like."

"Cheerleaders always win great prizes," Danae added, and offered Alekhsiy the cream. She'd sworn the result would be chai, the spicy brew that had fueled a thousand marches.

"Refuge of the lazy." Larissa made a very rude noise. "Freak-ing celebrity guest judges don't have the brains to look past tits and ass to find creativity, hard work, and solid research."

The great panels flickered, lingering on horizontal black and white stripes, not the audiovisual system's gaudy colors or crisp text.

Nora snickered. "So you can present Eowyn as a Rider of

Rohan, but not Eowyn as a simple princess," she contributed, clearly trying to offer a common example.

Alekhsiy took his first sip of chai and nodded, hoping he looked better informed.

"But everybody comes anyway, since GriffinCon is so old and big. Fifty years, isn't it?" Nora asked.

"Something like that," Danae agreed. "Plus, Hollywood's been finding extras here for years. They'll recruit them, shoot a battle scene or two at one of the local parks somewhere near GriffinCon, then come back the following year with the finished movie to find a ready-made audience."

The great screens hummed again. The stripes began to revolve faster.

"What with that and the photography prizes, we're almost as big as Comic-Con now. We even have a big international contingent." Larissa nodded toward a trio of girls armed with parasols and wearing frilly, short skirts. They tittered and bowed, then ran off, darting glances back at Alekhsiy.

"Gothic Lolitas," Larissa muttered. "They'll probably want their picture taken with you later on."

"Along with a gazillion other people," Danae snapped and yanked open her menu.

The panels reached a high-pitched whine. It sliced through all other sounds like the Imperial Armory's finest saw.

A girl yelped. Nora put her hands over her ears.

"What the hell?" Danae looked up and around.

The great screens keened again, higher and louder. The entire room went dark from its highest point to its lowest, from its farthest distance to its nearest. Even the golden balconies became only the faintest glimmer.

Women screamed in the fast-rising note of pure panic. Men

began to shout, some urging caution but others falling toward chaos

Alekhsiy shoved his chair back so hard it fell over and reached for his knife. He knew that noise all too well. Nothing on this world could create it. Yet, by the Red God of War, he should not draw his sword here.

The panels simultaneously flashed from solid black to the same vista of endless, ice-covered wastes. No land survived there, only barren ice and salt sea. Wind blew snow pellets across it, so bitterly that the crowd flinched.

A deep, harsh, disembodied voice laughed.

"Look at my deeds, fools, and know who you fight!" Azherbhai, the Imperial Terrapin snapped.

How had that thrice-damned spawn of Chaos come here?

Could he fight him? No, only a sorcerer or another imperial beast could do that, such as Khyber, the Imperial Dragon.

On the screens a single, small steading loomed up out of the storm, its chimney offering a small beacon of warmth and hope. A gust of wind blasted in the door and an earthquake ripped out the walls. The walls crushed a screaming babe, while its father struggled futilely to reach it.

Alekhsiy's heart lurched and he closed his eyes. Would he ever stop seeing his nephew's death in his dreams?

The images flashed past faster after that. The first skirmish by the far northern river, when Mykhayl's men had fought valiantly to protect him. Knowing now that Mykhayl had survived did not make it any easier to watch bloodstains cover the river's icy edge.

The trenches filling ever higher with the dead at the ice fortress's long siege; the nightmare forced march through the mountains when his men's flesh had been more carved by frostbite than wounds—at least until they reached the battlefield; the civil war's endless, futile battles between fools who had no claim upon the throne and only cost the land more blood. All of it pitilessly displayed, at a scale far larger than life, in a style designed to appall even the hardiest.

Several people became horribly, loudly sick somewhere close by.

Alekhsiy envied them. He'd had to school himself to block that escape from a young age, lest he fail his men in battle. Only the strongest could lead their troops past carnage wrought by Azherbhai's monsters.

Danae hid her face against his back, shaking. It was a canny move, since she wouldn't slow him if he needed to do battle.

He patted her hand, wishing he could offer more comfort.

Azherbhai laughed again. "You see? Your quest is hopeless, fools. Yield and send me my warrior!"

"Never!" Alekhsiy shouted. "Torhtremer forever!"

"Torhtremer!" Danae echoed him immediately.

"You have no hope!" The Imperial Terrapin roared, shaking the great lamps above the lobby. Icebergs spun through the panels, seeming to charge toward the crowd. They were covered with warriors who were both fighting scaly monsters from the deep and struggling to stay on the bucking, ice-covered sheets, lest they vanish into the mountainous seas.

"Torhtremer!" Alekhsiy shouted again, lest he start reliving that nightmare conflict.

"Torhtremer!" Danae was with him in the same instant and came to stand at his side.

"Torhtremer! Torhtremer!" First Nora, then Larissa joined in, the words deepening as if the Horned Goddess's three-part self was helping.

To Alekhsiy's complete shock, the crowd around them picked up the same chant. "Torhtremer! Torhtremer! Torhtremer!"

Music swelled, faint at first, then louder and louder, to pour into the lobby. Torhtremer's national anthem? How did they know it here?

The great panels hissed and popped angrily, then turned to black.

Lights began to wink back on, one by one, starting with the most distant sectors.

Praise be to all the gods, they'd somehow routed Azherbhai, the Imperial Terrapin—at least this time.

A half dozen helmeted men, garbed in gold, rushed into the lobby.

"Where's the fire?" their leader demanded.

"Well, that was a hell of a stunt to launch a movie." Somebody chuckled weakly. "I almost thought that really was Azherbhai, Torhtremer's ultimate villain."

If only it had been a trick. Alekhsiy swung around and dragged Danae into his arms, his heart pounding triple time. What would he do if—when—that brute returned?

FOUR

Corinne Carson shaded her eyes to look out over Bhaikhal's great harbor. The vista was still fresh and beautiful no matter how often she watched it. She loved seeing the boats dart back and forth between the great ships or the sun sparkle on the white marble dance floor, shining high atop the central island.

The temple there had been repaired since she and Mykhayl had fought Azherbhai, the Imperial Terrapin there seven years ago. No signs remained from when Mykhayl had killed the Dark Warrior. In fact, she and her husband frequently camped out there for a quiet night away from courtly protocol—or from their three growing sons.

Another breeze snuck into the harbor, bringing the taste of bitter northern ice. A ship staggered slightly, caught unawares by the unfriendly air.

Corinne hissed softly. So another enemy spy had tried to sneak in, had he?

She lifted her hand and banished him, using a spell she'd

grown far too familiar with over these last exhausting months—and one she'd used far too often recently.

The ship returned to its accustomed course, followed by its brethren.

Strong arms wrapped around her from behind and she leaned back against her beloved husband. He nuzzled his chin against the top of her head, his long red braids, brilliant with his beads of office, falling around them both.

Anything was possible, if undertaken with him.

"Where are the boys?" he asked, a not entirely idle question.

"In my garden with Mazur."

"You trust a *leopard* to keep them out of mischief?"

"Why not? Everyone else has thrown up their hands at least once. Even Yevgheniy—your *primus pilus*, your first spear, the most experienced noncom in Torhtremer, who can easily handle running the Dragon's Hoard's concubines for your officers and diplomats—won't keep an eye on all three of them."

"Point made—and taken."

She chuckled and mimed licking her finger and marking up a point. Jokes were all too few these days.

She turned to face Mykhayl, her silver and white dress drifting around her. It was her turn now to ask questions. "What of Khyber?"

"He hasn't landed yet?" He scowled. "I thought when he left on patrol this morning that he would return within minutes. He has spent too much time in the air since he dispatched Alekhsiy. Have you asked Svetlhana for news of Alekhsiy?"

"She's gone, too."

Mykhayl stared at her. "Can you talk to her?"

"As Tigerheart to Imperial Tiger?" Corinne shrugged. "Not really. She's a cat, even though she's a thirty-foot tigress. Have you ever tried doing anything with a feline who didn't want to?"

"Can you summon her, should we need to go to war?" the High King demanded.

"Yes, I expect so."

Mykhayl slammed his fist down on the balcony and started pacing. Corinne watched sympathetically, having long ago come to grips with her own frustration at Svetlhana's independence. So what if she'd shattered a few vases against the wall to get there?

"Is Khyber willing to talk to you at all?" Corinne asked quietly when her consort reached her side again.

"Only to ask his damned questions, which are designed to make me find new patterns in impossible situations." He leveled a disgruntled glare at her. "And before you ask, I am sure he'd come if I summoned him to war. So yes, we will have our two greatest weapons, should the Imperial Terrapin come once again in the flesh to Torhtremer."

"He can't do anything unless he's formally summoned," she reminded him, trying to look on the bright side.

"But his first task would be to destroy our sons, who are all potential Dragonhearts." Terror blazed for an instant in Mykhayl's golden eyes.

"There's nothing to worry about, darling." She wrapped her arms around him.

"Alekhsiy must destroy the potential catalyst and the sorcerer who can unlock the void's gate. Can you send a message to him?"

"He's only been gone for a few weeks, darling. Time may pass faster or slower for him across the void, as you know." She hugged him a little tighter, trying to blank out her own fears along with his. "Just you wait and see—he'll crush them both into dust."

GriffinCon
Friday Morning

Danae squeezed into a dark corner outside the registration area to let another torrent of newcomers pour past. Alekhsiy eyed them warily, his head swiveling to observe all comers. There was one good thing to be said for his blatant caution: Registration had immediately believed he was doing a LARP and hadn't bothered to ask for his quote-unquote *real name*.

She'd been coming to GriffinCon and other cons since she was born or, technically, while she was still in the womb. She knew all about no windows, low ceilings, and crowds dotted with eye-popping outfits. Even so, her skin was still crawling after breakfast's abrupt ending. At least she never listed her fanfic handle on her own badge, the better to protect her anonymity. Silly precaution, really, since she wasn't a big celebrity here for her dancing and she hadn't written enough stories to have a large following. But old habits of maintaining her privacy died hard, so she'd always kept her life as an author very separate from that as a dancer. Plus, she didn't want any dance producers to be embarrassed by anything she wrote.

She pulled her spare lanyard out for Alekhsiy's badge.

"I didn't know Azherbhai could travel between worlds," she muttered under her breath.

"He can't." Alekhsiy moved a little closer and lowered his voice to match hers, even though nobody else was close. "It takes dragon's blood or perchance . . ."

He stopped, his fist knotted around his sword's hilt.

"Or?" she prompted. She clipped Alekhsiy's badge onto the lanyard. At least he had one of the smaller on-site badges, not a gaudy and easy to read one from pre-registration, like hers.

His throat worked silently for a moment before he answered her. "Legend says sorcerers knew how to do so with the merest scrap of dragon's blood, so long as they had a great amount of chi to draw upon."

"Well, there's no sorcerer here." She put her hand on his arm and infused her voice with every bit of comfort she could.

"No, none of those men at all." A muscle twitched at the corner of his mouth.

"But that beast controlled the audiovisual system. That means . . ."

Really bad shit. A more elegant fanfic term escaped her.

She looked up at Alekhsiy. Nothing Corinne Carson had ever written covered this situation.

"The Imperial Terrapin can project his power to this world, but not his physical self." He squeezed her shoulder. "He can't hurt us."

"He took over some big-ass electronics. For a first try, it was pretty damn impressive!"

"We will manage." His voice deepened, sounding notes of command and complete reliability. It became that of the great general who alone had led Torhtremer's army at Tajzyk's Gorge for all those long minutes while Mykhayl had worked to summon the Imperial Dragon.

Somehow she believed him.

"Yeah, okay." She smiled a little shakily up at him. "Well, let me give you your badge so the local dudes don't get you in trouble. It's my spare, the one my dad always used; basically just a very high-quality chain."

Coming down from an adrenaline rush must be why she

was rattling on, especially why she'd mentioned her family to a stranger. She mentally kicked herself, hard.

"My thanks." The deep, melodic voice caressed her for an instant before he bowed his head.

She reached way up and carefully placed it around his neck. Her fingers somehow curved to pull him closer. But—in a crowd?

She stepped back far too quickly and too much and bumped into somebody shorter and softer.

"Hello!" a girl chirped.

Danae spun around. Alekhsiy pulled her back against himself.

Two bright-eyed examples of Spartan queens smiled at them, all glowing teeth, fake black tresses, and white dresses carefully cut and taped to display the maximum amount of tits.

"Hello," they chorused and wiggled to display their best assets. They ran their eyes down Alekhsiy again, greedily. "Can we please have our picture taken with you? I'm sure she"—one of them barely bothered to cast an edged glance at Danae—"won't mind taking it."

Danae gritted her teeth.

Alekhsiy had been infinitely polite to children, especially those dressed for the tae kwon do tournament. Watching imitation comic superheroes attempt to look impressive next to him would be fodder for years of jokes. His barely concealed shock at stormtroopers' plastic armor and the more bizarre attempts at anime outfits had left her giggling.

But this was different. These bitches didn't want to capture him on a few pixels; they obviously wanted to haul him back to their bedroom.

Alekhsiy hesitated.

Danae glanced up at him.

"Of course, if my lady is in the picture as well." He bowed. Their jaws dropped. "Well . . ." They looked at each other. "If you're sure."

"Excuse me?" A very creditable Jarred Varrain, Celeste Carson's cyborg hero, looked hopefully at their knot in the foot traffic, his black leather armor gleaming across his muscles.

"Could you help us, please?" Danae leaped for the chance of chaperonage. "These Spartans want a picture with the two of us."

"Oh, sure." He shifted his conference bag, clearly ready to accept a camera.

One of the bitches started to snarl but quickly wiped it away. "Thank you."

The other leaped for Alekhsiy's free arm. Boob-rubbing hussy. This photo op couldn't be over too soon for Danae.

Years of working with pros had taught her how to pull it off, though. She donned her merc warrior persona, which was at least fierce enough to ensure only one bitch had her hands on Alekhsiy.

Why was she being so prickly? She'd never given that much of a damn before about what a short-term fling did next.

"Very good," Varrain said approvingly. Several other people gathered around and handed him their cameras.

The greedy sluts departed, balked of their prey. Varrain slapped Alekhsiy on the back and thanked him for being such a good sport. "I'm sure I got some awesome pix. You can catch them on the Con website."

He strolled off, whistling.

"Will that bother your chi?" Danae asked softly.

"Not the photo-taking itself because people offer me their approval by doing so." Alekhsiy stepped onto the escalator like an old pro, nimbly dodging an orange and purple Renaissance soldier who hadn't yet mastered the combination of rapier and moving stairs.

"But?" Danae prompted.

"I was warned that physical images of me, whether pictures or words, wouldn't linger."

"Ooh, magic." She shivered at the mention.

He grunted, his expression abstracted and harsh. They stepped off at the next level.

"Where are you going next?" he asked.

"Larissa is helping to lead the costumers' intro to Griffin-Con. She wants me there as an example of a hall costume."

"*Hall* costume?"

"Something that's more or less easy to put together and very comfortable to wear. Judges roam the Con during the day. If they see something they like, they'll just hand out an award on the spot. It's much less formal than the masquerade."

She hesitated, studying his face. "Do you want to come?" she ventured.

"Thrice-damned busybodies, they'd probably fire off enough questions to occupy an army of Zemlayan fire ants! Isn't that what everyone else has done here?" A passing couple looked at him oddly and he lowered his voice. "I know I must accustom myself to scrutiny but I do not require an extra opportunity to have my undergarments publicly dissected."

Danae bit the inside of her cheek and nodded, as solemnly as possible. She could hardly disagree with him.

"I will join my comrades early, then learn how this tournament is to be conducted."

"Sounds good." She kept her voice clipped, trying to sound equally martial. "I'll meet you at McKinnon's smithy booth in time for the first Torhtremer panel."

*   *   *

Alekhsiy stepped onto the landing outside the bazaar and pulled the heavy gray curtains shut behind him. His fingers twitched with the need to return to Danae, his heart's lady, whose passion fired his blood. But he'd dallied too long with her already: He had to fulfill his quest.

This storage room was filled with chests and boxes, all labeled for the dealers hawking their wares in the pandemonium behind him. Large, ugly lights lurked in the ceiling. As pragmatic as a dungeon's arsenal of weapons, they'd only appear when and if needed.

Evan had promised nobody would come in here unless they needed additional supplies, which was highly unlikely this early in the Con. Even so, Alekhsiy found a secluded corner and dropped to his knee behind a mountain of crates.

He knew Turner would be the Imperial Terrapin's next ally, thanks to the serpent ring's warning prick at the villain's approach in the Dealers' Room. But he still needed to learn the second half of his quest—where to find the sorcerer who could open the gate into Torhtremer for that foul poison.

"Show me he who can take the next Dark Warrior into Torhtremer."

He blew on the silver tiger ring.

His breath frosted across it and shimmered away. Neither light grew nor heat burned against his skin.

"Accursed jewelry, I am only a few feet away from where you came to life before!" he roared and slapped the stone paving underneath him. "Why won't you show me the way?"

A small box rattled above him, until it almost teetered on the verge of falling.

He gentled his tone, cursing all imperial beasts and their arrogant ways. They'd lived for centuries. Couldn't they give men a few gifts, instead of making them stumble and fall when so many lives were at stake? Of course, thirty-foot tigresses had even more vagaries than dragons.

"Beautiful Svetlhana, thou art even more radiant than an Imperial Tiger could hope to be." He dragged the sweet words out from a very dry throat, hoping she'd hear them somehow and make the damn ring's magic start to work. "Please hearken to your admirer on this far world. Know that we both share the same goal, which is to save Torhtremer from another war with the Imperial Terrapin."

He cracked open an eye. Had the ring warmed a trifle?

"Thou hast infused thy magic and the great White Sorcerers' magic into this ring. Of thy grace"—what there was of it, anyway, given her notorious liking for games—"I beg of you, please light it now, that I might know where to find the man who holds the key to the gate. He is a traitor, both to his own world and mine, who must be crushed immediately."

The silver immediately turned ice-cold, searing his finger faster than frostbite.

"Ouch!" He tried to yank it off. It went instantly inert, more lifeless than scrap iron beside his father's smithy.

He glared at it. "By all the gods, now what should I do?"

If anything, the tiny silver tiger on his finger sneered at him.

He flung a very rude gesture back at it. Then he leaned his head back against a foreign crate, carrying who knew what hellborn oddity, and brooded.

Perhaps he should watch the Imperial Terrapin's potential ally. After all, that triple-cursed bastard son of Chaos would have to unite with the sorcerer somehow before he could go to Torhtremer.

Danae elbowed her way through the crowd, gripping Alekhsiy's hand tightly. He'd been oddly quiet since they'd reunited but that might be because there were so many people around—especially here. The multitude trying to get into this session was incredible. It made getting through the doors an exercise in tactics as much as patience.

She spotted another opening and shot forward, towing Alekhsiy behind her. Big or not, conspicuous as all hell or not, he was staying with her. He muttered an apology to yet another female trying to strike up a conversation with him and squeezed through the gap, to land with a thud against Danae's back.

His arm wrapped around her waist. "Shall we look for a seat near here?"

"No, the back rows fill up fast, especially for a really crowded session like this one. Plus, it'll be SRO in minutes."

"SRO?"

"Standing Room Only. It means there are usually more empty seats in the front."

He shuddered and eased her forward.

"Do you see Nora or Larissa?" She bounced on her toes.

"Uh, no."

"Damn." She checked her cell phone again, wishing Larissa was faster at texting.

"What are you doing?"

"Larissa should have sent me a message, saying where they're sitting, but she hasn't yet. Maybe they went to a different session after all. You know this will be the first time I've seen Turner since he canceled sponsorship of the dance show on PBS."

"That seems rather—impolite." Alekhsiy's arm tensed.

"Two weeks before airtime after a year of planning?" She snorted, her fingers still curving into weapons of destruction at the memory. "And arrogant and—well, you name it. Said he found better ways to showcase his new product."

"What happened?"

"We couldn't get anybody else at that late date, of course." Her stomach twisted like a washrag, remembering all the people who'd been laid off and dreams scattered like dust in a rehearsal hall. "We threw a private party much later when his new darling died."

"Chaos spawn." When Alekhsiy spoke again, his voice was calmer and louder. "Is that Larissa who is signaling from ahead of us?"

Danae glanced up and waved frantically back at her friend.

The room was a typical, albeit very large, hotel meeting room, decorated in gold with a spectacular carpet. Most of the panelists were seated at the head table atop a dais. The moderator, a famous female science fiction author, was pacing across the front, narrowly watching the aisles.

"*Third* row, Larissa?" Danae asked, kicking her Torhtremer backpack out of sight under her chair. Larissa was on her right, with Nora, then Colin beyond that. All of the panelists could clearly seen anybody in these seats, especially with the lights this bright.

"Sorry! I know you don't like to be filmed but Nora bribed Colin to save us seats. It's Jacobsen's first panel here and he might have some stills or footage from the new movie."

"Jacobsen?" Alekhsiy queried, solid as a rock on Danae's other side, beside the aisle. Good, she'd finally be able to just sit and enjoy his delicious masculinity in public. All solid, muscular shoulders, massive arms, deep chest breathing steadily, and strong legs.

"Peter Jacobsen, the movie producer from New Zealand. He and his wife wrote all the scripts," Larissa answered.

"And co-produced," added Nora, between gulps of water.

"Corinne Carson coauthored the first one and has story credits for the second," Danae corrected and snuck another look at

Alekhsiy's hands. Those beautiful, long-fingered hands clearly visible under the bright lights. How could they have so many calluses and still be so graceful?

"Oh, that's right. Of course, you're the fanfic author; you're always careful about giving credit."

Danae bit back a grimace. Crap, she never talked about that in public. Fandom was the one place where she was just Danae Livingston, not any kind of celebrity.

"Dammit, Larissa!" Nora muttered.

Turner swept down the aisle next to them, followed by a pair of bodyguards. The moderator stilled, but quickly pasted a plastic smile on her face.

"What?" asked Larissa absently, her attention completely focused on the billionaire who'd made his first fortune selling fast access to celebrity gossip from around the world.

"Hush." Nora squeezed her hand.

Larissa's head swung around. "Not until you tell me . . ." she demanded, her voice rising.

Turner stepped onto the dais without pausing to acknowledge the moderator.

"Oh crap, it's about Danae the author, isn't it?" Larissa gasped in an all-too-carrying stage whisper. People across the aisle and two rows down turned to listen.

"Shut the fuck up," Nora hissed. She spiraled a fingernail deep into Larissa's wrist, her usual brutally direct technique for dealing with her friend's loose tongue.

Larissa whimpered under her breath and fell blessedly quiet.

Turner's cold gaze swept over the hall, assessing then dismissing its inhabitants. His eyes lingered on Danae a little too long.

She stared straight ahead, maintaining a serenely impersonal expression of reluctant attention. She'd used the same attitude while a thousand auditions dismembered her.

Alekhsiy linked his arm with hers, silently offering her his strength.

She threaded her fingers into his and managed a more genuine smile. After all, she had much more exciting activities to look forward to, thanks to him.

"Ladies and gentlemen, we'll get started now with Torhtremer's first panel discussion," the moderator called cheerily. The excellent sound system made her words crystal clear, while both video and still photographers shadowed the proceedings. The entire room was brilliantly lit, showing that almost every seat was occupied, with more people standing along the sides. It was a gaudy space, designed to hold fancy parties, and many of its inhabitants' costumes lived up to that invitation. But most simply wore everyday jeans and T-shirts for comfort, especially given such an extremely hot Atlanta July.

The audience eagerly fell silent, watching the graying woman with the rapt attention others would pay the latest alt-rock band.

"I'm H. S. McCain, author of twenty published novels and fourteen short stories, for which I've won a few awards."

Somebody cheered and she flashed him a grin, briefly looking decades younger.

"But today, I'm here strictly as a fan. I read *The Leopard and The Lily* when it first came out, plus all of the sequels. I've seen every one of the movies at least four times."

"For which my accountant says thank you very much," came a Kiwi-accented voice over the PA system.

She snapped off a quasi-military salute, which triggered a few laughs.

"Our topic today is 'Who Needs Torhtremer's Seventh Book, Anyway?' Given that Azherbhai was defeated at Tajzyk's Gorge to end *The Raven and The Rose*, what plot remains to be told?

Since Corinne Carson tragically died in a fire, who could possibly complete her unique vision?"

She paused dramatically but the audience didn't answer.

"We have brought together four panelists who know more about the Torhtremer canon than anybody else. I'd like each one to introduce themself and give a brief answer to whether they think we need the seventh Torhtremer book. After that, we'll take questions, which I can see you're already lining up to ask. Peter?"

A strong masculine hand captured the mike.

"Hi, I'm Peter Jacobsen, the token movie producer." He waggled his free hand and the crowd waved back happily.

He was ex-army—some said ex-SAS—and was still addicted to military-style workouts and marathon running. He was also a devoted family man and science fiction fanatic, with a knack for making money. His five Torhtremer movies had only solidified that reputation, gained from his previous military-style action adventures.

"I was lucky enough to have Corinne Carson give me a story outline of the first six books—but not the seventh. I don't know anything more about it than you do."

A mass groan went up from the crowd.

Alekhsiy sighed softly beside her and Danae looked at him sharply. His expression was immovably polite, though, and she snuggled back against his wonderfully comfortable shoulder.

"I assume everybody here has read the book and thinks they know all about that final battle, where Azherbhai, the Imperial Terrapin, and the Dark Warrior are defeated. Well, Ms. Carson gave us a few extra details for you." He smirked. "You'll have a small taste tomorrow night."

The crowd's roar was quickly contained.

"Other than that, I can only say that if there was a seventh book, I'd buy it in a minute. I, too, want to read it and, legally, I alone have the right to make any movie from it. That's all."

He passed the mike during a loud round of applause.

"Hi, I'm T. Sanderson and I write fanfic, some of which is about Torhtremer. I also just had my first novel published, which I'll be signing tomorrow." The youngest panelist grinned and double-checked the microphone again. Too many authors shouldn't be allowed out in public but his day job was something to do with selling insurance. It had at least given him fairly flexible hours and regular people contact, so he could manage coherent sentences in front of a crowd. Unfortunately, it had also made his pudgy features into the face of fanfic for far too many people.

"A lot of you seem to think that the Torhtremer novels are mostly romance."

Larissa bristled. Danae gaped at the cocky newcomer.

"But they're really military sci-fi, with all those battles and so on. I've had a ton of positive feedback, writing fanfic like that."

"Truly?" muttered Alekhsiy. "Have you read any of them, Danae?"

She elbowed him in mock dudgeon.

"The sixth book ended with King Mykhayl not having a queen, just those hundred concubines. Well, I say nobody needs the seventh book. He can have a great time with all those women and fighting the occasional bad guy, now that he's kicked Azherbhai's butt."

He glanced around at his stupefied audience and snickered.

The next speaker clicked on the high table's second mike, causing everyone present to automatically sit up straight.

"Hello, I'm Xenia Murphy, author of *The Torhtremer Lexicon*." The five-foot-three, café-au-lait-skinned and magnolia-voiced terror of Torhtremer fandom was the Savannah librarian who'd helped Corinne Carson perform the original research. She'd later become her full-time research assistant and been left a very nice legacy in her will. What she didn't know about Torhtremer wasn't worth writing down. She'd spent time on the movie sets after Ms. Carson's tragic death, helping the entire cast and crew get it right. And if she thought anybody anywhere was trying to stray from Ms. Carson's intentions, she'd take them apart in a heartbeat.

Her great gift to fandom was *The Torhtremer Lexicon*, first an official website and later a published book, which contained information from both the books and the movies.

"Miss Xenia," the cowed audience murmured, addressing her by her handle.

"I'd like to remind y'all of the basic magic in Torhtremer." She gathered them with a glare, not sparing her fellow panelists. Alekhsiy was absolutely still beside Danae.

"Azherbhai is an imperial beast, just like Khyber, the Imperial Dragon. As we all know, it takes three things to summon them into being so they can fight: their unique magical weapon, the words of power, and most important, their catalyst or avatar."

"So what?" a man shouted from the back.

"The sixth book ends with Azherbhai, the Imperial Terrapin, still in possession of all three. He has the spear and his great ally, the Dark Warrior, who knows the words to summon him into battle. *Together*, the two of them can do battle at any time against Mykhayl and the forces of Torhtremer."

She glanced around the now quiet room and raised a superior eyebrow.

"Azherbhai may have lost a few monsters but they're nothing he can't replace, given time. The series, my friends, is incomplete—*until the Dark Warrior is dead*."

She clicked off the mike, having won yet another argument.

"Mr. Turner?" prompted H. S. McCain.

He captured the mike with the speed and swiftness of a striking cottonmouth, surprising for somebody who must be used to
higher-tech audiovisual equipment and minions to assist him.

"I'm Boris Turner, proprietor of the Dark Warrior's Iceberg,
the web's home for Hollywood and fiction's greatest villains.
I'd like to offer a different viewpoint from that of my esteemed
colleagues—Azherbhai, the Imperial Terrapin, as the great
underdog."

"What?"

"Are you joking?"

"What kind of stupid idea is that?"

"Please hear me out." Turner remained unruffled and much
more polite than Danae had ever seen him before at a Con.

The audience muttered unhappily but settled down.

"We are familiar with Corinne Carson's biography, of her
difficult childhood and traumatic marriage. Of how she only
got the first Torhtremer novel published with her beloved sister's
help. She was an underdog, who sympathized with our kind."

The third-richest man in the world, speaking of our *kind?
Well, he had started out dirt poor.*

Danae glanced up at Alekhsiy, who was observing Turner
with the narrow-eyed curiosity he'd give a poisonous scorpion.

"I agree that the sixth book ends with a perfect, albeit tem-
porary, balance between the two sides. I propose that she was
setting up for the world's greatest surprise ending, in which the
ultimate underdog, the Dark Warrior, wins it all. Torhtremer,
the Dragon's Hoard, everything!"

"You're crazy, dude!" The audience erupted into objections.
Even H. S. McCain forgot her moderator's impartiality and
stepped forward to argue with him.

"Proof . . . pay . . ." Turner was shouting into the mike.

"Let him finish!" Jacobsen roared and pounded on the table.

It took five minutes to reestablish order and get everyone to sit down.

"Mr. Turner? Please complete your statement," H. S. McCain commanded.

Turner smoothed down his black polo shirt, with its *Northern Wastes* logo in the shape of an alligator snapping turtle. His cold eyes scrutinized the room.

"Corinne Carson is no longer here to complete the Torhtremer Saga. However, some here are skilled authors who have also explored the Torhtremer Universe. Surely one of you can write the seventh book and give us an answer."

"It's already been tried—and failed." Miss Xenia sniffed loudly and folded her arms.

"Turner, you know Carson's will says no seventh book unless she writes it." Jacobsen snatched up the other mike. "Can't even complete it from her notes, not that she left any."

"Her publisher paid a million-dollar advance to an unnamed *New York Times* bestseller to finish the series. That tells me what they thought of the prohibition." Turner stayed in the fight, completely unruffled.

"Yeah—and his house burned down, taking the manuscript with it. Author returned the advance and said no deal," a man shouted from the back.

Alekhsiy snickered softly.

"There have been other authors and other deals." Turner shrugged the incident off.

"One author whose car crashed on the way to the post office with an outline, another who broke her hand, an agent whose office computer system shorted out when asked to review the deal . . ." The middle-aged moderator almost spat. "Face it,

Turner, by now there are no reputable authors or agents willing to touch this project because it reeks of bad karma."

"Were you asked?" Miss Xenia inquired softly.

"I've got a better agent than that."

"There are other authors," Turner insisted softly and looked at T. Sanderson.

"Me? Are you kidding?" The debut novelist almost dropped his water glass on the floor. "I would never . . ." He tried again more slowly.

"Corinne Carson was very cool about fanfic, which is pretty unusual for a big author. Oh, she didn't read any of the Torhtremer stuff. But she was okay with it, as long as you followed the special rules she laid down. Isn't that right, Miss Xenia?"

"Correct, Mr. Sanderson." She nodded approvingly at him. "No underage sexual content, no intimate contact *ever* between Mykhayl and any of his siblings . . ."

"Blessed Mother of All Life . . ." The breath wheezed out of Alekhsiy's lungs and he closed his eyes. He was very pale.

Danae patted his leg comfortingly. She'd never considered writing anything between him and Mykhayl.

He locked his hand in hers.

"The biggest one for me is no—none, nada, zip—stories set after the latest thing she'd published." Sanderson sat erect, looking completely respectable for once. "I have never, and will never, write anything that occurred after the sixth book."

"Even for five million dollars?" Turner inquired silkily.

The room was stunned into complete silence.

"Five million?" Sanderson looked off into the distance, then shook his head. "Nope, won't do it. Nasty things happen when you break the Torhtremer rules, like what happened to those other authors."

"Ten million?"

Sanderson's eyes grew rounder below his spiky hair but he shook his head. "Dude, nobody has ever successfully broken any of the Torhtremer rules. You can't even post your story on a board. Your hard drive will fail first or your ISP will lose your payment and kill your domain. Something, anything, but you'll be dead out there in cyberspace."

Danae's throat was very tight and Alekhsiy brushed his cheek against the top of her head.

"Hey, CrystalTiger has pulled it off!" somebody shouted in the next section.

Larissa started to say something but squeaked instead when Nora bent one of her fingers back.

Turner's dark gaze snapped to her.

"She's a damn good writer, too!" Somebody else added—but not Larissa.

Danae folded her lips together and prayed for the floor to swallow her group up. Instead the proprietor of the Dark Warrior's Iceberg winked at her. Her, not Larissa.

How much did he really know?

Needing privacy as a writer to be herself and escape from celebrity—and spend time with Alekhsiy—was one thing. Losing it under these conditions felt like losing her only coat in a blizzard.

She stared stonily ahead, refusing to acknowledge any reason for his interest. Damned if she'd admit to him she'd written a short story set immediately after Tajzyk's Gorge.

Alekhsiy growled softly.

FIVE

The crowd surged forward the minute the panel officially ended, eager to question Jacobsen and Turner. They spilled into the aisles and blocked the gap in front of the panelists' table.

"Come on." Alekhsiy pulled Danae to her feet in a single smooth lunge.

"I'm so sorry," Larissa began in the same instant.

"Save it for later, stupid." Nora yanked her up and into the opposite direction. "Can't you tell when you've said enough?"

"But—"

Nora lifted a few fingers in good-bye. Alekhsiy tightened his grip on Danae's hand and sauntered into the aisle, slipping into the flow of traffic as if he'd been attending conventions for years. How could such a big man blend in so smoothly?

They'd reached the back of the room before they heard the man shoving his way forward and the people grumbling about his tactics. "Excuse me? May I please have a few words with you, ma'am?"

Oh, Lord, that clipped British accent. Had Turner sent one of his bodyguards after them? She really didn't want to talk to them.

She didn't look back. Any man willing to pay ten million dollars to dictate a book's ending or pay the millions it took to cancel a show at the last minute was nobody she wanted to do business with. Far better not to start negotiations with him than to balk at his demands and be ruined, the way her friends had been.

They made it through the doorway along with the mob and into the hallway. Alekhsiy continued to use the others for cover, always edging toward the group's outskirts. When they reached a corner, she tugged slightly on his hand and slipped out of the crowd.

They faded into the shadows and down a long corridor. She began counting intersections, learned during so many Cons here.

"Ma'am? If you're down here, Mr. Turner would simply like to have a few private words with you." The voice echoing down the hall after them didn't sound cordial at all.

Danae's skin tried to race ahead of her for safety.

Alekhsiy's knife appeared in his hand.

Five, six . . .

She stepped into a small alcove and pushed on the hidden door, praying her luck would hold. It swung silently open and she stepped quickly inside, followed immediately by Alekhsiy. An instant later, the door closed as quickly and quietly as it had opened.

A man's footsteps rushed past outside, barely audible through the heavy wood. "Ma'am?" he called again.

Danae glanced up at Alekhsiy. Her heart was pounding harder than during any rotten dress rehearsal.

He shrugged wordlessly, his expression more dangerous than the knife in his hand.

They were in a small restroom, its marble countertops and floors testifying to the high-class customers the hotel expected to serve here. It was immaculately clean, down to the faint aroma of expensive forests. Next door was the associated executive conference room, rarely if ever used during GriffinCon.

She flexed her fingers, not daring to pace, and forced her pulse out of her throat and into her chest. Dammit, she usually did better than this when faced with an attacker. Was the need to protect Alekhsiy making her more nervous?

The footsteps came back, faster and heavier. "Sorry, sir. I must have missed her in the crowd."

Danae and Alekhsiy exchanged looks in the mirror. Their pursuer must be talking into his cell phone.

"No, sir, I couldn't read either of their badges. Didn't the other women say anything? Damn. Yes, of course we can hack into GriffinCon's computers and find her somehow."

Danae tilted her head back against the wall. If nobody else came by, they should be safe. This suite was normally reserved for VIPs' private meetings with the media, something those hard partygoers didn't do frequently.

"Don't worry, I'll keep you free," Alekhsiy whispered.

She whipped her head around to stare at him.

"It is I who'll keep you safe! You're the one who's lost far from home."

"But you've never fought brutes like him before."

She snorted in derision. "You haven't seen the neighborhoods they put ballet studios in. I didn't get a black belt in kung fu because I use those moves every week on stage."

"You've been attacked." He cupped her shoulders.

"Three times." She shrugged, still slightly chilled by the

memory. "I was sixteen the first time. I'd decided a long time earlier that if I was attacked, I'd hit back. They didn't expect that out of a prissy little ballerina."

She grinned, her fingers curving into claws. "It felt good to fight something and win for once, instead of being *just a kid*."

"My dangerous little dancer." He kissed her forehead. "That is why you understand warriors."

She shot him a startled look. "No, I just couldn't stand how Corinne Carson treated you. My God, every time she had a dirty, nasty job, she'd dump it on you—and never give you any pleasure or rewards for it! If there was a hundred-mile forced march through high mountains in the winter, she'd give it to you—especially if you had to fight the enemy at the end. So I tried to make things a little easier for you."

"Ending with the night after Tajzyk's Gorge . . ." His mouth curved smugly.

"Enjoyed it, did you?" she asked and tilted her head, watching him curiously. Her beautiful man, who she'd made love to so often on the page. A dozen stories, always told from his lovers' point of view.

"Definitely one of your best efforts, sweeting, although I prefer the night before the ice fortress siege lifted. I believe the hope you gave me then saved a thousand lives."

"Thank you." She flushed, moisture pricking her eyes. "I didn't know you were real but your emotions always affected me. Oh . . ."

She wrapped her arms around him and buried her face against him. He immediately pulled her close, their heartbeats thudding together.

"We should be careful how we hold each other, dearling. Or . . ."

"You'll stamp chain mail on my leather?" Enchanted armor might be useful but warm skin was more pleasant.

"I'll slide my hands over the bare flesh that beckons to me," he whispered in her ear. "Like so." He eased his hand under her vest and stroked the small of her back.

Danae arched toward him and purred. *Oh yes, indeed.* She leaned up and kissed him enthusiastically. "But you need to take off your tunic and armor, Alekhsiy."

He rumbled disagreement and kissed her again, twining their tongues together. His fingertips seemed fascinated by the boundary between her skin and the black leather—her waist where her trousers rode and her ribs where the cropped bottom of her bustier sat. He teased and explored, lifting just a little but never enough to let cold air inside, only guiding his warm fingers in to swirl and fondle more enticements than she'd known of.

She whimpered, writhed, and tried to move closer. She clung to his arms and cursed his armor in multiple languages.

He chuckled softly and pressed onward, dipping his hand deeper down her backside. She moaned into his mouth and lifted her arms so he could remove her vest. Heat flickered through her and danced across her skin wherever he stroked.

He petted and played up her spine, shaping her to fit his big, rough hands. Contrasts flooded her—his calluses, her leather, her sweating skin, her heartbeat drumming under her skin where he touched, the cool marble under her hands, her cream building between her legs.

"More, please, more, Alekhsiy," she begged against his mouth and kissed him again.

He unlaced her bustier and eased his hand in. His warmth honed in directly on her heart, seeming to draw it into the palm of his hand, and lancing it with fire. Hunger pulsed through her blood, sparking between her breasts and her core. She twisted her hips, aching to rub her cream over his cock.

"Danae, dear heart." His tongue swirled over first one nipple, then the other. When had he removed her vest? Or her bustier? Who gave a damn when he teased her veins and areola so well? Her breasts swelled to meet him, making her breath catch in her throat. She was a creature blazing with sensation, trapped between his mouth and his hands.

He untied her trousers and dragged them slowly down to her knees. Somehow his big hand crept inside and found her clit with first one, then a second big finger. He teased her hard, possessively seeking out her entrance and widening her ruthlessly.

She gripped him heedlessly, eager for fulfillment—desperate for him. "Alekhsiy, please finish me!"

He choked out a laugh and sucked his fingers. His eyes closed in ecstasy.

"Dammit, Alekhsiy!" She clawed at his shoulders, threading his long, silky hair between her fingers.

"Condom?" His blue eyes considered hers, barely sane.

She snatched one out of her vest's side pocket, reaching to where he'd tossed it over the stall's partition. He rolled it onto himself with a speed and rapidity that suggested he'd watched her very closely the night before.

Then he yanked her trousers the rest of the way off, unzipping them at her ankles to take them past her boots, and spread her wide. Her stupid heart kicked into triple time at the naked yearning—no, surely it was lust—on his face.

He rubbed his thumb through her folds and she threw her head back, moaning. How could anything be so rough, gentle, and sweet at the same time?

His hands gripped her hips and he pulled her down onto

him. She sank home easily, every inch full of him. Even her skin and bones were so overwhelmed they sparkled with lust.

"Oh my." She wrapped her legs around his hips, latching her boots against his mail-covered ass. Oh dear God, only her warrior's hands and cock were bare; everything else was still hidden by tunic and armor. His blazingly hot skin and iron-hard strength fed into her.

She tightened her channel around him and squeezed his cock hard in welcome. Hers, dammit, *hers*.

"Danae!" He plunged into fucking her, thrusting strong and fast. His hands molded her hips, holding her close, bracing her against the counter. He was wild and deep, driving her up and onward.

She sobbed, hot fire spilling through her bones. Her hair spilled down her back, sweaty and tangled and as uncaring as her emotions.

He twisted and hit a slightly different spot.

She gasped and climaxed, consciousness and pleasure tumbling together into an enchanted whirlpool. Alekhsiy shouted an instant later, his own hot climax accelerating the spin until time itself meant nothing and only pleasure existed.

She needed to rest her head against his shoulder for far too long before she could even start thinking about getting dressed again. At least it was a high-end washroom with real towels for cleaning up.

She blinked and took a deep breath, ready to start becoming presentable. After all, she needed to get ready for tonight's Torhtremer Masquerade.

Presentable.

She reconsidered the immaculate washroom. She'd never had sex while standing up in her own hotel room or in her tiny Manhattan apartment. There was no way to find enough vacant floor space near a wall.

This had been fun. Hell, this had been damn good. Even worse, Alekhsiy had been just as wonderful when they weren't having sex.

Don't get sentimental, Danae. This is a one-time affair with a particular guy.

Right.

She took a deep breath and prepared to leave his arms.

"Would you ever write the seventh book?" he asked above her head a few minutes later.

"Of course not!" This was an easy question, something she'd thought about and dismissed long ago. "I'm not that kind of author, for one thing, to figure out an entire book's complicated plot. I write short stories, dammit. And it's Corinne Carson's saga and I don't give a damn about King Mykhayl's love life, for another, even if I do want to know how Azherbhai gets whacked."

"Turner offered a large sum to the new author." Alekhsiy sounded all too neutral. He was facing the door, politely careful not to watch her get dressed.

She blew a raspberry, hoping he understood its sheer rudeness.

"Turner couldn't buy me if he tried. But even if he did, he hasn't mentioned a sum I'd listen to. I inherited enough when my family died, thanks to insurance and lawsuits, so that I don't need to work. And being a prima ballerina pays pretty well, especially when you don't get injured."

Even the bad angle the mirror gave her showed how his shoulders relaxed.

"He may well try force next." He leaned back against the wall.

"In a public place like this? He wouldn't be so stupid!" She gestured impatiently with her hands, then retrieved her bustier. "No, he'll prowl around and check out every fanfic author that's here. There are hundreds and he's unlikely to find me."

"Why?" The single word came at her like a bullet.

"Fanfic authors generally use fake names, or handles, not their real names like other authors. So you have to go through their ISP, or Internet service provider, to find out what their real name is."

"What difference should that make?"

How did she explain the Internet to an axe-wielding barbarian? Probably easier than wiggling her trousers back on, over her boots. Should she take them off first or just figure that if they'd slid off over those high-heeled numbers, they'd slide back on over them, too? Yeah, right.

She marched into a stall, smacked a lid down, and settled herself to do battle the straightforward way.

"Just think of it as being coded, okay?" Oh, Lord, she hoped this explanation worked. Dating a paranoid banker had taught her a few things.

He waved her on.

"The usual code is based on where you live. Most fanfic authors have at least one layer of encryption, maybe two. However, I have at least two layers, more often three, whose codes vary all the time because I travel so much. And they change unpredictably."

She dumped the last boot on the floor and started to pull on her trousers.

Alekhsiy frowned, his brilliant mind clearly revolving around a new and fascinating puzzle. "Decoding your identity would be very difficult."

"Probably not impossible," she admitted, tying the laces at

her waist, "but it should hopefully take longer than this week-end. Once I'm out of here, I'll be back in my well-guarded Man-hattan apartment and he can't reach me."

"'Tis only a few days away." Alekhsiy's expression turned bleak.

"I'm hiding in plain sight among fifty thousand other people here and he doesn't know my name. 'CrystalTiger' isn't even mentioned on my badge. The only link to me is verbal, a few words mentioned by people who know me." It'd take a while before she referred to multiple friends. Larissa had shot her mouth off before, but this time hurt more since she'd done it so publicly.

She stomped her feet to check her boots' fit. It was a pity she couldn't use Turner as a target.

Alekhsiy was pacing the tiny room like a caged panther, poor darling. She needed to free him.

"Which gives us through the weekend to charge up your am-ulet." She cupped his face. "Right?"

He tilted his cheek into her palm, his wintry eyes looking into a future so harsh she didn't want to question him. Finally his expression shifted into something closer to joy. "Of course we will."

He slid his arms around her waist and pulled her against him.

The small cage's doors finally opened later that evening—an el-evator, his lady called it—and released them into the corridor's tight confines. The mass of people still inside quickly rearranged themselves to take advantage of the extra space.

Alekhsiy dragged in his first grateful gulp of air in far too many candlemarks. By the gray gods of Chaos, the shield wall's close-packed formation, which permitted no spear to pass through, was a wide-open plain compared to these folk waiting for an elevator or crammed into one. He shuddered. And Danae had assured him they were in a quiet wing on a spacious floor . . .

Thud, thud, THUD. Thud, thud, THUD. Her next-door neighbor was having a very noisy party, threatening all who passed by with something called Celtic rock music. Blessings on the Goddess, Larissa had the room on the other side so there'd be some quiet tonight.

Danae twirled beside him, rocking her arms in the air. Her feet traced intricate patterns across the carpet, following the last song the band had played. She wore the green and gold of the High King's personal guard's uniform, which Larissa had created for tonight's Torhtremer Masquerade. It had lost to an extraordinarily gaudy—and inaccurate—version of the Amazon's war costume.

Afterward, she'd hauled him off to a concert where they'd danced and danced. And danced.

She bumped her hip against his. "Hey, hey."

"Hey, lady." He smiled and wrapped his arm around her waist. His musical rendition was a little closer to the actual notes than hers, although he didn't understand what many of the words referred to. He easily matched steps with her and sashayed out of the lobby into the hallway.

"You're a great dancer," he murmured to his lady.

"I'm far better with the right partner—like you."

He came to a halt, only a few paces from her door.

"There's no need to flatter me," he warned her.

"I'm not." Her green-gold eyes were direct and honest. "And I wouldn't, not with you. The truth is the greatest gift anybody can give you."

"Thank you." His heart flipped over in his chest.

"Now please open up the door, big guy, before we get interrupted again. We need to be up early tomorrow morning and I've got plans for you tonight." She ran her tongue over her lips.

He silenced her red, pleading mouth by the simple act of bringing his mouth down over it hard. She answered him eagerly, surging into his kiss as if they had all the time in the world, until he nearly forgot they were standing in a hallway and not in his room.

He dragged his head away and shoved the key into the slot, then kicked the door open.

Something hissed and popped in the bathroom. An instant later, two more of them did the same in the bedroom, followed by others in the sitting room.

Alekhsiy pressed Danae against the wall with his arm and immediately drew his axe. What thrice-cursed devil's spawn had crept into their rooms?

A faint, acrid odor touched the air.

The door fell slowly shut behind Danae. She sniffed. "What on earth?"

"No demons, at least." His axe's blade glowed faintly blue-white. He didn't sheathe it, though, since he misliked the scent lingering in the air.

"Should your axe be that bright?" Danae asked with the slightest of stammers.

"No. It's reacting to traces of evil, probably from evil's aides." He swept it slowly from side to side, searching for where it would grow brightest. "Wait here."

"But . . ."

He stalked into the bathroom, where his blade promptly blazed brighter. An instant later, it pointed to a small cream box lodged in the wall.

"An outlet adapter?" Danae queried and flipped on the light switch. He tried to hold her back but she swatted his arm aside. "Ease up, big guy. I'm the one who understands this world."

She squatted down to look without, praise the Red God of War, touching it.

"Well, I'll be damned." Her finger lightly traced a path over its top, marking a slightly seared patch.

"What?"

It's a bug, she mouthed silently. *But I don't know if it's dead or just damaged.*

He gestured his confusion.

A listening device, she explained, still not making a sound. She was very pale. *Turner probably wants to confirm that I'm CrystalTiger. It's cheap and easy for somebody in his celebrity-watching business to do.*

Turner. That greedy, thrice-damned spawn of Chaos's gray gods! He'd rip his heart out and roast it! He'd tear him apart with two teams of sacred oxen—no, four! How dare he try to eavesdrop on the most beautiful lady in the world!

She blinked at him, clearly not following his lapse into the cruder forms of Torhtremer soldier talk, then shrugged. "Come on. We've got to clean up both rooms."

The music next door surged into keening bagpipes, underlain by brutal drumming.

They found the other bugs easily enough but she blessedly allowed him to pluck them out of the wall. He dropped them into the wastebasket and raised an eyebrow at her. "Where to?"

"The trash chute, if we can reach it unnoticed. He's probably bugged the hall, as well."

A few minutes and several back corridors later, she led him to a small, ill-smelling room. She opened a panel in the wall and he listened with great satisfaction to those three invaders go rattling to their doom far below. Their destruction would not permanently deter Turner but should serve as a warning that his lady was not entirely unprotected.

Back at their room, Danae stared at the quiet normalcy of the tidy bed and her jumbled belongings. Tears welled up in her eyes but didn't spill.

She pressed her hands to her mouth and rocked herself, shaking slightly.

Alekhsiy wrapped his arms around her. Thrice-damned coward, to have sent such loathsome surrogates instead of coming himself.

"Everything looks so calm," she muttered.

"Can you rest here? Do you want to ask for another room?"

"No, I'll be fine. He made his money on the Internet, selling software to find things. There's no place I can go where he couldn't track me down." She roused herself enough to smile at him. "Hey, this is where we killed the little beasts. We're better off staying here, especially since we've got good neighbors. Larissa won't let him take over her room and we'd know in an instant if he booted out the partygoers on the other side, to eavesdrop from there."

"True." He dropped a kiss on her forehead and reluctantly let her start making tea. It seemed to be her way of healing both herself and the person she fetched it for.

"Do you know what destroyed them?" he asked, trying to sound relaxed. He needed to understand their enemy in order to protect her.

"It's so far-fetched." She sighed and looked up at him over her box of tea bags.

"Try me."

She hesitated unhappily.

He longed to kiss her until her mouth turned upward, but not yet. "If he will invade your room, what else will he do? Where will he stop?"

"This is madness." She almost slammed the box to the floor but her eyes were completely sane when she looked at him. "Are you wearing an anti-scrying spell? Something that would stop an enemy from spying on you?"

Why was she asking such an elementary question?

"Yes, of course. It's part of every general's armor."

"Well, there you are." She sank onto the bed as if her legs had no strength. "Your spell's magic worked just as well here as it would in Torhtremer. But it acted according to Earth's laws. The bugs shorted out, giving us an ozone smell and slightly scorched plastic."

"Why is that so difficult for you to believe?" Her explanation made perfect sense for him.

"Because up until now, I could pretend you were just a really sexy dude that I was shacking up with for GriffinCon! Sexier than usual and much better mannered but still basically here today and gone tomorrow."

A festival love, good for a few nights pleasure and no more. Pain barreled into his stomach and exploded in his heart, carving away any hope he'd mean as much to his little dancer as she did to him.

He forced himself back under control. The threat here was bigger than anything to him alone.

"Danae . . ."

She pulled her hair out of its tight queue and shook it loose. How much longer would he be able to run his fingers through it? The amulet would yank him back to Torhtremer once it was fully recharged.

"And now I must think about this crackpot billionaire who

wants me to write a book for him. I'll have to talk to him tomorrow and explain why I agree with Sanderson."

"There's more at stake than that, sweeting."

"What do you mean?" She spun to face him, her fingers poised at her tunic's throat.

"You never asked me what happened after Tajzyk's Gorge, Danae."

"I don't want to know." She started unbuttoning but he caught her hand. That was the last reaction he'd expected.

"Why not?" he demanded.

"Because if I knew, I might be tempted to write something that would change your future. If you've got a happily ever after going with the Dark Warrior dead and Azherbhai banished, then you should enjoy it," she responded fiercely, her green eyes boring into his. "You have more than earned it, after what that bitch Corinne Carson dumped on you."

His throat tightened. *Blessed Horned Goddess, please give my lady joy after I am gone.*

He kissed her forehead in thanks and tried yet again to memorize her scent. She sniffed and held on to his hands.

"Mykhayl killed the Dark Warrior—"

"Thought so!"

"But Azherbhai hasn't disappeared."

"Oh shit, is he still causing trouble in Torhtremer?"

"Yes." Alekhsiy's mouth quirked reluctantly at her description.

"What about his catalyst? He needs one to be really nasty."

"He doesn't have one *on Torhtremer*—and hasn't been united with him yet."

Danae rubbed her thumb over his knuckles, her gaze abstracted. "Potential catalysts are rare, even for the Imperial Terrapin?"

"Correct."

"So he'd have to hunt one down, which must have pissed him off. Served him right, too, after all the hell he's caused."

She affectionately kissed Alekhsiy's wrist, warming his heart. He'd build what memories of joy he could, while he was here. He waited patiently for her to find the answer.

"Is his intended catalyst here on Earth?" She stared at him. "The one guy who can summon Azherbhai into existence and make all of his magic come to life."

"Aye, sweetheart."

"Boris Turner." Her fingers had turned chilly around his.

"I've come to do whatever is necessary to stop him from joining the Imperial Terrapin."

"You can't stop him—he's obsessed with Azherbhai! He used to be a three-hundred-pound pudgy jerk. Now he's super fit and one the world's top experts with a sword or spear."

"Or staff?"

"Or that," she agreed promptly. "He pays big sponsorship money to Cons, just so he can show off his likeness to the Dark Warrior."

Alekhsiy's breath rattled in his throat. Her eyes locked with his.

"The height and the body type—he looks like the Dark Warrior, doesn't he? Stocky but very fit." She pulled herself away from him and began to pace.

Alekhsiy nodded grimly, reluctantly admiring her skill at dodging the room's disarray.

"Those fighting skills and his obsession . . . Oh hell, he would make a great catalyst, wouldn't he?"

Alekhsiy nodded again, watching her pace back and forth.

"But even if I thought Turner would be a good target, he'd still need to somehow go to Torhtremer. And your amulet is the only way to travel there, right?"

"Correct," Alekhsiy agreed. He started to consider her argument from every possible angle.

"So all we have to do is keep you and your amulet out of his hands? Which is easy."

"Except that if he somehow kidnaps you, after I'm gone"— *oh, hellish hour*—"and forces you to create a story, everything you're worried about will take place in Torhtremer."

"Don't be ridiculous, darling. I wouldn't do it."

He needed to make her take the threat seriously. If Azherbhai believed Turner was a suitable catalyst, then his depths of depravity had to be very deep. "What if he threatened Nora or Larissa?"

"He wouldn't dare." Her denial came a little slower.

"Or attacked Evan or Colin?"

"Oh, no!" Her eyes changed to pure gold, glittering with horror.

"My lady, you are a sorceress. Everything you have written for me to do, I have done—and I have enjoyed, thanks be to the gods."

"I could never let anything else happen, Alekhsiy, even if he harmed somebody I loved." A single tear gleamed on her cheek. "To hurt you, or Mykhayl, or Yevgheniy, or . . . ? No. I don't think I could even set pen to paper, I'd be so consumed by thoughts of the agony someone I knew was suffering." Her lip trembled. "I swear to you that I couldn't write such horror. It would self-destruct, be null and void—a spell that died ugly and ill-formed without drawing breath."

He caught her against him and cuddled her. She wrapped her arms around him and clung to him as if he were the only stability in a chaotic world. She was so small yet so strong, like the finest steel from his father's forge. Her trembling was more heartbreaking than seeing a named dagger shatter without warning during a duel.

"We have to believe that Turner will eventually see reason and give up." She sniffled and straightened up.

"Why?" He cocked an eye at her, genuinely curious.

"Hollywood failed to create the seventh book and he can't begin to offer the same prestige they can."

"But he is willing to pay more money, is he not?"

"Exactly. Readers would always think a billionaire had dictated a plot so ridiculous, only millions of dollars could get it published. They wouldn't want to read it, let alone spend money to buy it."

"Authors can strut more if they imagined everything on their own, which the movie would let them." Truly, bards on the other side of the void lived by a different set of rules.

She nodded, shoving her hands through her hair until it fell forward over her face. "I just hope he figures that out fast. I hate giving up my kung fu summer camp, but I'll go straight back to Manhattan if that's what it takes to keep everyone safe."

Return to Manhattan and the golden pool of light where she'd dance, never to be touched by him again.

He pinned a merry smile on his face. "Then let us prepare for bed, my lady. The dawn comes early, bringing your practice time."

Danae eyed him, wondering what had brought on that hideous excuse for a grin. Of course, coming face-to-face with twenty-first-century espionage would be a rude shock for anybody, even if they didn't come from a world of dragons and wizards.

"May I help you get undressed?" That should distract him—and her. They were both doing too much thinking.

He shot a surprised glance at her, having already almost finished removing his leather braces. "My gear is complicated," he
warned her.

She hooted at him, her first true laugh since entering her room.
"And just who do you think you're talking to, big boy, hmm?
Some silly virgin who's never seen cold steel or chain mail? Not
somebody who's been hanging around the stuff since she was
born. Ooh, horrors!" She shielded her eyes with her sleeve and
promptly scratched her nose with the glittering gold embroidery
of her High King's personal guard's uniform. "Ouch!"

She rubbed her face and looked at her fingers. If she'd gotten
any blood on it, Larissa would have her hide.

Alekhsiy chuckled.

She glared at him, daring him to say anything unkind.

He cleared his throat with a distinct effort. "Sergeant," he
began.

She blinked at him. *Sergeant?* Oh yeah, right, that was the
rank Larissa had assigned to the costume.

She snapped hastily to attention. "Sir!"

That was the correct way to do it, wasn't it? She never did a
LARP at Cons and she'd never been asked to dance a military
role. Or did they salute differently in the Torhtremer movies?

Alekhsiy thumped himself on the arms and broke into howls
of laughter. She crossed her eyes at him and stuck out her tongue.
He laughed harder and she joined in, well aware their mirth was
at least half reaction to their earlier terror.

"So remind me," she cooed, when they could both speak
again, "just how do you salute in Torhtremer?"

He thumped his right fist against his left shoulder, which was
remarkably hard to do when she was seated on his lap.

"Shit." She pursed her lips. "Obviously I haven't watched
the movies in far too long."

"But your expression . . ." He choked and she eyed him in mock suspicion. "Sweeting, sergeants don't customarily look at their general in such total surprise."

"I'll bet they do, especially when the general says they don't know how to get him dressed or undressed. Just who do you think really runs an army, hmm? Not the generals, surely. Of course I can manage your wardrobe."

"All of my weapons, too?" He raised an elegant eyebrow.

"You bet." She nodded firmly. Did he think she'd been so crazed with lust last night she'd completely forgotten everything he'd done? Well, quite possibly but she had learned a few things elsewhere. After all, she was a theatrical professional and she knew costumes.

"If you have to give me any clues, then I'll have to pay a forfeit," she added.

"Such as?"

"I don't know; you're the one with the temple sex games."

"Suck my rod down your throat?"

She should probably pretend that would be a hardship. She flickered a glance at him from beneath her lowered brows. "If you give advice just to insist on a penalty later, I'll cry foul," she warned.

"Agreed." His voice sounded stern but his cock was definitely an eager ridge under his mail.

Her uniform featured a knee-length, close-fitting, emerald-green silk jacket, brocaded with golden tiger designs. The ornately cut collar and sleeves were further embellished with gold embroidery showing her supposed rank and battle decorations. A narrow black belt carried a reproduction Torhtremer dagger, courtesy of Kyle. Black silk breeches and black boots with very ornate tassels completed her outfit.

She extracted herself from his lap and circled him, considering the best place to start. Next door, they'd changed the playlist to a set of Celtic ballads, sweet and lyrical.

"Do you plan to remove your boots?" he inquired. His voice's seeming casualness was belied by his fingers' restless drumming on his knee.

"Do you want me to—sir?"

He choked and surged to his feet, a hungry glitter in his eyes. "A better viewpoint may help you, sergeant."

"Thank you, sir," she answered demurely.

Sword first, then dagger, not boots. She set to work on the buckles.

"I'm glad you're no longer openly displaying your axe, sir," she remarked to distract him from her fingers' clumsiness. How could she be fumbling so much now when she'd only just started and there were so many layers left to go?

"Why shouldn't I?" He planted his feet a little wider apart and looked down at her.

"Most here don't carry three weapons. They use only axe and dagger, or sword and dagger."

"They'll expect me to fight with a sword."

"Probably." Weapons and their harness gone, she knelt to take off his leather ankle boots.

"I'm looking forward to seeing their different styles of fighting," he commented and ran his fingers through her hair.

"Mm-hmm." Her scalp tingled and she leaned her head against his leg for a moment. *Oh my, that felt good. Almost as sweet as his presence.*

He stroked her again and she had to force herself to move away, lest every cell in her body turn boneless.

She unpinned his cross-tied indigo garters and swiftly unwrapped them, humming softly to herself as she neatly wound the yards of cloth into a ball.

"You've done this before," Alekhsiy commented.

"My eldest brother had a Robin Hood obsession, which included that kind of clothes. It was a toss-up for a while whether the family would wear Star Wars or Robin Hood to GriffinCon." For once, it didn't hurt to talk about them, not with Alekhsiy still gently massaging her.

His trouser legs ballooned away from his legs, far fuller above his knees than at his ankle, having been carefully pleated into those garters. They were made from a wonderfully lustrous silk shantung, finer than the best suit James Bond ever got to wear. It was obviously a lot easier getting Alekhsiy out of his clothes than into them, especially if tidiness was desired.

He smelled wonderfully masculine, too, of sandalwood and a little sweat.

She rubbed his calf, kneading out any aches from a long day on narrow metal chairs and edging through crowds. Big men like him should be striding through courtyards and swimming under waterfalls.

"Lovely." He sighed and relaxed into her touch, his hand resting gently on her head.

Poor darling. How many people gave him simple relaxation without asking for anything more? She continued to work on him, first one calf and then the other, using the skills she'd learned through years surmounting the demands on a dancer's body. She eased up his thighs, staying gentle and free-flowing. He needed healing and to bring the earth's energy into him.

She could almost sense where a knot would be, or an old scar, before she found it. She couldn't do as much as she'd like to. She wasn't a trained masseuse, and this wasn't the best position. But she could help.

And in that room, her fingers flowed instinctively along his muscles and tendons. Even their breathing matched, aided more than hindered by the faint music from next door.

His breath sighed out, deeper than a mountain spring.

She closed her eyes. She needed to move on before matters went too far while they were still dressed, even if his mail and tunic were slit down the front. She pressed a kiss to his thigh and came up onto her feet.

"Danae!" he protested, his eyes slumberous. Lust sparkled over her skin wherever they rested.

"Would you want a sergeant to fail in her duty, sir?" She managed a teasing grin.

He groaned. "Of course not."

"Your helmet . . ."

"Is already removed and stowed in its magical pouch," he returned sharply. "As is my mail coif and the linen coif underneath it."

"Gloves, too, sir?"

"Yes, sergeant, they are."

"I'm glad to hear that, sir." She circled him, daring to run her hand lightly over his hip. Narrow hips, too, leading to that hard sweep of muscular ass. She gulped and yanked her palm away.

He shuddered and swayed slightly toward her.

"May I ask, sir . . ."

"Yes?" he demanded.

"If you are wearing a leather codpiece under your armor, sir? I would want to treat it with all consideration, sir." *And pray my fingers don't fumble so hard I break the laces in my rush to take it off.*

"Codpiece." He closed his eyes. "Mother of All Life, she asks me about a codpiece—and she expects me to stand here calmly?"

Danae's pulse shot into triple time.

"No, I am not wearing one. General's armor renders that unnecessary since it's enchanted, thanks be to all the gods."

"Uncomfortable, is it, sir?" She could tease a little now and try to ignore the tightness in her chest.

"They are not shaped to fit all occasions, sergeant—such as the present circumstances."

"In that case, perhaps we should remove your surcoat and armor, sir. So you can be more at ease," she suggested.

"Certainly." He bowed slightly to her, allowing her to lift off his dark green field tunic, which was made from heavy, textured silk. His mail was formed into a long shirt, or hauberk, which reached to his knees and elbows. The links were so finely made they shone under the light like the tiniest of fish scales rippling under the sea, a dream impossible to catch—like spending a week or month or lifetime with a lover like him.

Her cream melted, heating her aching cunt. She dragged in a breath and reached for the next piece.

Danae ran her finger along the intricately braided strip of leather, which made a stand-up collar for the hauberk and protected his neck. She'd seen its like before hundreds of times, making it far more comfortable to admire.

"Beautiful. That's the finest made one of these I've ever seen."

Her hand brushed his hot skin and tugged gently at his long hair, which he wore loose now. He leaned his head into the caress and rumbled something, which didn't translate. She glanced up into his eyes.

"Pray, continue—sergeant." His voice had turned deep and slow.

She nodded hastily, her skin hot and dry under her thin chemise and heavy brocade jacket.

The hauberk came off easily into her arms and she quickly

folded it, trying hard not to think about whether or not it was enchanted. It was far better to consider Alekhsiy, standing there with his chest heaving under that paler green tunic.

"You need to get rid of those tigers, sir, before they jump off you." Surely a joke would ease her.

"Jump off me?"

"You're panting." *Well, so was she, but why mention it?* "Plus, the gold trim doesn't really flatter your breeches, sir."

Actually, she'd rather look at him in just the trousers.

He peeled the tunic over his head, balled it up, and threw it into a corner.

He propped his fists on his hips and lifted an eyebrow at her. His quilted tunic—or gambeson—emphasized the width of his shoulders, the depth of his chest, and the narrowness of his hips. If she could see the pattern more closely, she knew it'd be protection spells. No woman should have to see him in such garb and remain sane.

Her nipples promptly hardened into desperate arrowheads of lust, pointed straight at him.

"Sir!" She gasped in a last-ditch attempt at self-control.

A wicked smile played around his lips.

She wanted his mouth on her lips, on her breasts, on her . . . She gulped.

He began to unbutton his tunic. "I believe I should remind you, Sergeant, that you appear overdressed for this occasion."

She blinked at him. Why was he mentioning her clothing?

"Boots and jacket?" He clucked his tongue.

He couldn't have said anything she agreed with more. She sat down on the armchair and stripped off her boots and socks. The knots down her jacket's front took longer.

"Excellent, Sergeant." Alekhsiy purred.

"Sir?" She glanced at him over her shoulder and her mouth dropped.

He was seated on the bed, wearing only his linen shirt and drawers—and fondling his cock. Very slowly, up and down.

She watched him desperately, her breath condemned to match his every move. Up and down, in and out. Up and down . . .

She managed to turn around and unbutton her breeches. She was wet, so very, very wet.

He squeezed himself, showing off how very engorged his cock's head was.

Up and down . . .

She dropped her breeches and her thong in the same movement, before snatching a condom out of the party box.

"Why do you call it a party box?" Alekhsiy asked.

"Huh?" She dropped the foil wrapper into the wastebasket. "It's actually a variety pack, showcasing a bunch of different styles. A gay friend of mine bought two for a party he was throwing for his lover."

She dropped to her knees before him and swirled her tongue over his cock. And those fat, plump balls of his that nestled into her hand.

Her hips rocked toward him, aching to join them. God, she was so fucking wet.

She'd bet a mortgage payment he had no STDs—but she wasn't about to gamble on a baby. Dear Lord, he tasted and felt almost good enough to take a chance on riding bareback. Beautiful, beautiful Alekhsiy.

Better remember the moral of the story.

"They broke up before the party took place. So I bought the two party packs from him."

She rolled the condom onto him, lingering to pet and stroke

him. The fat mushroom cap, the generous shaft, the golden hairs gilding his balls . . .

Hunger shafted her lungs.

"You're very generous," he gritted out.

"I try to help my friends." She looked up at him and smiled shakily. God help her, he was quickly becoming too much more—for a man who'd be gone in a few days.

"Am I that?" He caressed her shoulders.

"Always." She immediately came up to kneel astride him.

"Dear heart." He pulled her back to the center of the bed and tucked his legs into a lotus position, stabilizing them both.

She promptly slid her legs over his hips and giggled at him. His rampant cock was so very neatly nestled against her cunt. "Friends—and lovers?"

"But of course." He caught her mouth with his, sucking her lower lip. She yielded happily and threw her head back for the series of kisses and gentle nips he bestowed on her throat and shoulders. Everywhere he touched, fire built, driving into her spine and lungs—and lower down, too, until it burned even hotter in her core.

"Danae, lady of golden light." He scraped his teeth along her collarbone.

"Alekhsiy," she moaned and clawed at his shoulders. "Please."

He kissed her again, deep and slow. His hands gathered her up and she sank down onto his cock. *Oh yes, finally.*

He thrust lazily and she tightened herself around him. "Alekhsiy, darling."

"Sweeting." He kissed her again, demanding more, linking her to him, heart and soul through their mouths.

Waves of delight rocked through her bones, into her blood, and back up to him. More, she wanted more. She rode him recklessly, heedless of anything except the man who was the fire in her blood.

Her breath sounded in her ears and came back to her from him. Her blood raced in her veins and echoed through his hands. His cock filled her core and brought heat and stability and . . .

He suckled hard on her nipple. Pleasure, more intense than pain, shot straight to her heart and down to her core.

Danae shrieked and climaxed, wracked by waves of sheer delight that shattered and remade her, like being swept into a giant tsunami. Alekhsiy growled and climaxed with her, the one sure thing in that ever-changing world.

Afterward, she was too exhausted for small talk. She certainly wasn't about to comment that his amulet had become so much lighter. Enough had happened that evening that all she wanted to do was sleep—and cuddle him as much as possible.

Alekhsiy tucked the covers more firmly around his sleeping lady. She deserved her rest after the night's terrors—and all the chi she'd poured into his amulet. It wasn't enough to take him home, but it was much closer.

He eased himself into bed. She promptly turned toward him, threw her arm over him, and rested her head on his chest, all without waking up.

His bruised heart eased a trifle. He smiled and allowed himself to twine a lock of her hair around his finger.

He'd willingly bound himself to her for life when he drank her intimate liquors, those carnal delights of a sorceress. He loved her gallant generosity more every day and her occasional flashes of arrogance and temper simply made her human. Yet she'd made it more than clear she saw him as little more than a pleasant bed partner—he, who half of Torhtremer's maidens pursued avidly, if only for political gain!

Yet,even if he had wanted to stay, he dared not, lest more magic leak across the void and draw the Great Terrapin after him.

Azherbhai and the catalyst he desired, the man who could make all of his evil become real—Boris Turner. And Turner hunted Danae, hoping to have her make all of Azherbhai's dreams come true.

She didn't want to do that, of course. But would Turner or Azherbhai allow her any choice? He couldn't afford to have her fall into Turner's hands or for Turner to make any threats against her loved ones. There was simply too much at stake, both on this side of the void and at home.

He'd have to stay very close to her, while he was here. No longer could he leave her alone for an hour or two while he visited McKinnon or fought in the tournament. No, he'd have to either travel with her or make sure she came with him, using whatever excuses were necessary. It might take a little wheedling but surely no outright lying would be needed.

No matter what the cost to himself or anyone else, he had to ensure that everyone remained safe.

SIX

Danae gave her soy latte one final stir and sealed the lid, humming the guards' theme music from the Torhtremer movies. Two steps down and one step back up, all syncopated just like Fosse might have done. There was nothing like a big flight of stone steps to inspire a dancer, even this early in the morning.

She snapped her fingers to the beat in her head and repeated the pattern again, wishing she'd had a little more time for her exercises. Or maybe not. Alekhsiy was a magnificent distraction who wouldn't be around for very long.

Yeah, just keep telling yourself that. Like you won't wake up the first morning he's gone and reach for him . . .

"That's a very complicated step. Do you want me to hold your cup so you won't spill any on your uniform?" he asked, obviously being careful not to mention the horde of attendees clumping down the stairs beside them.

"Not at all. I'm used to dancing in crowds and my cup is a lot smaller than yours," she pointed out virtuously and managed a very brief pirouette. She landed on a larger block of stone that created a small terrace and curtsied, safely out of harm's way.

"Bravo, my dear. Bravo." He joined her and lifted his gigantic cup of chai high in salute.

"Do you think you'll finish it before we have to take our places in the parade?" she queried mildly. "Or will you be the only royal Torhtremer cadet carrying a modern, eco-friendly container?"

She wore the cobalt and silver cadet's uniform, which looked like a cross between an ancient Chinese military uniform and a West Point uniform. Her hip-length tunic was made from intensely blue brocade, woven with silver tigers in a variety of martial postures. Heavy silver braid trimmed the collar, center front, hem, and cuffs. The riding breeches were made from heavy silk in a matching shade of blue and tucked into calf-high boots, adorned with an ornate silver tassel.

Alekhsiy's embroidered pouch, the one marked with a crossed spool and scissors, had produced a uniform for him that matched hers, except for the knee-length jacket and ornate dragon embroidered on the shoulder. He'd chuckled when he saw it, commenting that he'd always wanted to command a cadet brigade. He'd even strutted a bit like an ecstatic teenager when he first put it on.

"Certainly I'll finish my tea. Would I waste it by throwing it away?" He took a long, clearly ecstatic swallow—one of the very few sensual actions she'd seen him do in public. Adam's apple moving up and down in that strong throat, framed by the long blond hair, between the jutting jaw and the silver metal of his uniform. Hot skin begging to be kissed . . .

Don't start something now, Danae. Just keep matters platonic, even though Larissa's well-designed tunic could be taken off far faster than Alekhsiy's damn armor.

"Now that you put it that way—no." That sounded logical,

right? And he was becoming addicted to Indian teas, at least the dark and strong ones that made the best chai.

The hurly-burly of the parade's first moments swept around them, isolating them in a bubble of noise and movement on the hotel steps, as GriffinCon attendees organized themselves to march in full costume through downtown Atlanta. Many would join prearranged units, like the 501st who dressed like Star Wars' stormtroopers in their smooth white armor. Others would simply wear what suited their fancy, such as the many elves, Varrain fans, or myriad Star Wars variants. Some had spent months or even years on their wardrobes; others had rented their outfit, while many had simply picked up a T-shirt or an accessory to fit a theme. All would have fun.

The towering high-rises and red brick palaces of a bygone era looked on tolerantly. The police watched them cautiously and probably thanked their lucky stars this conclave took place early on a Saturday morning rather than late at night.

Two old acquaintances appeared beside them, hovering on the stairs as if uncertain whether they could enter the small terrace. Too many years of friendship—and her mother's ghost—booted Danae into acknowledging them. Making up after one of Larissa's more spectacular examples of shooting off her mouth usually came after a couple of days, not the next morning.

"Good morning, Larissa." Danae nodded politely, a little surprised at the other for making the first move. She was far better at sulking and dodging the spotlight than opening herself up to a public rebuff.

"Good morning, Danae. Alek." Larissa nodded nervously to Alekhsiy. "This is my husband, Sasha, who got in late last night from Dallas."

Uh-oh, Sasha the cop was furious and trying to put the best possible face on it. Had she told him what happened yesterday?

"Pleased to meet you, Alek." The two men shook hands, testing each other's grip carefully. Obviously satisfied with the result, the ex-cowboy gave Danae a tentative smile. "How're you doing, honey? Dance business been treating you okay?"

Larissa must have told him something or he wouldn't be so cautious. "Doing great. My agent negotiated a new contract with the troupe and I've even got some great guest gigs coming up. How's the kid?"

"Growing fast! I tell you, we buy him clothes one day and we're putting him in new ones a couple of weeks later. If we didn't have hand-me-downs from my brothers, I don't know what would happen." Larissa had garbed her cowboy in the popular merc's black leather costume, giving him the boon of letting him fade into the crowd. Given any choice, she'd dress her very fit husband in far more spectacular gear.

"That's so great. You'll have to send me some more pictures of him; I don't want to miss a moment of my godson."

"You should have one of your own. You'd make a great mom." The beaming enthusiasm of every new convert broke out in Larissa's smile, making Danae shift her feet uncomfortably.

"Oh no, I'm a dancer. Us gypsies do airports, not babies." She couldn't stand to leave a kid behind whenever she hit the road, the way she'd seen others do. Dancing had kept her alive through the worst of times and still kept the blood pounding through her veins. Children didn't fit into that.

"Oh yeah, that's right, no entanglements ever." For a moment, glimpses of the old Larissa who'd talked her through long, hard nights of agony flashed between them.

Alekhsiy made a low, raw sound and gulped some more chai.

Danae frowned briefly, then shrugged. Any daylight agreement with Larissa's comment would make it more solid.

Larissa and Sasha exchanged an unreadable glance before she shook out her heavily decorated skirts.

"Well, we—we don't want to overwhelm you with pictures or gossip or anything," Larissa demurred, hanging on her husband's arm. "Sasha's explained to me how a little bit of talk can get picked up and be blown into something really big. Especially in cyberspace by somebody who knows how to manipulate it."

Danae blinked. She hadn't heard such a carefully calculated tone of voice from Larissa since they'd been ten.

Alekhsiy glanced at Sasha, then silently sauntered onto the steps, cutting off the only easy observation point for eavesdroppers.

Larissa stared at Danae, as if willing her to understand. "You know, really nasty stuff?" she added. She glanced around and Danae followed her look. Nobody was anywhere nearby.

"I'd be very sorry if anything I said hurt somebody I cared about. Please forgive me," she whispered. She blinked fiercely, willing back a tear.

Danae's heart clenched and she quickly put her hand on her arm. "Yes, of course."

"Thanks." Larissa gave her a quick hug, sniffling.

"You can see more of our son after we get home, when I upload some more pictures." Sasha gripped his wife's elbow.

"Watchers? Even here?" she hissed.

"Turner? Damn right," he retorted under his breath.

Danae's stomach dropped out from underneath her soy latte. She'd found a little soot above the electric plug in the bathroom this morning, making last night's scare a reality rather than a nightmare.

Alekhsiy slipped his hand into hers, giving her strength.

"We'd better be going." Larissa looked over their heads

from the step below them. "Jenny's shaking out the banner and Feodor is pumping up his bagpipe."

"Coward!" It felt good to tease Larissa again. "Just because you're not marching in the Corps this year doesn't mean you get to skulk indoors for an extra fifteen minutes."

A smile broke across her pal's face. "Oh yes, it does—if it means I don't have to listen to Feodor massacre 'Scotland the Brave' again. Although I heard he's finally managed to memorize the 'Homage to the Red God.'"

Alekhsiy spluttered and choked on his chai. Then he signed himself, using a Torhtremer rune, and bowed his head in prayer.

The line of warriors shuffled forward again, like a Zemlayan millipede sauntering across the desert sands, lazily certain it could destroy anything who challenged it. It was a smaller parade than the one that had filled Atlanta's streets less than an hour ago. In some ways, this group down in the earth's bowels formed the kernel for that gaudy procession.

They were compressed into a single narrow corridor, supposed to be cowed by decades of administrators' maxims. Yet they joked and aided each other to appear their best, tweaking a leg guard here or retying a gorget there to better protect a vulnerable neck. They ranged from youths fretting over their first bout to narrow-eyed veterans looking to add one more to their roster of accomplishments. They all had the same goal—to appear their best and be authorized to fight in GriffinCon's great tournaments.

They were going to war against bureaucrats and tasteless bits of paper that sought to rob a warrior of his chi. Surely they would win, with the Red God of War's blessing and each other's aid.

Alekhsiy stepped to the other wall and assessed them yet

again. Good men and women, by and large, certainly of character and solid fodder for an army. If he could take them back to Torhtremer . . .

His lady giggled very softly and his heart lifted. How long had it been since he'd enjoyed her? An hour? Too long, at any rate.

She shifted slightly, readjusting the paraphernalia hanging from her waist. She was his squire at this event and therefore wore the straps and belts with all of the magical pouches containing the gear he didn't need for battle. After last night, leaving it in the room had seemed the poorest of options. Fire Wind, his axe, had been forged in dragon's breath. Legends surrounded it, as much as the imperial armory's trappings had when Mykhayl gave it to him. It had settled far too easily into its pouch, bespeaking the generations of magic around it—more swiftly than Ice Wolf, the sword his father had created for him. Heart's blood had gone into that and an ocean of love—but no spellworking except that of a master smith.

Alekhsiy hadn't been surprised that his warrior's gear looked well on Danae's cadet's uniform. He had been considerably startled that it had accepted her. But it was bespelled to understand battle necessity, such as the need to match the strange materials used in this tournament. Similar pragmatism must rule its choice to hide itself against her.

"Danae!" The deep young voice rang through the hallway, utterly joyous and completely sure of its welcome.

Alekhsiy immediately, thoughtlessly, drew his dagger and whirled to face the challenger. No man, however young, would take her from him.

She was so beautiful, so strong and supple. Her elegance was so perfectly summed up by her swan neck under her intricately braided hair—clean, graceful, and yet complex.

"Hi, Colin!" Danae jabbed Alekhsiy in the ribs hard enough to be felt through unenchanted chain mail. "You sound great—and so adult," she added sotto voce.

Ice crashed his veins and his hand shook, making it hard to sheath Finger Nipper. Somehow the gray gods of Chaos had not been watching and only Danae had noticed his folly, not his fellow warriors. Had their hours of passion so deepened her sorceress's hold on him that he guarded her more ferociously than any white-collared lynx circled its mate?

At least he didn't have to worry about her wanting another man's child. Although if he thought she'd willingly bear his own, he'd happily hatch a thousand plots to destroy those condoms she always insisted on.

"Colin." He forced himself to hold out his hand.

"Awesome." The youth pumped it thoughtlessly hard, more interested in staring at his armor than Danae. "Your mail looks incredible without the surcoat over it. How heavy is it?"

"Enough." Considerably heavier than it had been, since it had apparently deemed the lightness spell inadvisable for the tournament.

"What are you doing down here?" Danae queried. "Aren't you in the youth tournament?"

"Oh yeah, but I've already got my papers."

Braggart. Alekhsiy reminded himself again not to be jealous. Every warrior surmounted the different stages in his own time.

"Morning, all." Nora strolled up. "My pushy son wants to ask you about your GED."

"Now?" Danae's eyebrows flew up. "And why's that?"

"If it doesn't bother Alek," Colin said hastily. "I wouldn't want to distract him before a bout."

"No, of course not." Danae had already filled out the paperwork for him and the practice bout with Kyle should be pure joy.

"It's the only time I could be sure to catch you," Colin added.

"If it's okay with Alek, it's fine with me. Why do you want to know? Are you thinking of leaving school?" Her usual vivid openness had changed to the steady discipline of an experienced bureaucrat, all wary eyes, thin mouth, and still hands. Why such a difference?

"To work with my dad and grandfather. There's more than enough business now, what with the Torhtremer reproductions and all."

Nora crossed her arms over her chest and tightly folded her lips.

"I know Mom has advanced degrees but she says you don't. And you're the one who became a professional ballerina. So what's in it for me?"

Danae flinched subtly, shadows flickering through her green-gold eyes.

Alekhsiy quickly calculated the distance to the end of the line. Not soon enough. He should have followed his first instincts and gutted the assertive cockerel.

"I got serious about ballet when I was thirteen and took so many dance classes I basically forgot about high school. I was a full-time dancer by seventeen, at the company where I met your mother." She slipped her ring out from inside her tunic and stared down the hallway, turning the heavy gold over and over.

Her voice was so soft Alekhsiy had to strain to listen.

"They had a program where you could mix ballet with school. You could come out of there with a Bachelor of Fine Arts or you could leave with a GED, no ability to even balance a checkbook, and the prospect of a broken-down body in a few years because you'd performed so much." Her voice trailed off into pain-shadowed huskiness. "I chose dance before all else."

"That won't happen to me!" Colin protested.

"Want to bet?" Danae hurled back, looking him in the eyes for the first time. "Do you know how many charities specialize in helping people who are injured and out of work? Do you know how many high school dropouts are helpless and starving because they can't read or write or handle money?"

"You can make bucks without school," he protested. "Besides, I've got family to help."

"Oh crap, Colin." Nora rubbed her forehead and closed her eyes.

"That's right—but they can disappear at a moment's notice." Danae's voice lurched into heartrending pain, like the memory of tears shed for so long they'd stamped themselves into her vocal cords. "When I was twelve, my family called to say they were picking me up at dance camp. Next thing I knew, they'd been burned to death on the interstate and I had nobody."

His poor, poor darling. Alekhsiy's heart lurched to a stop. How could she have endured so much and still survived? His mother and younger sisters cried extravagantly at the least threat to their loved ones. But his lady was lost and utterly alone. He couldn't imagine such darkness.

He wrapped his arm around her waist, giving her the only comfort he openly could. She leaned against him, strands of dark hair drifting against his mail like ghosts. The warriors around them had turned away slightly, giving them an illusion of privacy.

"I'm sorry," Colin offered. "I forgot."

"I'm luckier than most." She shrugged and brought herself erect, tearing away a piece of his heart.

"Getting a GED was easy because I already had a very good education," she stated brusquely, as if restating an old argument still sharp-edged by ancient grief and anger. "I figured out how to beat the system and became an emancipated minor. It wasn't that hard to pull off, since I had no parents and was living on my own, and the trustees didn't want the hassle of looking over my weird contracts. Plus, I had plenty of money from the insurance settlements after my folks' deaths."

"Trustees had a field day suing the bastards who caused the accident," Nora muttered, her lips pulled back in a snarl.

Alekhsiy nodded to her, baring his teeth slightly in perfect agreement. Money was not enough of a penalty for him. He'd have chosen something more creative, such as boiling tar or slow poison. Still, if that was how this strange world chose to mete out justice, he'd reluctantly accept it.

"And left you alone with paperwork for family," Nora grumbled.

Danae frowned at her.

"Hey, I'm working on my college degree. So don't think I've given up on school just because I pretty much live, eat, and sleep ballet."

"You are?" Nora gaped at her.

"It's a bitch, but correspondence classes help. All of us kids promised Dad we'd do it, and how do you say no to a Navy fighter pilot?"

Of course, she'd be a warrior's daughter. Alekhsiy tilted his chin a little higher and forced his thoughts away from her heart's emptiness.

"That's why you wear his Annapolis ring. Cool." Colin looked like he'd found another new horizon.

"It survived Vietnam and the fire that killed my dad. It's got gold from other family class rings and my great-grandfather's diamond. Plus, it's been baptized in every ocean. I figure it'll see me through my bachelors' degree." Her jaw jutted stubbornly.

"I'm sure you'll make it." Nora hugged her.

"You'll be a superb scholar." Alekhsiy gave her a quick hug, laced with gentleness.

"Thanks. It's got to be easier than writing my first story was. That one took me a dozen tries to come up with anything I liked."

"Your first with Alekhsiy, where his lover was that temple priestess. I loved reading how she got that uptight soldier to loosen up. Yum." Nora licked her lips.

Alekhsiy stared at Nora, then shuddered. She knew about that episode, too? How many women—and men—had read Danae's stories, anyway? Did Nora and Larissa, perhaps even Sasha and Kyle, know everything Danae did about him? He'd always enjoyed having his little dancer share his adventures but how many strangers? And especially that moment in his life.

Bhaikhal custom dictated that every highborn male and female mastered the carnal arts, as if it was another skill such as swordplay or music. Northerners, like his clan, did not set a similar premium on its formal knowledge and he'd been too consumed by warfare—in the academy and the army itself to pay much attention. Plus, his own fastidiousness had kept him well away from camp followers and most hasty liaisons with other soldiers. But after Mykhayl had emerged as the heir, Alekhsiy's lack of high-level carnal skills had become a vulnerability for spies to exploit. Yet once again, his little dancer had protected him with one of her most sensual and lengthy adventures. He'd greatly enjoyed flaunting himself to her—but he could cut out the eyes of anyone else who'd seen it.

"And there was the one where Alekhsiy got involved with that tavern keeper's wife. Oh yeah." Nora hummed a dance tune, a beatific smile floating across her face.

Alekhsiy suspected he shared a similar expression. He

wouldn't have foregone those adventures for a thousand dragon rides, even if it meant occasionally displaying himself.

"No, I visited Torhtremer in my original story," his lady announced.

"What?" She'd traveled between worlds? Hell-born terrors sank their claws into Alekhsiy's skin.

"Really?" asked Nora. "I never read it. What did you do?"

"I wanted to be present for the muster of the clans in the first book, to actually see and feel it. But there wasn't much plot so I destroyed the story."

Praise be to all the gods. The tale could not have been significant, else he would have felt its events. When he returned home, he'd sacrifice a hundred—no, a thousand baskets of the finest red and white roses on Bhaikhal's high altars.

"I'd have liked to read it. Your writing is so vivid," Nora mused.

"It happened the night Corinne Carson and her sister were killed in that huge condo fire. In all the panic and excitement, I forgot to tell you about it."

"Well, that explains it." Nora pursed her lips. "And when you say you destroyed something, you go all the way."

"Mom, how good would my grades have to be if I wanted to attend Annapolis?"

All three adults stared at Colin.

"Superb," answered Alekhsiy, the first to recover. If that was the academy that had trained the warrior who'd bred his lady, then only the finest need apply there.

Or here. They turned the final corner and came face to face with an open foyer, backed by a solid desk. A man and a woman, dressed in sheets of armor rather than woven links, stood on a colorful carpet. Two men, dressed in brilliant, flowing linens and silks, sat behind the desk, rapidly scribbling in what Danae had termed "laptops."

They had finally reached GriffinCon's marshals. Alekhsiy's mouth went a little dry, despite years of experience in dueling.

"We'll see you upstairs." Nora clapped him on the arm. "Good luck; I'm sure you'll be approved in no time."

He tucked his conical helmet in the crook of his arm and advanced to meet his judges, hoping the spell would successfully color Ice Wolf's edge and not take the amateurs' safety requirement as an insult to its honor.

Boris Turner took another swig of vitaminwater and surveyed the gymnasium, his binoculars close to his hand. He could observe all of the approval bouts from the stands, although normally he wouldn't bother.

Swords hissed and clanked against each other, accented by the crowd's ebb and flow of conversation and applause. New sweat lightly stung the nose, like the promise of pain to come.

GriffinCon had used the standard tournament setup, including the high platform with the stupidly expensive floor he'd donated to this stuffy local college. Just another one of the little things he'd done to make sure ConComm would listen to logic for once this year. The overall conference committee had to come to its senses sometime.

Next year he might donate better seats for the gymnasium. Solo bouts on Saturday and team bouts on Sunday, with finals on Sunday night at the big arena—hell, no, he didn't spend much time in these stands. But that didn't mean he enjoyed squeezing his ass into a steel-and-plastic trap, either. Losing all that weight had helped but not enough. The publicity from improving everybody else's comfort might finally win him a place on ConComm, too. *Prissy bastards who didn't recognize a good argument when they hear it . . .*

Dammit, he'd built his empire off good technology—whether using, creating, or selling it. He knew how to make a winning pitch, whether it took sweet words or a strong arm. He'd get GriffinCon to change its programming so others could start hearing the truth about Torhtremer, no matter what it took.

And he'd have the right seventh book written for them to read, too. The loser finally wins it all, gets the crown, and *all* the girls.

Boris grinned. He paid for women regularly but what would it be like having a Dragon's Hoard at your beck and call? A hundred women just begging to do anything you want, any time you want it? And next year, when you get bored or they wear out, there's another hundred more on the way to liven things up all over again.

Oh yeah, baby.

He replaced the bottle in his duffel bag and picked up his binoculars again. The current approval bout featured a duel between two Torhtremer personas, who were both fighting at full speed—or close to it—while their squires watched from the holding area.

He'd never thought to see Danae Livingston, the proud dancer and veteran of so many GriffinCons that ConComm sought her advice at least once a year, waiting submissively behind ropes.

She broke into applause, followed a moment later by people in the stands.

He gritted his teeth and refocused his glasses.

Harrison slid into the seat next to him.

"Well?" Boris demanded, certain nobody was close enough to listen in. The rest of his men would see to that.

"No news on what happened to the first set of bugs. The second set died this morning—"

"Exactly when the targets returned to their room after the parade?"

"Yes, sir. But we don't know where those electronics went either." Harrison's voice was as carefully colorless as the rest of his appearance. It was only one of the reasons the FBI had taken so long to put him between bars. "So I can't confirm the identity of CrystalTiger, although no other candidates have appeared."

"Trash chute." Boris put down his binoculars this time. "They must have thrown both sets into it."

"Probably. But this set was much smaller than the first. Frankly, I don't see how they could have found them. They show no signs of having the necessary specialized equipment."

"Friends?"

"Unknown, sir." Harrison shrugged.

Boris frowned. Harrison's brain was almost as sharp as his own. "What about a probe?"

"From the neighbors? One side is planning a large party and has declined to move, no matter how big the incentive. They've already sent out the invitations and say it would be too difficult to change the location."

"The lazy, stupid cows!"

"The connecting room is occupied by the targets' friends, a Texas policeman and his wife. He's not an electronics specialist but he quickly showed signs of unease when I spoke to him. I did not want to press the subject in case Miss Livingston had mentioned the bugs to him."

"Crap." Boris drummed his fingers on his very expensive optics. "Can you get better gear?"

"Already on the way."

Boris stared at the two men advancing and retreating across the floor below, flashing steel weaving a web around them. Harrison waited patiently, his eyes on their attendants, the clever man. Of course, he also knew who'd bought his probation.

"What about when they're in public? They did march in the parade this morning."

"We were unable to get a fix on them, sir. Our expert believes there's too much crowd noise and background electronics to isolate them. We're also limited in our selection of directional microphones by the need to be discreet."

"True."

He might have to act without solid data and he hated that. Damn, damn, damn.

"What do you know about her companion?"

Harrison, thank God, already had the answer. "He's here on a live action role play, as Alek Alekseiovich."

"And a very boring name." Boris snorted in disgust. Fellow should have put more creativity into it.

"Is it, sir?" Harrison sounded genuinely fascinated for once.

"Oh yeah, it's close to some of the names in the saga. What else?"

"There is no record of his real name anywhere. He registered for GriffinCon using only his persona and paid cash."

"Really?" *Was the man trying to hide?*

"Actually, Miss Livingston paid for him with cash. He obtained cash through barter for some hair ornaments and has never paid in plastic for anything."

"No credit cards?"

"None have been observed, sir."

Boris sat back and stared at Harrison. That was the most unusual behavior he'd ever encountered. Everybody had credit cards these days, even if they cleared up the balance each month.

Still, the guy would have to leave a paper trail someplace else. "Hotel room or insurance?"

"He's staying in Miss Livingston's room. We have not yet checked the insurance policy shown on his tournament registration."

"Do that."

"Already in process, sir; we only hacked into that database five minutes ago."

Boris grunted acknowledgment and scanned Danae Livingston's companion more closely. Why would she, Miss High-and-Mighty-Spirit-of-the-Law-Contractually, go out of her way to help some dude skate through a conference without leaving a paper trail?

"He's pulling his blows," he muttered.

"Sir?"

He watched for a few minutes longer to gather more data.

"The approval process has three parts," he began, still studying the man. "First you have to convince the marshals that your armor's okay and that you're not stupid enough to act badly."

"Very cautious fellows, these marshals."

Oh yeah. But they were human and humans could be bought.

"Then you duel a well-known fighter at half-speed."

"Still proving you can behave yourself," Harrison filled in.

"And that you can call your own blows and your opponents."

"What?" Harrison squeaked.

Boris allowed himself to savor the first time he'd ever startled Harrison. Then he put down his glasses, satisfied with his conclusions.

"Yes, each fighter decides how severe a blow is."

"But that means . . ." Harrison frowned, a world of implications spinning behind his pale gray eyes.

"It's done for safety."

"But the marshals?" Harrison's full attention came back to him.

"Can step in, of course," Boris purred, "should they feel the need. But that's very, very rare."

Harrison understood immediately, of course.

"I'll have them all profiled immediately, sir. With special attention paid to personal weaknesses."

"I knew I could rely on you, Harrison." Boris folded his hands and watched his future opponent block a thrust with a lightning twist of his shield.

Harrison's gaze followed his. "Might I venture to say, sir, that I believe you're faster than he is?"

"Thank you. And yes, I am"—he smirked privately—"Even at times like that one, when the dude countered at full speed. However, if you continue to watch him, you'll notice . . . Ah! See that round?"

"Where he started with his sword held high and wound up staggering back?" Harrison frowned. "I'm no expert with the sword"—he was, in fact, a third-degree karate black belt—"but didn't he hesitate until the last second?"

"Yes, and basically lost the exchange."

"Perhaps it's because he's dueling his troupe leader."

"So? Would your sensei approve of you holding back under similar circumstances, especially when this is only for admission into the tournament?"

"Not at all." Harrison's answer came promptly.

Had Alekseiovich just glanced up at the stands and nearly slipped? Was he afraid of the much more powerful Boris Turner?

How very delightful. Maybe he did have time to order a pair of prostitutes before the first bout after all, even though it always took extra time to pay them off.

Boris cracked his knuckles one by one, like the way his true sword could shatter that fool's rattan weapon.

"My guess is he's very aware of his audience in the stands."

"It has been a long time since I've met anyone of his caliber, sir." Harrison's jaw tightened.

"That brute is essentially Miss Livingston's bodyguard. One way or another, I will speak to her and she will write my book. Nobody, but nobody, is allowed to refuse a deal with Boris Turner or I wouldn't have my business. If he doesn't understand that, then he simply has to leave the scene, one way or another."

"It will be a pleasure to assist you, sir."

SEVEN

"You're limping!" accused Danae. Of all the stubborn, thick-headed beasts on this earth, men were surely the worst. "You can't tell me that a man who danced for hours last night walks like this. This is not your normal gait."

Alekhsiy raised an eyebrow at her and followed her into the hotel lobby.

"And a one, and a two, and a—" he chanted, swaying his hips in one of the dances she'd taught him and deliberately emphasizing the syncopated beat.

She choked back a laugh. Vikings—or, more accurately, northern Torhtremer generals—had never been idolized for their ability to cha cha cha. In fact, anyone who'd seen six feet four of muscle, covered with chain mail and bedecked with sword and dagger, would probably have run shrieking to see him swivel his hips to an imaginary beat.

Or grabbed him for a taste.

"Any injury left untreated will only grow worse." She forced herself back to her original topic.

"Sweeting, let us first celebrate your award for a beautiful hall costume and my acceptance as a warrior of GriffinCon." He scooped her into his arm, and neatly dodged a trio of peacock-blue clad Kyristari troopers from the Varrain universe clustered around a virulently green Incredible Hulk.

"With a drink in the bar? You need a long, hot bath." Besides, she'd much rather wait to snuggle him until his armor convinced itself to do the silk thing again, rather than being woven steel rings. They'd already privately stowed his shield into the proper pouch and told Kyle they'd sent it back to the hotel with friends. "Your opponent thwacked you a good one across your thigh. Do you think a dancer doesn't notice these things?"

He broke stride at the bar's edge and shot her a slightly sheepish look. "I didn't expect how much force it would take for the required laming blow to send me to my knees."

"Do you mean Kyle surprised you?" Surely he had far more combat experience than her friend did. And the smith was even afraid of spiders, although everybody had their phobias.

Like the rest of the hotel bars and restaurants, this one looked down and across the hotel lobby's multiple terraces, which were filled with hundreds of people. Above them, an enormous Lucite sail pulsed green and yellow, while a huge TV showed the latest images from GriffinCon. Smaller TV screens were scattered around the edges, offering updates on schedule or prizes won. Bartenders strutted and posed, pouring drinks like works of art. Their clientele was an even more widely varied cross-section of humanity than the rest of GriffinCon, ranging from T-shirts and jeans to those so heavily costumed it wasn't clear how they sat down, mixed with expressions ranging from harried and sleepless to dazed bemusement. Mental attitude, as ever, had nothing to do with the amount or quality of clothing.

"Somewhat." Alekhsiy shrugged. "The business of fighting from the ground is a new one for me."

Her mouth rounded into an O. "He did surprise you! Just wait until I tell Nora." She chortled softly

"We need to find a private table." A muscle ticked in his cheek and he surveyed the golden room. Suddenly he came up onto his toes and then cut through the crowd, taking ruthless advantage of his height and intimidating presence. They slid into a small booth moments ahead of the next contender.

"Poor darling, you really don't want to go back to the room, do you?" Danae cooed and petted his thigh out of sight and under the chain mail.

He raised an eyebrow at her. "Will you take shameless advantage of me here, my lady?"

"Certainly I will." She batted her eyes at him and widened her grip. Could she find where he'd been hurt? Maybe a little massage would help.

Or maybe a little foreplay would be better. Just a little more to the center and up a little higher, under the crease of his mail to where his cock nestled.

"Minx," he said feelingly and wrapped his fingers around her wrist. "There."

Ah, he wanted his bruise attended to instead. Well, that was certainly much more acceptable in public. She rubbed it gently, concentrating on healing thoughts.

The enormous sail, three stories high, rippled like a black and white test pattern—or an Arctic snowstorm—and filled the bar with shadows.

"Can we be overheard?" Danae asked softly.

"Eavesdroppers?" Alekhsiy responded, equally quiet. He

shook his head. "Not a chance. Whether they try to listen or watch, my armor will protect us and punish them."

"With what? Another electric shock?"

"No, I suspect it destroyed the bugs because it knew not what else to do. Instead it will visit the spies with a hangover, stronger and faster depending on how mightily they strive to watch me. Their heads will ache and their stomachs knot until they cannot concentrate. It is akin to that suffered by those who have indulged in riotous liquors for far too long."

"Is it very bad?"

"They will seek their chamber pots for hours if they hunt me too fiercely." His blue eyes were clear and calm as his sword's razor-sharp edge. "It can kill."

"You're joking." *A deadly spell?* Here and now, next to her? Her fingers flexed with the need to either push him away or pull him closer and explore more of the chain mail she'd thought she understood.

"I tested a general's tolerance once as a cadet."

"Once, huh?"

"Only once." He raised an eyebrow at her and she swallowed hard.

"Okay, you're not joking." She couldn't touch it, not here, but she could ask about it. "Does it guard a large conversation with you?"

"It is far nastier the smaller the group, such as the two of us."

Okay, that sounded closer to something like a microphone with a limited range. She understood those.

"Would you like me to order you a beer?" Danae asked softly.

"Gods, yes." He closed his eyes, his hair spilling along the cushions. "But I can manage the phrases."

So he could, could he? His spells had odd quirks if they could produce the names of liquid refreshments but not protect his limbs. She snorted in disgust and went back to massaging him.

Or maybe magic was intuitive, like dancing. Something that leaped into being with luck and skill and talent, rather than from a formula.

The waiter arrived and departed with their order, silent testimony that Alekhsiy could enunciate alcohols.

"What did you think of the other bouts?" she asked to change her thought's direction. It was better than yelling at his damn spell.

"Kyle is very, very good. His archers are excellent, as are his wrestlers."

"Oh, the karate dudes?"

"Is that what you call the style? I would like to learn it. I recognized more of the other one that your friends used."

"Kung fu." She nodded. "It includes a lot of schools, plus weapons." She gently kneaded Alekhsiy under the chain mail, pressing and releasing.

He hissed softly.

"Sorry. I must have pushed a little too hard." She stretched her palm out, crooning to him silently.

The TV screens hissed and popped.

The gold chain holding Danae's father's ring scratched her neck. *What the hell?*

She'd worn the same chain every day since she was thirteen and had slid the battered ring onto it the night before her parents' funeral. It had taken months for all the blood and scorch marks to wash out from the accident. Some of the dents never had. She liked to think that the water of Earth's seven seas, which it had been baptized in, had kept her safe during auditions. Her skin and bones certainly knew every kink and twist in the chain perfectly, so well that she had to consciously remember to take it off before a performance.

She used her free hand to lift it out from inside her tunic and drape it down the front, over the silk. The old diamond flashed briefly in the light, a legacy from her great-great-grandfather's tour of duty on the China Station.

"I need to heal quickly," Alekhsiy said under his breath and tossed back a large draught of beer.

"If Kyle's team is so good, why?"

"Because Turner's team is equally skilled." He eyed her sideways. "And Turner himself is fast, very quick indeed."

His tone sent a shiver down her spine.

"Just how speedy are we talking about, considering you've only seen him in a demo this morning to open the tournament?" she demanded.

"Damn near catalyst fast," he said flatly and finished the rest of his beer. "Far quicker than I am, certainly. And the tournament is seeded so that The Northern Wastes will meet Yevgheniy's Spears in the finals."

"Are you sure?" she asked faintly, crushed ice having taken the place of her vertebrae.

He shot her a telling look and signaled for the waiter.

"Okay, that was a stupid question. You've probably come face-to-face with the Dark Warrior more often than anybody else except Mykhayl."

The great sail went dark, followed an instant later by all the lights.

"Wretched mortals!" boomed a very deep voice from somewhere underneath their feet. And yet it seemed to echo through their bones as if it came from everywhere and nowhere. "Welcome to my world, fools!"

Alekhsiy sprang to his feet, his axe in his hand, its blade glowing brilliantly blue.

The enemy? Here?

"Shit!" She elbowed him hard and he stowed it back in his pocket before anybody else noticed, cursing under his breath.

A man shouted and somebody else pointed to the air overhead.

Danae vaulted onto the tabletop so she could see better.

A giant alligator snapping turtle swam over their heads, uglier than sin and more powerful than the worst nightmares. Its beak alone looked large enough to swallow a man whole whenever it chose. Its edges sparkled and the building's other side could only be faintly glimpsed through it. But when it dived onto a balcony, everybody there screamed and ran for cover.

Azherbhai? Danae's stomach promptly converted itself into knots.

The Imperial Terrapin chuckled, infinitely old and evil. The temperature in the great lobby promptly dropped by thirty degrees. Teeth chattered amid its helpless audience.

"Begone, foul brute," Alekhsiy shouted and ran out of the bar. "You have no place here."

Danae dropped a couple of twenties on the table and followed him, the ring glowing softly on her chest. This was worse than performing at Lincoln Center with a drunken partner when she never knew what would happen next, only that it would probably be more appalling than the last dance step.

"Foolish ones, anything I see is mine." Azherbhai chuckled again, chilling the air even further. "Deliver up my creature and I may choose to depart. Or perchance not."

He circled lazily, snapping at anybody foolish enough to stand erect on an escalator. They flattened themselves, shrieking, and he laughed.

"Begone!" Alekhsiy roared from the balcony overlooking the atrium.

Oh shit, Larissa and Nora were caught on the escalator.

God willing, Alekhsiy had a plan. Danae rushed up to his side and shook her fist at Azherbhai. "Begone!"

Other people's eyes shone and they raised their arms in defiance. "Get out of here!"

Did they think this was a game? Another lead-up to the new trailer? Well, if it got the chi flowing, who cared?

Azherbhai started to dive once again.

Alekhsiy grabbed Danae's shoulder. "Get down!"

"Like hell." She shook her head ferociously at him and he glared at her. But he didn't have time to argue.

How had they banished Azherbhai the last time? "Torhtremer forever!"

Azherbhai was coming closer.

"Torhtremer, Torhtremer, Torhtremer!" Danae chanted, filling her voice with everything she'd ever learned in a lifetime of performance. She wasn't a cheerleader but she could bring an audience to its feet. *Come on, crowd, join in!*

Azherbhai was coming closer.

"Torhtremer!" Alekhsiy was white but he echoed the chant, followed a moment later by Nora and Larissa, then the rest of the crowd. It swelled through the atrium in an instant, the echoes singing to each other like a massed choir.

Danae pictured a wall of shields rising between the people and the Imperial Terrapin on the lobby's every level, like the interlinked shields protecting a Viking ship. The fists were spears, charged with fiery chi and ready to go war.

"Torhtremer!" The ring pulsed warmly against her heart.

Azherbhai swooped down. Down . . .

Varrain look-alikes and Kyristari warriors, Star Wars stormtroopers and the dragon riders of Pern, superheroes and pointy-eared swordbearers, anime characters and time-traveling Brits and more stomped their feet and clapped their hands, driving their feet into the building's bones. "Torhtremer, Torhtremer, Torhtremer!"

Shields shimmered into being along the golden balconies, green and gold overlapping silver and blue. Spear tips bristled between them in fiery scarlet.

Azherbhai pulled out at the last minute, only inches above Alekhsiy's sword. He clacked his great beak until it sounded like a machine gun and disappeared in a puff of foul-smelling black smoke.

Danae collapsed against the railing and commanded her lungs to start breathing again. In and out. In and out.

Alekhsiy slammed his sword back into its sheath and snatched her against his chest.

She held on, grateful for the brutal reality of rough chain mail and steel-buckled leather. He needed to heal as quickly as possible.

"What was that all about?" Nora and Larissa rushed up to them, agog to learn the news.

"Hell, if they spent that much money on holograms for promo," a female Southern drawl pronounced, "the movie should be spectacular."

Alekhsiy choked and Danae closed her eyes, unable to respond. Hollywood was a better explanation than the truth, anyway.

Danae's hotel room was a blessed oasis of peace and quiet after the hubbub outside. Even the elevators, normally a whirlwind of multiple conversations, had focused on only one topic—the amazing *special effects*, whatever they were, needed to produce Torhtremer's great villain.

Alekhsiy groaned and kicked the door shut. He could guess what had produced Azherbhai: Somehow the sorcerer was coming closer and closer to Turner, the Imperial Terrapin's future catalyst. The hungry beast could sense the swelling chi across the void and had sent his own in search. If the two life forces ever linked up and the catalyst jumped, there would be bitter war once again in Torhtremer.

Alekhsiy smacked the wall, furious at his own failure to find the sorcerer who held the gate's key. But if Danae was tortured into creating a tale where the Imperial Terrapin destroyed Torhtremer, all was lost, too.

Hiss, pop! Hiss, hiss, pop, pop!

"Guess our friends came back while we were gone," Danae announced and pointed at the desk lamp's base. A delicate plume of smoke drifted into the air and vanished, followed by the now-familiar acrid stench.

"Thrice-damned spiders, spinning their webs where any man can see." He yanked his axe into sight, biting his lip at the resultant twinges. Within a minute, he'd found all the hidden bugs.

"They're smaller this time," he pronounced with disfavor. "A flea would be comelier."

"Turner respects us more." Danae hung over his shoulder to see them but was careful not to touch them. "These must be much more expensive. They're probably state-of-the-art."

"Do you mean the best he can obtain?"

"Quite possibly." Her ring flashed briefly, as it had when Azherbhai visited, and fell quiet.

"I will remove them to the trash chute." And then seek sweet oblivion in her arms.

"Don't." She caught his arm and he swung back to face her.

"Why not? We do not want such foulness near us."

"Turner's men have probably tapped into the hotel's surveillance system."

"Spies and corruption there, too? Faugh!"

"I'll wrap them up and put them in Larissa's room. They can go out in her trash, which Turner probably won't search."

"Her husband might notice." Sasha was a man to journey with on a long hunt or to stand beside in a shield wall.

"Not if I use a fast-food bag. She's very fond of that stuff." She started hunting amid the clutter on her floor.

"Very well." Truth be told, he was too tired to argue.

Seconds later, he could have flung back his head and howled. By Chaos's gray gods, there was no justice in this universe. How could her appalling clutter yield up what his immaculate quarters would never have provided?

She knotted the tiny black dots into a clear plastic bag, bedecked with colorful characters and foreign lettering. Then she disappeared through the connecting door, still grinning triumphantly.

He shook his head and reached over his shoulder for his axe. "Ouch!"

He doubled over, unable to fully lower his arm. Kyle had nicked him more than once on his arms and ribs. Plus, there'd been the void's brutal kick onto that filthy box in the back alley.

"Accursed spawn of demented scriveners! Filthy rules fit only for drooling idiots!" If it hadn't been for the absurd need to be approved—him, war leader for all Torhtremer—he'd never be in this predicament. And he hadn't yet tried to take off his breeches, covering where the much harder blows had landed.

He gritted his teeth and fought his arm back down to his side.

"Poor baby," Danae crooned, reappearing at a flagrantly inopportune moment. "Do you want me to fetch a doctor?"

"A chirurgeon? No, it's not necessary." By the gods, he wouldn't tolerate any such furor. "My armor will—"

"Heal you?" She clucked her tongue at his nod. "Pity it can't make itself even more useful and take itself off."

"Don't be absurd," he protested. "That would be impossible. It only heals the worst injuries, enough to keep me in battle."

"I will never understand magic," she muttered. "Come on, let's get you out of all those layers. I've got a ton of Earth remedies to help you, or just a basic massage. You've got to be one hundred percent for tomorrow."

"One hundred percent?" By the gods, the language here was enough to plague the most skilled scribe. Why would anyone wish to combine a "per" with a "cent," let alone multiply them a hundredfold?

"Completely healed, buster, if at all possible." Her lovely jaw was very firmly set.

"Aye," he agreed, "one hundred percent." He would agree to anything, so long as he didn't have to tax his brain with it. His lady had recovered far quicker from Azherbhai's assault than he had, praise the Mother of All Life.

She was a very puissant sorceress, indeed. She'd built the assembly's chi into a wall capable of stopping an imperial beast's chi with amazing speed. Then she'd leveled it at the Imperial Terrapin's projection and stood her ground, thereby forcing him to retreat. Oh, Alekhsiy had had the joy of standing at her back and he'd taught her the chant yesterday. But 'twas she who'd stood in the forefront and his chi that had been drained.

But she eased off his armor as if she was a mother duck, tut-tutting and cooing over every bit of stiffness he showed. Surcoat, hauberk, gambeson, undertunic—she took them all until he was left in only his shirt and chausses. Once they were gone, he'd be bare to her for the first time in daylight. Did he have the energy to pursue that pleasant thought?

She'd closed one set of curtains, allowing a pale, diffused light to fill the room. She glowed under it like an ebony and ivory goddess. She'd stripped off her own uniform and wore only a slim, tight-fitting chemise and trousers, with her ring. She'd adjusted the temperature, making the space feel like a warm spring day.

He was the High King's brother and hundreds had fought for his attention. But how many people had ever paid attention to him and his comfort of their own free will, without hoping to gain something from it?

Yes, she understood the need to fight Azherbhai and his allies but she could have healed him for that purpose with magic. These arrangements were a gift from her heart. His own heart flexed and allowed itself to open up, just a little.

She dropped to her knees before him.

Shock brought his breath rattling to a stop. A sorceress kneeling to him?

"May I?" she asked sweetly with a sidelong glance at his fly, hidden now under his shirt.

He dragged air back into his lungs. "Certainly," he agreed with what grace he could. His rod warmed and laid its head high on his thigh to watch.

Danae unlaced him quickly and eased his chausses down over his hips. Her tenderness with his rod and balls was capped by a quick kiss before she stripped the linen all the way down to his knees and ankles. His brain flew south.

"Step, please?" she asked.

He rested his hands on her shoulders and stepped out of his chausses, unable to speak or even think well.

"You have beautiful legs." She encircled one ankle and then lightly rubbed his calf.

He shot a disbelieving look at her. But no wise man would argue with a lady under these circumstances.

She attended to his other calf as well, leaving warmth and slow relaxation behind. Her hands moved upward to his thighs, finding every place where he'd been battered. She stroked gently, her thumbs always moving upward toward his center.

His rod swelled a little more but not urgently. His breath settled into the same slow, sweeping pattern as her hands.

She shifted, still on her knees, and kneaded the backs of his calves as delicately as a cat making itself at home. Higher, still higher.

His eyes sank shut and his legs instinctively widened to keep his balance. Bards at the Phoenix Court sang of houris like her, who brought bliss beyond compare.

"Come on." Danae laid her head against his thigh. "Let's get you out of this shirt and down to where you can relax."

He unbuttoned it but she eased it over his head. She pointed to a spot on the floor near the window.

The cozy nest he spotted made his eyes widen in shock. It wasn't what Torhtremer would provide but it was far better than anything he'd hoped for on this dismal, metallic world. For once, both of their neighbors were out and their hotel room was entirely silent. Even the usual roar of the machines from the street was distant and muted.

"By all the gods, what did you do?"

"One comforter from the bed, plus the extra sheets and my massage oil. It's not the greatest massage setup in the world but the best I can manage and they'll put any damages on my bill." She hesitated. "Will it do?" she inquired more tentatively.

"It's delightful," he assured her, his heart leaping like a starred antelope at play.

"Good." She placed both hands on his shoulder blades and gave him a small shove through his shirt. "In that case, how long do you want to stand here?"

He chuckled hoarsely and lifted his arms for her to remove the last garment. Then he dropped down into the nest on his stomach, turned his head to watch, and waited. His pulse rumbled happily through his body.

"You look like a kid in a candy store," she teased.

He didn't bother to deny it, especially when she lit a scented candle. The scent of forests drifted into the air, achingly tangy and barely sweet. She drizzled unscented oil over his legs.

"Hmm." His eyes began to sink shut.

She gently rubbed his feet, taking the time to start slowly, and handled his ankles with the same respect. She stretched them and arched individual tendons until every element felt reborn and utterly relaxed.

She kneaded and stroked his calves until they purred in delight. His knees, too, became her slaves after receiving her attentions. She clucked briefly over his thighs, a sound that barely penetrated the pleasant haze he floated in. His ass was the subject of equally thorough attention, until he vaguely wondered how much she knew about that old cavalry charge.

His shoulders decided she was a goddess and his neck and scalp would have followed her into the farthest northern reaches, simply to stay close to her hands. The ancient headache, always arguing with him unless he was swimming in the western rivers, began to disappear for the first time since he was a cadet.

"Roll over, please," she whispered.

He blearily gathered the strength to do so, his arms and shoulders moving easily for the first time in hours.

He was completely asleep before she finished massaging his face, his bruises and tension completely gone.

The immense ballroom was only dimly lit, its rows of ruthlessly arranged chairs ready to hold an awestruck audience. The stage loomed above it in the front, its starkly neutral spotlight ready to assist or deny the next contestant's attempt at selling himself. A few spectators whispered comments in the back rows and kept their eyes cocked for a juicy tidbit.

It should be heaven, absolute heaven. Theaters like this had protected her for years. The only true differences between them were the people.

Danae glanced down at her watch again and frowned.

"Next, please!" Andrew, the longtime technical director, thumped a few keys on his new PC. Jenny, the costume coordinator, shared more chocolate with her assistant.

"Countess Ramona's portion of the *entr'acte*?" he added. Technically part of Saturday night's showcase but not competitors in the masquerade, they'd perform while the judges deliberated.

"Here!" Danae came down to the front of the stage. Drat it, where the hell were Larissa and Sasha? He was supposed to be the other half of the Saturday night showcase. Had Larissa delayed him somehow? That woman couldn't tell time in units less than days.

Alekhsiy rose from his seat in the first row and sauntered over to her. He leaned his elbow on the stage's apron, putting his head and shoulders beside her feet. His color had definitely improved since his nap and he was moving much more easily.

"Oh hi, Danae." Andrew gave her a small wave. They'd chased each other through GriffinCon's backstage more than once as kids. "I didn't realize you were the model."

"I'm honored to have the opportunity."

Andrew shot her a sidelong glance, clearly wary of her tone, but mercifully kept his mouth shut.

"That's a two-person *entr'acte* on Saturday night and a two-person entry on Sunday." Jenny licked her fingers off and tabbed through her laptop. "Good to have you back, Danae."

"Thanks, Jenny." Danae waited patiently, her hands submissively clasped behind her back. With any luck at all, the candy would keep her sweet tempered enough to overlook any infraction of the rules for once.

"Lord Sasha is supposed to be the other half of Saturday's entry. Where is he?"

No arrival noises from backstage and no visuals from out front. What the hell was Larissa thinking of? Sasha was reliable, even if she wasn't. And Danae was supposed to have met him early enough to have practiced the dance so they could feed cues to the tech crew.

She gritted her teeth and smiled sweetly. "I'm sorry but he hasn't arrived yet. I'm sure he'll be here any moment to assist us." She tried to sound as reasonable as possible, using a tone that her mother, that born-and-bred Southern belle, would have approved of.

"I suspect his job as a law officer may have detained him." Was that last touch too much?

"Danae, your mother wrote these rules."

Oh shit, now came the real lecture. Danae nodded her head meekly and waited.

"Every participant is required to show up for tech rehearsal or another act will be given the opportunity. According to this, you represent a White Sorceress in tiger form and a Torhtremer warrior linked together by chi."

Alekhsiy made a strangled noise. She quickly glanced down at him but he was staring straight ahead, not at her.

"Do you have the costume with you?"

"Mine is body paint." *Stall, Danae, stall.*

A frosty glare greeted that response. "I am sure *you* have managed to make your attire capable of meeting GriffinCon's decency standards. But there's more to costume than that. Can you conduct technical rehearsal right now?"

"Yes, but . . ." She was *sooo* going to strangle Larissa.

"I will be the other half of the act." Alekhsiy came to attention. "Countess Ramona is responsible for my costume."

What the hell was he doing? Panic ripped through her lungs. But this was the theater; she couldn't run.

Jenny's sharp eyes measured his scarlet silk surcoat, pristine chain mail, indigo tunic, and stunning weapons. "Very well," she agreed slowly.

Thank God. At least Larissa would get the credit if they earned any awards for her.

"LED collar and leash, linked to an LED cuff," Andrew read off. "How bright are they?"

"Very. They're made from that LED fabric. Got them here." Danae acquiesced to fate, her stomach playing a roller coaster between her ribs. How the hell could Alekhsiy look so calm?

"Will you be dancing?"

"Brought my own music." She held up the CD.

"And you're going to need some fancy light effects, starting with a fade in?"

"Or maybe very simple—starting with that fade in."

Alekhsiy vaulted onto the stage to stand beside her. He put his arm around her possessively.

She glanced up at him. "Are you sure?" she whispered.

"Nobody else is permitted to touch you, especially in the silver bond."

Why did he call it that? Corinne Carson had never given it a special name in the Torhtremer Saga.

EIGHT

TORHTREMER, M.R. 13

Igoryok struck a flint and lit his torch, careful to shield it from the biting wind. It roared into full life with the sweet sound of old pine knot and the smell of rich tar, which had long been stored in the village's armory. Priests had blessed it years ago, consecrating it to the service of the Realm.

A few men flung up their arms to protect themselves from being dazzled, their white sleeves ghostly against the midsummer snowfall. But they and their northern fellows stared stolidly back at him, their axes and spears as steady as their gaze.

"How many have come to aid the Rock of Tajzyk?" he demanded of the next village's headwoman. Zhenechka was a good woman, even if far too inclined to value her clan's horses over anyone else's.

"Friends, both men and women. They have traveled from here to the Gold River, and from the Plains of Dawn to Tajzyk's Gorge." She paused, her scarred hand steady on her katana's lethally businesslike hilt.

So far? The gods be praised that any had listened to his dream.

"You said to come quietly and prepared for a long journey," she prompted.

"There is trouble in the Realm and all must do what they can. The High King will protect Bhaikhal and the young princes at all costs. But my dream says General Alekhsiy will fight in the north. We cannot reach Bhaikhal in time to help the king but we might be able to aid our former general."

"The king will not like losing so many fighters," she countered fiercely.

"We asked for only those who are free from obligation to family, village, or king. I and my friends will travel north, in hopes of aiding the man who saved my son's life." Into the worst weather since the Dark Warrior was slain. "We are grateful for any who choose to accompany us. Many may not return from this quest."

Igoryok spread his hands in the most courtly bow he could manage. He preferred to let his horses perform the fine tricks, not his bones.

The wind whistled around them, taunting him with the prospect of failure. Zhenechka studied him, her thoughts unreadable behind the many scarves wrapped around her face. Their audience was silent and immovable, almost invisible in their white hunting tunics.

May the Hunter bring them onto the trail leading north . . .

"Then let us make haste and begone, Cousin Igoryok." Zhenechka seized one of the torches from the basket at his feet. "I have a mighty hunger to raise my sword once again beside General Alekhsiy."

She touched her torch's tip to his. It lit immediately with a flash of green and gold, the High King's colors.

The great sign of favor from the Red God of War made Igoryok's jaw drop. But he quickly recovered to join in the cheer. "Torhtremer! Torhtremer! Torhtremer!"

He vaulted onto his horse's back with a young man's fervor, still holding his torch high. His favorite gelding sidled but steadied quickly and soon settled into its smooth, league-eating walk. Zhenechka rode beside him, also carrying her torch aloft.

The others each picked up a torch and lit it from another, one by one, in the ancient tradition of a rescue expedition. The armory's enchanted baskets would ensure a sufficient supply, no matter how many came, and thus the clan's sacred fire would accompany them.

Igoryok swung around in his saddle at the first rise to count their number. A river of fire followed him, brilliant against the snow and darkness, rippling through the river valley as far as the eye could see. Their travel song awoke echoes from the night and warmed the heart.

No doubt they would travel more quietly very soon since the battle ahead would be perilous.

But for now? The hot red lust of the bloodshed to come stirred once against in his belly. He would fulfill his debt and protect a friend, no matter what the cost.

GRIFFINCON
SATURDAY EVENING

Backstage was all shadows and dark corners, waiting to give birth to light. A few bright red LEDs flickered, marking time and readiness. Stage ninjas moved smoothly past, with purpose and joy, careful to stay out of the white lines. The stage was friendly tonight, humming with the crowd's enthusiasm. Tonight's masquerade was for historical and children's costumes, during which Danae and Alekhsiy would provide a brief intermission.

She flexed her shoulders and hands and allowed herself to sink deeper into her inner tigress. She wore a flesh-colored tube top and thong bikini, plus a cap to protect her hair. Her ring nested underneath a patch of white at almost the center of her heart. She had a long, tufted tail that perfectly matched her body. Even her fingernails were black.

But all that mattered now was her performance. She was an Asian tigress, looking like something straight from an ancient Chinese scroll painting—all slender, swirling exotic golden stripes that were only barely outlined in black. While she'd blown those whirling lines onto her body, fire had flickered and leaped hotter and brighter into Alekhsiy's eyes.

She gazed up at him now, ghostly in the faint light from the stage manager's desk. His armor had remade itself into a foot soldier's uniform from an earlier age, with more leather than silk to protect his skin from the mail's heavy iron. His pendant lurked underneath, all gold and brown like a tiger's eyes watching from the forest.

"Me-row," she purred as softly as possible and mimed dragging her claws down his shoulder.

His eyes lit, blazingly blue. "Kitty, kitty," he drawled, a promise and a threat in the same erotic phrase.

Her knees went weak.

"This should be easy," she stammered. She'd planned a very martial bit of choreography, built around some strutting and ka-rate *katas*, or formal exercises, which Sasha the cop should have been able to do without thinking. He and Larissa were watching from out front. They'd arrived in a flurry of excuses and blushes, just in time to catch the end of tech rehearsal.

Alekhsiy twined his fingers through her leash, the silvery metallic fabric oddly delicate against his callused hand, and gave her the lightest of tugs.

Heat floated into her, from his wrist into her throat.

She came eagerly and leaned up to him, totally forgetting they were the next entry to go on. "Purr?"

Her heart was thumping in her chest.

He delicately stroked her under the chin and she arched closer like a blissful cat.

Ah, warmth, such warmth was filling her. She'd had a good warm-up, but this was better than anything she'd ever experienced.

The stage manager tapped him on the shoulder, a reminder which somehow she felt. Drat.

Her eyes slitted shut and she did her best to ignore the previous entry's exit under the few bits of lukewarm applause. Time for the *entr'acte* to bring the audience back to life.

The theater's lights dimmed again. She and Alekhsiy hit their mark on the stage.

A single flute played a call, hauntingly sweet.

Danae flipped on her collar and leash, answered an instant later by Alekhsiy's matching cuff. Brilliant white light gleamed between them, symbolic of the legendary life bond between a Torhtremer soldier and the White Sorceress who'd fought the Imperial Terrapin centuries ago.

And she was suddenly, completely the tigress, teasing her warrior lover and being pulled back to him.

Alekhsiy growled something, not in English, and she laughed. Her pulse was pounding and it was hard to remember the precisely timed choreography.

She ran a paw down his back and whirled away but was caught by a single glance from his eyes.

She tiptoed back, flirting her whiskers. He ran his tongue over his lips.

Fire sparkled through her skin, into her lungs, and down to her toes. She was lighter than air.

The music grew stronger and bolder, echoing their magnetism and the light pulsing between them. The audience began to clap their hands, echoing the primitive drumbeat.

Alekhsiy's eyes were intent and dazzlingly blue. He captured her and held her, poised for display with one hand in the small of her back—more perfectly than any tango dancer.

Danae stretched her head back against his shoulder and laughed up at him, completely confident in her ability to escape or to remain and enjoy him and the heat melting into her bones.

How many thousands of years ago had men and women danced like this? Could they have had any more fun?

Alekhsiy lowered his mouth to kiss her and she spun away—but not too far, not with this pulse pounding through her veins.

The crowd roared, clearly enjoying every detail. The stage was brilliantly lit, yet Andrew hadn't brought up any of the overhead or side lights.

Alekhsiy tugged on the leash. His eyes were brilliant blue pools that she could drown in. The summons resonated in her bones, all the way down through her shoulders and ribs to her spine, far beyond her delicate collar's and leash's limits.

Something deep, deep inside answered him, where breath began. She came up onto her toes and crept toward him.

He tugged harder. She ran, the music racing through her blood, and leaped into his arms.

He clicked off her collar and his cuffs just as the curtain fell, and kissed her. She answered him, desperately trying to equal his claim on her with one on him.

The stage lights snapped on with a loud, electronic clank and the crowd outside let loose with a storm of applause.

Alekhsiy's head snapped up.

Danae blinked at her lover's face and closed her eyes.

That was one of the best dances she'd ever done. Pity she didn't know where its choreography or the lighting effects had come from.

Danae struck another pose, all arched back and angular limbs that amazingly resembled a white tigress. Clicking burst into life, like the arrival of a thousand cockroaches, inside the brilliant golden room.

"Look over here please, Danae!" called one photographer amid the horde clambering over chairs and crawling on the floor.

"Could you give us that last pose again?" cried another.

Alekhsiy glared at one who'd dared approach the dais a little too closely. He might no longer be of sufficient interest to warrant recording but that didn't mean he should be elbowed aside like a foreign king's despised courtier.

The lanky young fool with the very small box blanched and faded back, soothing Alekhsiy's twitching fingers somewhat.

The bards had sung of the silver bond for centuries but he'd never thought to see one, let alone experience it. It existed between a White Sorceress—or Sorcerer—and the Torhtremer warrior he or she fought alongside, a link that was both mental and sexual. But the Dark Warrior had massacred the last White Sorcerers and they'd become more myth than sword brother.

If he could call Danae a *sword brother*.

A reminiscent smile quirked Alekhsiy's mouth and blood stirred happily in his rod. Perhaps he could persuade her not to attend tonight's *movie*—whatever that was—if he told her a few details about that legendary order of sorcerers.

"Ready?" She gave him her hand.

"Always." He kissed her fingers and those scions of Chaos erupted into another storm of clacking.

He tucked her hand into the crook of his arm and headed for the door.

"Miss Livingston? May I speak to you for a moment, please?"

By Zemlaya's sandblasted Seven Hells, what was Turner doing here? He was dressed very simply by GriffinCon standards, in something called a *polo shirt* and *jeans*. His blazon was an offense to all mortal men, since it proclaimed his allegiance to Azherbhai.

Alekhsiy's skin crawled. He could locate every detail of Turner's armament and that of the three highly competent fighters with him. They hungered to kill him

His fingers barely twitched. He could have destroyed them before they grasped their weapons, but he couldn't touch them or their master, not with Turner watching Danae like a hungry wolf at a sheeps' fold.

"Turner." Her voice cut like a whip and a couple of the photographers turned to watch. Her eyes, ever those of the professional performer, flickered slightly. "What do you want?" she asked, a hair more graciously.

Alekhsiy maintained his exact knowledge of those bodyguards' weapons. Protect her first and hunt Turner later—after he'd found the sorcerer who could open the gate for that maggoty bastard back into Torhtremer.

"Can we talk in private?" Turner looked around openly.

"Sorry but I'm in a hurry. I've got barely enough time to change for the trailer's preview." She shot a dazzlingly false smile at everyone present, drawing in more onlookers.

"It will only take a minute." He truly sounded unaccustomed to being polite. "Or perhaps later?"

"You can call my agent. My schedule's pretty full at GriffinCon."

Somebody snickered and Turner all but snarled.

Alekhsiy shifted slightly, giving himself more room for movement.

"I've been considering the sad state of dance education in America nowadays."

Danae frowned, a reaction Alekhsiy shared. This was the last topic he'd expected to hear from Turner. "Really?"

"I've been interested in professional dance for a long time and I'd like to combine that with education. What would you think if I endowed a combination school and dance troupe?"

"What?" She blinked at him. Cameras erupted like a volley of Baluchistan slingshots.

"Where students attended both regular school and dance school to begin with." Turner advanced toward her, a ridiculously large smile on his face. "The better dancers would advance to the professional dance troupe, whose more experienced dancers would tutor the younger students. The more intellectual students would receive college scholarships."

"That could be very exciting." Her expression was completely abstracted, like a dreamer finally seeing her promised future.

By Chaos's great whirlpool, what was Turner's advantage in all this?

"I would need somebody to help me arrange all of this. A great dancer, who's widely respected, somebody like you." He tilted his head to observe her more closely.

"And I can guarantee you'd have plenty of time to write," he crooned. "Say, an additional ten million to finish the Torhtremer Saga?"

Her eyes widened. Crystalline terror shot down Alekhsiy's spine

"You could ensure that the underdogs come out on top, give Azherbhai and the Dark Warrior the victory."

"No . . ."

"Put all the money into an endowment for the school's students. Think about it, Miss Livingston. Chances to build a school like this don't come along very often."

He reached out to her, just as Alekhsiy pulled her away from him.

The silver tiger ring burst into glowing life, hidden from the public by the curve of her arm.

Danae could open the gate? His stomach knotted in his throat, worse than when he'd leaped through the void. But he was sworn to destroy the sorcerer who could do so.

His lady, his heart—the little dancer who'd given him joy and life time and again during the darkest of days—could make it possible for evil to destroy his world and everything he loved in life? Everything he adored except her?

The cameras exploded into volley after volley, like an army of accusations against Turner. The brute yanked his hand away, hot words frothing on his lips.

Alekhsiy instinctively tucked his lady protectively against him, ferocious as a Baluchistan wolf guarding its mate during breeding season.

"No, thank you, Mr. Turner." Danae's gaze was level and her spine straight. "I don't write that kind of fiction."

Turner's livid gaze measured their avid audience before returning to her. "A pity. Perhaps we can continue this at another time."

"Perhaps." Her tone offered him no encouragement. He left like an ill-tempered alligator, snapping and snarling, with his guards staying well away from his bite.

ConComm staff tactfully guided her and Alekhsiy out through a private door a moment later, before the media could ask any questions. Alekhsiy's head was spinning like an armorer's sharpening wheel, too quickly to form questions or thanks.

By the Mother of All Life, he was bonded to her, the only person who could destroy his family.

The music swelled to an ecstatic flourish, underscoring the larger-than-life king gazing desperately into the distance from the movie screen. A beautiful young couple faded out of sight, accompanied by saccharine prose, while two swordsmen fought for their lives against overwhelming odds in the background.

None of them could disappear too soon for Boris Turner.

The music ended, the room fell black, and the lights came up. The audience, packed into every nook and cranny of the immense ballroom in absolute defiance of fire department regulations, was completely silent.

The tall, thin, easily fit movie director bounded onto the stage. "Well? What do you think?" he asked with mock humility.

Anger raced through Boris, hot and enervating, flooding every cell. What the hell did the fool expect after the world's biggest ad campaign and a one hour preview? A chorus of boos?

The crowd released its tension into an explosion of whoops and screams of joy. Half of them stood on their chairs to make more noise. Many threw more confetti than they'd tossed during the film itself. They even began that disgusting cheer, "Torhtremer, Torhtremer, Torhtremer!"

Idiots. Didn't they understand they were being setup for the seventh book when Azherbhai, the Imperial Terrapin, and the Dark Warrior would come back from near defeat to win everything?

Boris roared his disbelief, unheard by the ecstatic crowd, and slammed out of the old-fashioned box, high above the ballroom floor. Dammit, he might have been stupid enough to watch the movie preview, but he didn't have to stay for the stupid cows' celebration.

Especially when Danae Livingston was celebrating with her boyfriend and friends only a few rows away from the movie director. Bitch. Nobody ever said no to him forever.

His bodyguards hastily fell into formation around him and cleared the way through GriffinCon's usual throngs. His people at least had the sense to obey him. The folks here, no matter how they were dressed, were slow—slow-witted and slow moving.

He shoved his way through, heedless of whom he stepped on or knocked over. If they didn't get out of the way, then they needed to learn how to look out for themselves. It was the law of the jungle, by which the fittest survived, and he wouldn't cry for any of them.

He dealt with the usual crowd at the elevators equally summarily. Wait a half hour—or more?—to go upstairs? For Chrissake, what a waste of time! No, he traveled as soon as he chose, where he chose.

A few extra glares and his bodyguards' strong arms gave him a private elevator. "Which floor, sir?" the team leader asked.

"Straight up to my room."

"Very good, sir." He punched the button and waited stolidly in the elevator, ever the most reliable man.

Boris drummed his fingers on the rail and counted floors. The filthy hotel designer had wanted passengers to enjoy the view so he made the elevators slow. The hotel's more recent management had compensated by installing monitors that detailed the latest news, mostly of events within the building.

His bodyguard shifted his stance, subtly checking the gun hidden at the small of his back.

If Boris never saw the fucking trailer for *The Raven and The Rose* again, he'd die a happy man. He'd survived the preview; wasn't that enough for one lifetime?

Damn, but Hollywood was so predictable these days! It was always so easy for the hero to win everything—the girl, the cute little neighboring kingdom's crown, the key move for the big battle . . . And if that starlet who played the heroine, High King Mykhayl's younger sister, had ever needed to lose more than five pounds in her life—well, he, Boris Turner, was Arnold Schwarzenegger's kid brother.

Couldn't the underdog win just once? How much money would it take to convince ConComm to give his theories a chance? Apparently more than he had, which was damned amazing. But for the Livingston bitch to turn him down, too, was intolerable.

The elevator monitor shifted images in a faint wash of sparks. Azherbhai's immensely ugly head appeared, immediately recognizable to millions from six movies—and Boris's dreams.

Boris's knees buckled and he barely saved himself from collapsing to the floor.

"Who are you?" he demanded instinctively, unwilling to publicly admit any weakness.

The elevator skidded to a stop.

"Your friend and inspiration." The beloved deep chuckle echoed through the tiny cab. "Who do you think I am?"

"Azherbhai," he suggested warily. How many times had he actually imagined what it would be like if Azherbhai were real? To meet this most misunderstood of all villains in the flesh? But surely this was a trick by some hacker who'd broken into the hotel's systems and wanted to use his well-known obsession against him.

"Are you certain—or merely pretending, little mortal?" The great Terrapin lunged forward and clacked loudly with its beak. For a moment, Boris thought the knife-edge was going to cut his throat or the elevator's cable and he shrank back.

The elevator shook violently, which sent him staggering closer to the glass window. He glanced around hastily to see if they'd been noticed but his bodyguard was still staring ahead stolidly. Incredibly, no other elevators were moving either, although they were all still brightly lit up. The escalator wasn't shifting waves of slobbering fools between lobbies either.

Oh shit, this was real. No hacker could have shut all that down without causing mass panic. His wildest dreams had come true and he was somehow caught between time.

"Azherbhai?"

"Correct, little one."

"What are you doing here? Are you only in the TV screen?"

"Your faith has brought me closer to you." The angular snout stretched wide in a lethal grin, displaying its massive jaws. He was so wonderfully deadly and magnificent that Boris reached out to stroke him. "Not yet, little Boris. You will have to travel to Torhtremer before you can join me."

As in, actually be there? Boris frowned. That was crazy. "How can I do that? Torhtremer is no place on Earth."

"Living stone can unlock the gate and bring you through."

Living stone? His accent was weird. Did he mean Livingston?

"The dancer?" He knew there was something unusual about her.

"You are an unfledged sorcerer but instinct still works. You will know by touch."

"That's not very clear, sir!"

Ancient dark eyes studied him, less hospitable than the mold at a dank well's base. "Come soon, my catalyst."

The screen snapped black and then began to scroll Griffin-Con's Sunday schedule. His bodyguard finished adjusting his belt. The tiny golden cab swung smoothly into motion, the other elevators scuttled onward like beetles, and the rats began to race between lobbies once again. Him, the catalyst for Azherbhai? After a final moment of disbelief, Boris pumped his fists into the air, triumph surging through his veins sweeter than any Wall Street–born high.

It was real. It was all real! *He* could defeat Mykhayl and rule Torhtremer. *He* could have his pick of the Dragon Hoard's hundred concubines. He could have it all! He just needed to get there. And wasn't that one hell of a problem, though. But he did know one man who should be able to help him solve it.

He flipped out his BlackBerry. "Harrison?"

"Sir?" The ridiculous amount he paid for the man to answer at any time, day or night, was well worth it.

"I need to speak to Danae Livingston privately, in person, as soon as possible."

"How soon, sir?"

Why was Harrison questioning him? Boris thought impatiently. Now that he knew her true abilities, he would stop at nothing to get to her.

"Tonight, preferably within two hours."

"Two hours, sir?" Caution from Harrison? "May I remind you, sir, of the numbers of police present?"

"Or four." He could be patient for that long, if necessary. "Any and all methods are approved, of course. Her big bodyguard will probably need to be distracted."

"Do you think so? In that case, of course, sir, I'll see to it right away."

Boris cast his eyes toward the sky. *What you had to do nowadays to drag an agreement out of your staff!* But Harrison had been hesitating. Maybe he should encourage action a little more.

"If you can accomplish it by sunrise, you will probably want to check your Zurich files before you rest."

Harrison's sudden intake of break of break was quickly turned into a cough.

"Thank you, sir. I'll definitely do my best to check those files before then."

That was better. Boris clicked off and stepped out of the elevator, which had finally reached his floor.

Harrison would work his ass off for a reward big enough to warrant a bonus directly deposited to his beloved numbered Swiss account.

And Boris would have Danae Livingston and the trip to Torhtremer to become Azherbhai's catalyst. What did he want to do first with Bhaikhal and the Dragon's Hoard? Rework that gaudy throne into something more modernistic and monochromatic? Or just start fucking the bitches?

Choices like that were the reward for a lifetime of hard work—and how many men had the brass balls to reach this high?

Maybe he could combine the two options: fuck the bitches in the throne room until they approved of his decorating scheme.

He began to whistle.

Alekhsiy slapped Sasha's palm to celebrate their triumph over the gods who controlled parking at GriffinCon. He could sing those praises, as he could for the dance he and Danae had performed earlier that evening, little though he remembered of it.

Moonlight flung a silver veil over the buildings, as distant and remote as his chances of returning home to help his family. Far closer was the feathering white light cast by the standing lamps, like a coming nor'easter blurred by a linen curtain. The distant world was etched in crisp stripes of light. Only dim, silent boxes watched from nearby, all masked in shadows. Muted hums and purrs, mixed with occasional loud whines, told of cars prowling the streets far below, their deeds as remote as their territory.

The stones here smelled less bitter than their distant brethren, as if the higher elevation had allowed the sun and rain to erase some of the machines' foul stench. But not enough to bring back honest scents, such as sweet meadows, barnyard aromas, or campfires' wood smoke.

Alekhsiy could recall more of the dinner party afterward, when Sasha and Larissa had sung their praises at a restaurant far from the hotel. The obviously insane judges had awarded him and Danae Best in Show—whatever that meant—for their dance at the *entr'acte*. Odd, very odd, when they hadn't even been official entrants, just performers.

He'd spent most of the time since brooding on the implications of Danae's identity as the sorceress who could transport Turner through the void. If he knew how great her power was, how soon would his enemy realize the same thing and act? He'd more than once had to stop himself from pocketing those sharp little knives—called *steak* knives for some unfathomable reason—as extra ammunition, in case the brute's allies attacked during dinner.

If Turner ever reached Torhtremer, he would bring war back

to the people who'd died in the thousands before, whose fields were only now returning to fertility, and whose children had only just begun to fill the schools again. This would be the first year since Alekhsiy's class that the North would have enough young boys to send cadets for the Imperial Military Academy.

Turner would raise Azherbhai, the Imperial Terrapin, into roaring life with his army of deadly monsters. Mykhayl would fight once again from morning to night, barely eating or sleeping, his golden eyes harsh with the knowledge that a realm depended on him.

And above all else, Turner would do his best to kidnap Mykhayl's young sons, those delightful rogues whose ability to work magic charmed everyone who met them almost as fast as the need to clean up the results irritated them. Since they could summon Khyber, the Imperial Dragon, if he held them, he, too, would be able to command Torhtremer's most potent weapon.

Clapping Izmir's Curse on Danae's slender wrists would deny him that prize.

Svetlhana, the Imperial Tigress, had not faced battle against Azherbhai in living memory and had always been unpredictable. She was a female cat who'd never served a male battle commander. Alekhsiy had devoted far too much thought to her possible strategy but reached no comforting conclusions.

The thought was almost as disquieting as his need to see Danae smile.

She chuckled and clapped Sasha on the shoulder from the backseat. "Are you very proud of yourself, now that you've found the last remaining parking space in the entire garage?"

"Hell yes!" He opened the door and climbed out, automatically turning back to assist his wife.

"Planning to use a can opener to get all of us out?" she asked tartly and accepted his aid.

Alekhsiy had to admit he'd seldom seen vehicles packed so closely together, even at the most crowded fairgrounds. Even slender, athletic Danae needed caution to leave the minivan, while he found it a considerable trial. He didn't draw a deep breath until he reached the main thoroughfare.

The boxes around them resolved themselves into dozens of cars, vans, and a few of what Sasha had termed "pickups," all of them far too large and stolid for a man who'd grown up with horses. They stood atop a ramp that circled down and around, again and again for hundreds of paces to the hotel's entrance. Only a few paces away, a large flat space opened up, which would hopefully lead to the true exit from this tower.

A shadow moved, then another, and a third, along the ramp.

Alekhsiy stiffened and his hand automatically curled around Finger Nipper. The others, even Sasha, casually turned to look.

Two of the shadows resolved into women wearing black trousers and coats that swept the ground, plus very angular eyeglasses.

"Oh, look, they're LARPing," Larissa commented under her breath. "They must be fans of that new TV series set in the near future."

TV series? Ah yes, the readily available set of tales told by invisible bards.

The two girls unleashed what looked like clumsy knives and briefly flailed at each other. Moments later, one yelled, "Killing Blow!"

Killing? Alekhsiy tensed to run toward them, hot blood surging through his veins. Danae clamped her hand over his and he stared at her.

"I can save her," he growled, keeping his voice down for some unknown purpose.

"Just wait and watch," she retorted. "LARPers don't want your help."

But *death*? He glared at her and she tightened her grip. He ground his teeth and waited.

"Ow! I'm dying!" The second woman slowly sank to the stone floor. She looked over her shoulder, brushed away some pebbles, then folded onto her side.

Her opponent tapped an impatient foot, her knife prominently displayed.

The so-called dying woman collapsed onto her back and flung out one arm. An instant later, she groaned and folded it in across her stomach. Finally she was silent and still.

Her opponent stood over her, one hand propped on her hip. Evidently satisfied the other wouldn't move again, the victor quickly dropped back into an effective crouch and went back to creeping up the ramp, always hiding in the darkness.

Alekhsiy glanced at Danae, not about to voice his question lest he be condemned as an outlander.

"This must be one of the first LARPs for *Black Rose*," Larissa commented.

"Yes, I heard they were going to game the Chancellor's assassination, the new modern day scenario," Sasha agreed.

"There are several dozen LARPers, aren't there?" Danae craned her neck to look a little more closely.

Alekhsiy reconsidered the moving shadows. If he saw them as but townsfolk with a few weeks'—or months'—training, then their clumsiness was understandable. But they knew the basics of finding cover and most moved boldly against their opponents.

He'd played similar games as a child and as a cadet. These folk might have potential, especially since a handful were far more graceful.

He turned to look into the garage's edges a little more closely, peering past the cloak of darkness.

"I'm for our room. Anybody interested in joining me?" Sasha leered hopefully at his wife.

She chuckled and whacked him on his ass. "You don't even have the key."

"Then I'd better bring you along, hadn't I?" He tugged her lightly by the elbow and she giggled again. "See you tomorrow, guys!"

They strode toward the elevator, talking happily amongst themselves and ignoring everything else.

"Do you want to watch?" Danae asked quietly.

"Will they mind?" Alekhsiy answered, equally reserved. His skin had chilled, more so than any breeze borne on this humid summer night could account for.

"No, not as long as we're quiet and unobtrusive. If they stopped for every set of non-players, they'd never be able to play here."

He grunted acknowledgment, still watching the shadows.

The elevator clanked and then whined, announcing Sasha and Larissa's departure.

Two men farther down the ramp were apparently trying to decide how to adapt their plot. "How do you fit in an Austrian assault rifle?" complained one.

Other LARPers continued to leapfrog up the ramp to the top deck, uttering odd cries of "Martial Attack" and "Martial Defense" to mark their attacks.

A pair of booted feet whispered across the stone for an instant.

Alekhsiy spun to listen more closely.

The first LARPer he'd noticed stretched, sat up, and rose to her feet, then trotted off to the stairwell.

Danae harrumphed disapprovingly.

"Poor sportsmanship?" Alekhsiy asked, more to make conversation than because he truly cared. Were three LARPers working together to move up the ramp, rather than singly like the others?

"She should have stayed ten or fifteen minutes to give the others a body to work around. It's a pretty large group, after all." Danae hugged herself, shivering slightly in a light breeze. "But she probably didn't want to get any dirtier or more uncomfortable."

Alekhsiy sniffed in disapproval but said nothing more openly.

"Have you played in many of these?" He slipped his arm around her waist and started toward the stairs. That trio was moving very fast toward the top.

"No, not really, just a couple since I grew up. My father preferred board games, like chess and backgammon."

She paused to allow some LARPers time to move out of their way and he ground his teeth. That trio was moving far too quickly toward the top.

A quick twist loosened Finger Nipper in its belt sheath, the only weapon he openly carried now. Using it would be an act of desperation, though, since it would sign his name to any wound. Few here had blades and the skills to use them in a fight.

He and Danae finally reached the top deck and turned for the elevator. The swift-moving trio peeled themselves out of the shadows among the cars on the other side. Two men ran toward them, while the third hung back

"Miss Livingston?" a burly man with a guttural, ruined voice asked. "Mr. Turner wants to see you. *Now.*"

He flipped back his long, black coat to show an unusual rifle, compact, ugly, and utterly unlike anything listed in Corinne's spell. It reeked of death, for all that he carried it casually on his hip. His companion sneered from a few paces farther away, just distant enough that Alekhsiy couldn't take them both out with the same strike, and briefly flashed a big, square pistol at Danae.

Two deadly projectile weapons, wielded by men more than willing to use them. No dart, however small or fast, could penetrate his chain mail. But no one else could claim such protection.

Alekhsiy's stomach jolted into his throat. *By the Hunter's long search, if anything happened to his lady . . .*

Danae froze, her green-gold eyes narrowing like a hunting cat's.

Far below, a loud whine and squeal of brakes screamed that a car was racing upward toward them. The would-be kidnappers had a means of escape.

The third man chuckled and flickered his green, woolen cloak to display the same gun.

Three enemies, all ready to shed blood, while he had but one knife and his body's skills to protect his lady. His flesh chilled, terror's sharp claws shredding the edges of his vision.

He began to calculate strike angles.

"Wicked, man," crooned a man who'd been answering questions by the LARPers. He started to walk toward their group. "I've never seen a gun like that. Can I see how you peace-bonded it?"

For a split second, the would-be kidnappers gaped at the interruption.

"Drop, Danae!" Alekhsiy hissed.

Red God of War be praised, she did so—but her foot simultaneously lashed out in a spinning kick. It cracked into the knee-cap of the villain closest to them, destroyed his balance, and slammed him onto his back.

Bam, bam, bam! His pistol roared a ribbon of fiery little lights and explosions across the ramp and into the sky. His head thudded against the pavement and he lay still.

Splat, splat, splat! The most distant brute fired his gun, sending a long, hot spray of death-dealing darts through the night.

Danae slithered under a car, disappearing in a blur more felt than seen.

The spokesman glanced desperately over to assess the new threat.

Alekhsiy grabbed him by the shoulders and whirled him back. He kicked him between his legs, slamming all the force of Torhtremer's finest chain mail into his privates.

The threat to Danae shrieked and collapsed in a boneless heap. His rifle clattered to the stone floor and he moaned, making no attempt to retrieve it.

Bam! Bam! The other element of the kidnappers hadn't run. He continued to fire at them from across the ramp.

People screamed and ran in all directions, across the deck and down the ramp. Others simply flattened themselves to the ground.

By all the gods, Danae could be killed! But if he couldn't let them end her life, how could he do it? There was no time for such worries now.

Alekhsiy dove to follow her. He squeezed under the car where she'd taken shelter. A small white hand, barely visible in the darkness, waved at him from another nearby.

He growled deep in his throat and crawled like a worm toward his lady. His pulse raced hot and hard, spurring him forward faster than any High King's strongest engineer.

Splat! Splat! Small dust devils erupted from the stone paving.

Success! His hand latched on to her hip and dragged her protectively close.

Her slender fingers, streaked with blackness even in the half-light, desperately twined around his wrist.

He twisted his arm and slid his hand into hers, silently offering what comfort he could. Words might cause their deaths.

She linked her fingers tightly with his and her breath shuddered into the same pattern as his. His chest rose and fell inside his mail, further constrained by the innumerable knobs and bars above them and his burningly hot amulet.

A series of strange, high-pitched, mechanical screams sounded from down below. *Sirens?*

The car below shrieked, paused, shrieked again, and started to fade away.

Ping! Ping! Metal resonated over and around them.

The thrice-cursed spawn of Chaos was shooting at the machine. Surely it contained enough bulk to keep them safe. Danae was quivering slightly against his arm but she hadn't made a sound, the brave darling. *May these thrice-cursed spawn of Chaos boil for ten thousand years in the lowest circles of Hell before they escaped to the realm of endless deserts!*

Alekhsiy petted her hip, offering her what comfort he could. Surely those sirens meant that help was coming soon.

Plop. Plop. Plop.

Liquid slowly dripped onto the stone from underneath the van, setting loose a tart aroma near their feet.

Danae jerked, then began to scrabble desperately forward.

By all the Red God's more harebrained battle tactics, what was she doing? The enemy clearly hadn't found them.

She grabbed his arm and he followed her. If nothing else, he needed to stay near her. They slithered out as quietly as possible to slip under the next car, before escaping into a small gap.

"Where the hell did you go?" The shooter muttered and bent down to look under the cars. "A million dollars is too much to walk away from, dammit."

Horror of horrors, Danae had blood running down her forehead.

Alekhsiy's heart was pounding in his chest like the High King's finest drum corps. Yet even at Tajzyk's Gorge, he'd always been able to think clearly and calmly.

Plop! Plop!

He closed his eyes and reminded himself once again he was a general. He knew how to fight and how to maintain his composure. He could control himself and bring them both to safety.

She tugged his hand and pointed. Two turns and a mostly-concealed gap should bring them to a set of stairs.

He nodded his comprehension, then bent double and began to creep forward.

Ping! Another deadly little dart whizzed past their feet.

BAM!

The van they'd hidden under exploded into a ball of fire. Alekhsiy and Danae staggered sideways and fell against the parking garage's wall.

BAM! The car next to it blew up, sending another pillar of black smoke into the sky.

Alekhsiy caught his lady up in his arms and bolted for the stairs, a few panic-stricken game players close on his heels. Fiery-hot air clawed his back like dragon's breath.

Danae squeaked and tucked herself into a ball, making it far, far easier for him to carry her.

Blessed Mother of All Life, may my beloved remain safe, even if it costs me my own chance at the Afterworld . . .

He slammed the iron door open with his shoulder and burst into a narrow turret. Scarlet flames butchered the night sky overhead and the stones underneath his feet shuddered.

He took a deep breath, forced his racing pulses to steady, and started down. He would be of no use to anyone, least of all his darling, if he lost his concentration.

NINE

The Imperial Throne Room, Bhaikhal, Torhtremer

"How many men did we lose?" Mykhayl snarled. He was pacing between the throne room's great marble columns as if they were enemies his sword could behead. Young Rhodyon stirred against his shoulder, large enough now that only adult men could easily carry him.

Tenderness, mixed with the memory of agonized terror, swept across Mykhayl's face.

Corinne started to leave her seat on the Tigerheart Throne to comfort him. But little Iskander's bandaged hand batted her arm and he whimpered.

Her heart turned over, once again, at the memory of the bloody wreckage in the practice fields. How had the boys and Mazur survived that brazen attack from the skies? Had it been a kidnapping or murder attempt? Who cared?

She crooned to her second son, the worst wounded, and tucked him back against her heart and into the blankets. The Tigerheart Throne was a cold silver couch underneath her, since

Svetlhana had disappeared on patrol once again. The throne room was the heart of the palace and Torhtremer's magic, where every object showed some aspect of the Imperial Dragon and Tigress's powers—if they were present. The boys were safest here but it offered little comfort.

Mykhayl adjusted the sleeping rogue and spoke again, gentling his tone. "Do we have any new word from the Tents of Healing about the casualties?"

"Less than thirty are dead," Ghryghoriy responded, his bloody bandage an obscenity against his raven hair. Normally Ghryghoriy was the Dragon's Claw but he'd set aside his black and gold uniform and his spying duties to take up his former lover's obligations as war lord.

"So far," added Yevgheniy, never one to spare his High King the truth. Baby Levushka, named for Mykhayl's grandfather, dozed on his shoulder, a chubby fist tucked comfortably into his mouth. His clean scarlet robe perfectly matched his idol's robes of office and also hid his few bloodstains.

Mazur, their beloved companion, slept against the dais, too numb from Corinne's spell to twitch even his tail. It was very, very hard to bandage a leopard who'd nearly been gutted. But he would survive, thank God.

Corinne briefly closed her eyes and reminded her stomach there was nothing left in it to hurl.

"Of the wounded?" A muscle throbbed in Ghryghoriy's jaw. "We have very few of those since most who took injuries died. They fought to the death to save the young princes from the chimera."

Mykhayl beat his fist against his leg. Even Yevgheniy couldn't find words to respond.

"The queen and wizards have done"—Corinne shot Ghryghoriy a ferocious glare—"*are doing* everything possible for them."

Mykhayl returned to the throne, his gaze as restless as the thoughts behind his eyes.

"Now we must consider where to array our forces." Mykhayl drummed his fingers on the Dragonheart Throne, as if trying to summon Khyber. "Before the Imperial Terrapin always aimed such attacks at the countryside."

"Aye, his monsters are ever greedy and eager to breed terror," agreed Yevgheniy.

"So why is he focusing on the capital?" Corinne demanded. "The chimera today, a hydra the day before yesterday, a manticore last week—and all of them right here. If he wants to have a war, why doesn't he go someplace else?"

"I believe he hoped to kill the two eldest boys and steal the youngest." Yevgheniy's deadly calm voice held too much brutal honesty to be ignored. Every one of his years and bitter battles carved deep grooves in his face. "Only Prince Levushka isn't a sorcerer, making it far easier for him to be manipulated."

Terror shredded her heart and ripped out her breath.

"He probably wants to draw our attention away from Alekhsiy." Ghryghoriy offered hope in his old friend's name.

"He's been gone for weeks." Mykhayl looked almost as old as Yevgheniy. He gripped Corinne's shoulder and she quickly covered his hand with hers to give them both comfort.

"Time flows differently there," she reminded him and herself. "He could think he'd only been there for a few hours or days."

"He might not have found the new catalyst."

"He certainly hasn't killed him yet." Yevgheniy kicked a blameless piece of dust.

"Can we build wards that will protect us until next spring? When I can take an army to finally destroy that scum?"

Corinne flinched, thousands of hideous visions flooding her author's brain. Could Mykhayl kill Azherbhai or would he only cause his own death in battle? Perhaps she could cast a spell, which would keep him at her side.

"Corinne?" her beloved husband turned to face her, their son nestled in his arms.

But if he didn't take an army north, wouldn't their children be killed? How many women through the centuries had ever needed to watch their husbands march out to fight for their babies? If only she could ask Svetlhana's opinion now . . .

She was cold, so cold. Even the heat coming through the great seal of Torhtremer set in the marble floor didn't help warm her.

"We'll need both Khyber and Svetlhana's help to build any wards that could hold off the Imperial Terrapin," she said, stalling for time.

"True, two imperial beasts are always stronger than one," Mykhayl agreed.

"Pity Khyber can't roast that monster in his shell," Ghryghoriy snarled.

"No imperial beast can kill another, only their catalyst." A lesson she'd learned all too painfully once before.

"May the gods lead Alekhsiy to do so quickly, lest we must do so here." Mykhayl surveyed the small gathering, measuring their resolve, and nodded. "We will prevail."

God willing.

ATLANTA
LATE SATURDAY NIGHT

The street below the parking garage was an insane mixture of milling police, firefighters, TV crews, and gaping Con-goers—every single one of them standing on wet pavement.

Danae took off the singularly ugly brown blanket provided by the Red Cross and returned it with thanks to the ladies still passing out doughnuts. She wasn't cold any more, especially since she hadn't gotten wet. Besides, if she had to hang around in this circus, she'd rather do so in her own clothes. Her hoodie and jeans were eminently suited to urban late nights.

The firemen had had a field day pouring water onto so many burning cars high atop the garage. And all that liquid had had only one place to go—down, down onto the street, across the asphalt, and into every drain it could find. For a while, it had looked like Noah's Flood was running below the Krakatau volcano.

Alekhsiy still stood where she'd left him, a pillar of strength, albeit somewhat streaked with grease. A lot of LARPers were in similar condition, down to the whiteness around their tight mouths.

A slow curl of something far more than affection rolled through her gut. Alekhsiy had hit the man with a rifle, even after that other guy's pistol had gone off, and he'd carried her out of a burning building. He'd saved her life.

"Hey, big guy." She wrapped her arms around him and laid her head against his chest. Two seconds with a paramedic had taken care of her scraped face but Alekhsiy had needed longer than that to stop shaking.

He immediately hugged her until he held her so close she could hear his heart beating, even through the chain mail.

"How much longer do you think they'll be?" he asked, and jerked his head toward the cops. Like all of the LARPers, the bystanders in the street, and the late-night gym attendees, they had to talk to the police.

"Not too much more." She craned her head around his shoulder to look. "There are only one or two people ahead of us in line."

"How can you tell?" he hissed, clearly horrified.

"Dance studios are not located in the best parts of town, darling. Do you know how many seedy industrial areas I've been in? To say nothing of the New York City subway system at the worst hour. And the police reports afterward."

"Too much crime." His arms tightened until she almost gasped. They immediately loosened slightly.

"Let's just say I've seen more than my share of real-life cops and robbers. I decided a long time ago I wasn't about to be a victim." *Like after the first attempted mugging when I was seventeen and on my own in New York. If my father hadn't taught me so well . . .*

She shivered and moved closer.

"That's why you immediately fought." His voice was barely a breath against her hair.

"Yeah." She inhaled, reassuring herself with the faint spiciness that was uniquely Alekhsiy. He didn't carry any special toiletries, either. She'd miss it when he was gone.

Gone. His chest was warm under her hand, very, very warm in one particular spot.

"Your pendant!" She stared up at him. "It's so hot. Does this mean it's fully charged?"

"Yes, sweeting." He nodded, his mouth very tight.

He could leave tonight. But she'd thought he'd stay for the entire weekend. She wasn't ready to say good-bye yet.

Unaccustomed moisture dampened her eyes and she blotted it away impatiently. She did *not* cry over men. At least she never had before, for any significant amount of time.

Something flashed through his gaze but she couldn't read it very clearly. Surely it was a trick of the bizarre light here, a mix of streetlights, hotel signs, and TV klieg lights.

Stick to business, dammit. She needed to arm him for the upcoming interview. "By the way, your name is Icelandic."

"Ice Land?"

Thank God he had kept his voice down. Even an anti-scrying spell probably couldn't cope with a full-fledged bellow.

"Yeah, it's a country in the North Atlantic Ocean. Their names are old-fashioned Viking ones, where men's last names are based on their father's first name."

"As they should be."

She harrumphed in mock disgust and he winked at her.

"In that case, I must not be carrying my passport, because I'm in costume."

"Correct. You're very quick on the uptake, you know?" She leaned up to kiss him on the cheek.

"Passports. Shootings." He nuzzled her hair. "Dancers working in fear of their lives."

Huh? She leaned back to stare at him. She was close to her profession's top and things were easier now for her. She opened her mouth to correct him.

"Brutes determined to capture you."

She shuddered, her objection dying away on her lips. Well yeah, there was Turner. Three armed kidnappers, two of them with rifles for God's sake, were a whole 'nother matter and a very scary one.

He dropped to his knees before her.

"Will you marry me and come home with me?"

"What?" she squeaked. People around them turned to stare but he barely glanced at them.

Kneeling must be so unmistakable that his anti-scrying spell wasn't trying to hide his words.

"Stand up, you fool." She tugged at him but she might as well have tried to lift the Empire State Building by herself.

"The fire tonight showed me how much I love you."

What? They were just having a quick weekend affair, right?

"Will you marry me? I'll build you a fine house of your own."

"Oh, how sweet," somebody murmured. More people began to watch. Two stormtroopers leaned against each other and cooed, their white armor making them look like tall turtledoves under the streetlights.

She flushed.

"Aleks . . ." She stopped and gritted her teeth.

"Alek, stand up or I will never speak another word to you again, so help me God!" Her voice rose to a shout on the last word and hot color flooded her cheeks.

He came to his feet, graceful as a hunting cat despite the layers of tunic and chain mail. He scowled and spun on his heel to glare at any overly inquisitive neighbors. Their audience promptly found numerous other items nearby much more entertaining than they had been. Several even scampered back toward the hotel.

Danae buried her face in her hands.

Alekhsiy was a great guy—strong, caring, great sense of humor. Heck, she knew him pretty well, thanks to writing about him. He wouldn't lie about loving her.

But that was not the same as agreeing to spend one's entire life in another world. As an author, she knew all too well that she only glimpsed parts of life in the universe she wrote about and then exaggerated them.

How could she leave Earth? She might be able to recite entire passages of the Torhtremer Saga by heart but that didn't mean she knew how to live there. How did one shop for groceries, anyway? But that was trivial, compared to big picture stuff.

And to go without dancing . . . Never, ever again to hear the orchestra come up on a Robbins ballet or wait in the wings, heart beating just a little fast, for the first syncopated beat of a new piece? Or spend hours in a studio, her legs burning, until the choreographer finally declared he'd found his vision for his new work? Or stay late after class so she could help a young dancer practice?

And never, ever see her friends again? Not Nora, nor Larissa, nor their children. No more shrieks of laughter and stupid gossip from Larissa, mixed with dozens of baby pictures. No more wickedly dry political cartoons from Nora or tales of her sons' exploits in the Boy Scouts. To say nothing of her friends in Europe and New York, too.

Or visit her family's grave on the anniversary of their death?

Maybe somebody better than she was could do it but she had too much here to walk away from.

She shook her head and looked up.

"I'm sorry, Alekhsiy, but no."

"Is it that you don't love me?" A muscle in his jaw jerked hard.

She started to deny caring for him, then stopped. She owed him the truth, however painful, if nothing else.

Nobody was watching, right? Good. She took the plunge.

"I'll miss you like hell when you're gone. But Torhtremer is too damn far."

"You've written about us for years," he insisted and caught her fingers.

"That's not the same thing as giving up my life and friends here to make a home there." It was all too easy to let her hands lay limp and unresponsive in his grasp.

The lines around his mouth deepened before he nodded and let go of her. "As you wish."

"Sorry." She gave him a meaningless little smile. The night

had not suddenly turned cold, dammit, and she did not need to retrieve that blanket.

"Ma'am? Detective Brown would like to talk to you now." The rumpled policeman nodded to her, his experienced gaze coldly impersonal.

She blinked at the interruption, then nodded back. Oh yeah, she had to put on the mask of just another poor, innocent passerby who'd happened to be caught in a shooting. It wasn't a lie, just editing a few things that a little luck would keep them from asking her about. Hopefully they'd think any fumblings in her story were due to her recent—and undoubtedly well-witnessed—lovers' spat.

Alekhsiy folded his arms and waited, for once less troubled by facing the local police than his dealings with Danae. He'd played a big country yokel before during a few spy missions with Ghryghoriy. His ability to do so was part of why he'd been asked to come here.

But Danae? He couldn't believe she'd willingly harm Torhtremer but the stakes were so high. If Turner forced her to choose between Nora's sons and writing a book that savaged Torhtremer, which would she choose? Or between Larissa's little baby and Torhtremer?

Would the danger to Torhtremer be as real to her as it was to him? Of flooded fields and people begging for sun to dry their grain that their children might eat and not burn to death of fever?

Of Mykhayl, blood streaming down his throat from the ice serpent's bite, yet lifting Dragon's Breath again to strike another blow?

Or the nightmare of his nephews' battered bodies, lying crumpled in the queen's garden under Azherbhai's monsters' claws?

He could not take the chance.

She pushed her long dark hair back from her face, baring her lily white neck.

His breath hung in his throat for an instant. His heart's delight, even if he'd never tasted her carnal liquors and bound himself to her for life.

He forced himself to drag in another taste of the sour, machine-tainted air. It was another aspect of her world and therefore something else to remember her by once he was gone.

Marriage would have bonded her through him to Torhtremer but she'd refused.

His High King had ordered him to kill her, the dreaded sorcerer. The only option left to bar Turner from Torhtremer was Izmir's Curse.

The Plains of Vasyugan, the northern border of Torhtremer

Igoryok drew his horse to a halt on the hilltop and sourly studied the craggy peaks looming ahead. The day was fair and sunny, as if the gods mocked them with clear sight of the difficulties to come and the homes they'd left behind.

"Are those the Biysk Mountains?" Zhenechka stopped beside him. Her horse sniffed the air, clearly little troubled by the hard pace they'd set. If they returned—no, *when* they returned—he'd trade for more of its kind to add stamina to his breeding stock.

"Aye. There's the famous five-pointed peak, with the broken rocks underneath." He'd studied the ancient scrolls during too many long winter storms not to recognize that formation.

The river below them was broad and shallow, little troubled with rapids, and bordered with a wide, pebbled beach. It flowed gently toward the south, its source hidden by white snows and gray clouds.

"Truly the gods have favored us to bring us this far in safety." She sighed ecstatically, a remarkable sound from those perpetually pursed lips.

Igoryok flashed a sharp glance at her but could find no hint of blasphemy in her expression. Indeed, they'd only lost two men on the journey and those to a drunken fall. Their horses had survived and Zhenechka had promptly searched and confiscated all other potentially dangerous liquors and drugs.

There'd been no trouble since. Even so, he'd be more comfortable if he thought such luck would hold.

The rest of their little army gathered around them, filling in the line along the hilltop.

"Do you think the enemy is watching?" Jeirgif asked quietly, running a soothing hand along his big dapple's neck. He was one of the best at looking after his mount.

"Undoubtedly," Zhenechka answered, equally softly. "But probably only the monsters can take physical shape."

"Only?" Jeirgif managed a credible snort.

Igoryok's mouth quirked over his remaining teeth. But as much as such chatter warmed the heart, it was time for deeds, not words.

"My people!" he raised his voice slightly and the faint clatter of weapons and gear immediately died down.

"As you can see, we have reached the farthest borders of Torhtremer. Those are the legendary Biysk Mountains and beyond them rolls the Tungur Sea. There, on the Chulym Beach, is where the Imperial Terrapin will come to spawn. I will force none of you to come with me."

Some of his troopers broke into shocked murmurs. One startled horse sidled when its master nearly stood up in the saddle. Another bucked when his rider yanked on the reins in astonishment or far too understandable fear.

Despite all the commotion, nobody broke the line to turn south. Most troopers simply went a little whiter about the mouth.

Igoryok wryly watched all his nightmares pass through their eyes. It had taken him weeks before he'd been driven to send out the summons to come here. His people were faster about accepting its inevitability than he'd been.

Zhenechka made an ancient rune and her lips moved silently.

Igoryok waited patiently. They'd need all the protection the gods would grant if anyone was to have a chance of returning.

"This river will lead us into the mountains but we must leave our horses behind," he announced.

"But . . ." Zhenechka began, then stopped.

"They cannot go where we must," Jeirgif said simply, his gaze tracing the high snow blowing off the needle peaks like smoke. He stroked his beloved mare's neck. "They are far safer here."

She sighed and swung herself down.

ATLANTA
SUNDAY MORNING

Danae rolled over and pulled the comforter higher over her face. But the single ray of daylight glowed like fire behind her eyelids.

She grumbled and flopped onto her back. Surely Alekhsiy would close the curtains tighter and she could go back to sleep.

Alekhsiy. Sleep. He'd needed to rise early so he could reach the tournament on time. She'd been such a supportive girlfriend that she hadn't even tried to seduce him after they returned to the hotel so late last night. Well, this morning actually.

She grunted discontentedly and pushed the covers away from her face.

A broad gold bracelet on each wrist dragged across her skin. Her fine hairs prickled at the unaccustomedly heavy rub, since she wore very little jewelry except her father's ring. But her sleep-dazed brain refused to consider it.

Of course, there had been the scene when she'd refused his proposal. But he hadn't mentioned that later when they were alone, just seemed glad to go straight to bed. He'd even cuddled her like an angel.

She shoved her hair back from her face and sat up. Hugging her knees wasn't nearly as much fun as holding him but it was better than being totally empty-handed.

She'd have liked to wish him good luck this morning.

Dammit, why hadn't he woken her up? Okay, so she slept hard—enough that her brothers had always teased her about it—but she'd have been very willing to get up for Alekhsiy. They still had a day or two left to enjoy their friendship. She wasn't about to give that up.

She swung her legs over the side. She'd go down to the gymnasium and wish him luck there. Nora would tell her how to get into the back room or maybe bring him out for a couple of seconds. Yeah, that should do it.

She stretched luxuriously, her eyelids falling over visions of their reunion. Just a few more hours to dodge Turner's machinations and enjoy Alekhsiy's company before everybody went their separate ways. Anything felt possible today.

Her arms came down and pointed at several sheets of hotel notepaper, covered in Alekhsiy's bold handwriting.

For the first time, ice whispered across her skin. But surely that was folly. Alekhsiy wished her only the best, right? Of course right.

Even so, she picked the note up very gingerly and held it at arms' length. Hotel stationery was notably boring from a style perspective but this didn't smell like good news.

My dearest Danae—

I came to Earth to destroy the future catalyst. But you have never asked me how he can reach Torhtremer. Dragon's blood and a spell of power are needed to cross the void in the flesh, both of which the Imperial Terrapin lacks. The future catalyst needs a sorcerer who can perform this magic, a sorcerer as rare as the catalyst.

You, my love, have crossed to Torhtremer before. You are the key that can unlock its gate.

Crossed to Torhtremer before? Did he think one short story where she'd witnessed the Muster of the Clans qualified her to haul somebody else across the void?

Danae glared at the innocuous bit of paper as if it was a laptop throwing sparks.

Heck, she'd been such a newbie author, she hadn't bothered to make up a character. She'd just written it in first person. She, Danae Livingston, had seen and done everything connected with the Muster of the Clans.

Oh, shit. Maybe that was what he meant.

If being an author meant she was a sorceress, as proven by her ability to tweak events in Alekhsiy's life, maybe she could tweak things in her own life and somebody else's.

It still seemed crazy. She'd have to prove she could work magic here on Earth before she'd really believe it.

I have sworn to destroy both the catalyst and the sorcerer, lest my home be cast into war once again. I cannot end your life, even though my High King expects it.

Kill me?

Danae sank into a chair, her legs too weak to hold her. Alekhsiy was strong-minded enough to kill a woman, if he felt it necessary.

At least he'd decided not to slay her but her heart wasn't beating very strongly yet.

Therefore, I have placed Izmir's Curse around your wrists. Please believe I have taken this step to protect you. I cannot accept any chance that our enemy might compel you to harm my home. But I cannot kill you, either.

Izmir's Curse? He'd locked her up in Izmir's Curse? The pair of handcuffs that kept mad wizards from killing themselves or anyone nearby? But that was a pair of bracelets.

Weight dragged down her wrists.

Two heavy, wide, gold bracelets, covered in runes, looked back at her.

She ran her fingers over them but found no seam. She could get her little finger under one but nothing more.

Five minutes of hard work with the bathroom soap left her very clean and the gold still gleaming above her hands.

The damn jewelry was there to stay.

You bastard! She threw the washcloth at the mirror. It hung there for a moment before sliding down and blurring the glass behind it like the path to her future.

The cuffs will stop you from working magic of any kind and can only be removed by me or the High King. However, you will still be able to enjoy a happy life and love whomever you choose.

You should be safe to move through GriffinCon if you remain close to Larissa and her husband, Sasha, who's a policeman. He is already wary of Turner.

Please believe that I will always love you.
Alekhsiy

The arrogant bastard!

Danae balled up the note and threw it at the TV.

Who'd appointed him god and ruler of her life? Didn't he understand she'd never do anything for Turner? That she'd rather die than hurt Torhtremer?

Son of a bitch! Well, maybe not, since she really liked his mother—but goddamn prick at the very least!

She dropkicked a pillow across the room to relieve a little more of her anger. He'd better not show his face anywhere around her again or she'd give him a real piece of her mind.

Besides, Izmir's Curse was high magic, which had been made by the White Sorcerers long ago. Surely it wouldn't work here on Earth, unlike the wizards' low magic that powered his armor.

Goddammit, the least he could have done was say good-bye to her face, instead of leaving a stupid note.

She snarled again and stomped back into the bathroom. If she broke something there, she could at least flush the remains down the toilet—which was exactly where Alekhsiy belonged, too.

TEN

"Thanks, Sasha, for being such a good workout buddy." Danae gave him a genuine grin, her key poised above her lock. He'd actually helped her forget about Alekhsiy for five minutes of the last sixty.

"I should thank you for educating me. I always forget dancers do so much cardio." He tousled his sweat-soaked hair, his hooded cops' eyes seeing far too much inside her face.

"Five hours of class per day, plus performances. How do you think we fuel all of that?" She gave him the old tease. "Heck, right now, I'm on vacation."

"Just blowing away some cobwebs or some nightmares." His mouth thinned.

"Something like that." Larissa had mentioned his bad dreams. Danae patted his arm. "You'd better get into that shower so you can take your old lady down to brunch. She gets cranky when she's hungry."

"Doesn't she just? No matter how much she talks about

dieting, that girl loves her food." He chuckled, genuine amusement ringing out for the first time. Then his hard fingers gripped
hers. "Thanks for providing our room, Danae. We couldn't have
made it this year without you."

"Hey, where would I be without my favorite wardrobe assistant?" She tried to keep the tone light. "And gossip source?"

"You know we'd do anything for you." His gaze bore into
hers.

"Feeling's mutual." She squeezed his hand. "Now go on and
look after your wife, will ya?"

"Glad to. Give us a call when you're ready to show off the
last hall costume, okay?"

"Sure thing." She waved at him and escaped into her room.
Last night's flameout in the parking garage had obviously left
him with a bad case of overprotectiveness.

Or maybe he was worried about what she'd say to Alekhsiy
when they met again. She had most of a really good speech already drafted in her head but she needed to let it simmer.

She leaned against her door and considered her options. She
could wander through GriffinCon without Sasha—which was a
very bad idea, given Turner's track record. That meant she had
to stay up here for the next few hours.

What could she do? E-mail? Maybe but nobody expected to
hear from her during the Con. Write? Not when she was in this
mood.

She should have something packed somewhere in her trunks
to keep her busy. She sauntered forward to take a look.

The curtains were open, allowing brilliant morning sunshine
to spotlight every object, whether it was on the table, desk, or
floor. For the first time, Danae saw her pad through Alekhsiy's
eyes and she shuddered. Her father would have killed her.

Crap. What was half this stuff? Could she even walk in here? She'd have to pile things up to reach her trunk and clearing off the table probably meant dumping stuff onto the floor.

What a pigsty. At least housekeeping had made her bed but she couldn't just lie around. If she did, she'd start thinking about Alekhsiy, the sweet talking son of a bitch who was so damn good in bed.

Maybe she could do a workout in the sitting room, using one of her exercise DVDs. She was accustomed to five hours or more of class and rehearsals, plus performances, each day. She'd never spread out her junk in the other room, since Larissa had used it for fittings.

A few minutes later, she finished unrolling the all-too-demure yoga pad and stood up. It should not be so hard to find something that large, dammit. Still, all she needed was an hour.

Izmir's Curse working magic through her on Earth, indeed. Alekhsiy had simply given her some unique jewelry.

She plopped the dance-inspired exercise DVD into her Mac. The drive hummed and lights rippled. She backed up and widened her stance, then stretched her neck.

"Good morning, ladies! And gents!" Danae's old friend Karen chirped in her best award-winning and money-making voice. Equally perky music rolled through the speakers.

Danae waved back through the mirror. God grant that all dancers do so well in retirement.

"Now, we'll take this first stretch very slowly," Karen cooed enthusiastically. "And, one."

Danae bent over a split second later.

That was odd. She knew this music very well and she was supposed to hit that move exactly on the beat.

"And, two."

Danae was even slower. Worse, her arms were awkward, angular sticks, instead of gracefully floating into the air as thousands of hours in the studio had taught her.

She began to watch every move in the mirror, just as she had in Miss Wilson's School of Ballet when she was five.

She was music—and when music came to life, so did she.

"Three and four. Don't you feel better now?" Karen cheered.

"No, because I could dance better when I was four years old, bouncing on the sofa for my parents!" She could feel the music but she couldn't express it at all—and that ravaged her soul.

She threw a pillow at the wall. Then she stalked off to hunt more DVDs.

Four exercise routines later, she slid down the sofa and onto the floor.

Dancing was magic. Period. It always had been, even before it saved her life and sanity after her family was killed. She could feel it in the air, draw it out of an audience, catch it in her bones, and weave it into greater things than herself.

She was a dancer.

But dancing now felt like lifting an elephant when she used to blow feathers, or being lost in blackness when once she'd painted stars.

The man who loved her had taken everything she had, everything that had kept her happy, everything that had kept the darkness away. Now she truly was completely, utterly alone.

Danae buried her face against her knees and wept.

Alekhsiy rotated his arm to remind his muscles exactly how much true armor weighed. His hauberk had apparently decided it could no longer pretend to be knitted silk, which was probably safest, and had resumed its true metallic heft. An arrow or one of those small, heavy darts called bullets couldn't have pierced it.

But the change meant his body needed to remember all the little details about fighting, starting with armor's heaviness and the sweat. The spell would help somewhat but not completely, lest he be noticed as an oddity.

Most of the knights here were very observant. Some of them had combat experience, too, which could make them more interesting during a duel. All of them were gathered in a loose enclosure, where they could see far too much of each other's preparations. At home, they'd have been neatly sequestered in separate tents.

None of that mattered, so long as he reached the finals and Turner. All he needed to do was kill that brute and he'd save Torhtremer and Danae. He'd left her safe and Torhtremer protected, however bitter those wards.

A muscle jerked in his cheek and he started loosening up his other arm.

There'd be no other woman for him, ever. The brazen hussies here at the gymnasium, snuggling against the fighters to have their picture taken, had made it very clear they thought him fair game with her gone. His rod had been more flaccid than sea grass and his stomach had all but retched. He'd quickly sent those chits on their way.

The stands here at the gymnasium were half full, although he'd been promised crowds would swell later in the day and the great arena that night would be full to overflowing for the finals. The crowd's chatter was friendly now, filled with rustles and soft exclamations when one knight or another was pointed out.

Mistress Nora watched from there with young Evan, who was holding his own very well in the tae kwon do tournament.

"Your sword, sir." Colin bowed and offered Ice Wolf, which

was stretched across his palms. He was dressed in scarlet and gold tunic and leggings, which matched Alekhsiy's uniform. Wonder of wonders, he'd scrubbed until everything visible shone and now acted with all due seriousness, despite the eager glitter in his eyes.

His father was training another squire and Alekhsiy had barely hesitated before accepting Colin's services. He certainly needed a servant who would stay alert to the goings-on in this strange competition.

"My thanks." Alekhsiy bowed equally formally and buckled his beloved sword on. His father had forged it for him when he'd been given his officer's commission. Its constant reminder of his father's love had often steadied him during those long, early years when he'd been young and terrified, and dared not show his doubts in front of his men.

Fire Wind, his axe, hummed quietly from its pouch on his weapons belt. It had come from the Dragon Mountains so long ago that no man knew the date. But it was deadly and implacable in the Realm's service.

The knights were warming up on one side of the platform, while the unarmed fighters prepared on the other side. Each team was readily identifiable by their heraldic blazon and colors. Kyle had chosen Torhtremer's green and gold for Yevgheniy's Spears, surmounted by the entwined dragon and tiger of Torhtremer's great seal.

Turner's team, The Northern Wastes, wore black and white parti-colored tunics, so irregularly assembled they seemed an attempt to dissuade the eye from following them. None of the other men talked to them.

Alekhsiy settled Ice Wolf on his hip, making sure no ungainly folds marred his surcoat's smooth display of Torhtremer's great seal. Let the enemy know who hunted him.

Kyle rounded the corner along the trail from the unarmed warriors, his face so expressionless it was harder than his helm. Trouble haunted his footsteps.

Alekhsiy stepped into his path. "What brings you here with unease riding your shoulder?"

"Hamish is confined to his hotel room with the twenty-four-hour flu." Kyle scowled.

"That's stupid!" Colin protested. "I saw him at breakfast and he was fine."

"Whose task was he performing?" Alekhsiy demanded. "And keep your voice down."

His harsh voice made the stripling's eyes widen but he obeyed. "He was talking to the guy who's always with Turner. Called Harrison, I think," he whispered.

May he roll in Chaos's razor-sharp bed for eons to come in exchange for interfering with honest sport!

"Shit." Kyle punched his fist into his palm. "I don't have another unarmed fighter."

"Will you accept a wrestler?"

"It'll be Greco-Roman style."

Alekhsiy nodded. Surely the gods would be good to him and guide him in whatever manners were necessary.

Kyle's eyes lit with hope before he pursed his lips. "You're heavy combat. Do you have the energy to do both?"

"Yes—and I can't be bribed." Alekhsiy put all his determination into his voice.

"Very well, I'll tell the marshals. Colin, see about finding him some gear, in case he didn't bring any."

Danae paced back and forth across her hotel room, her costume's skirt flapping against her trouser legs like pieces of shattered resolutions. The snug torso had long, tight sleeves and an ankle-length skirt, which was slit up both sides to her hips. Straight trousers were tucked into brocade boots, which matched her torso's lapels. Everything was made from a symphony of flame-red silks, supposedly because she came from the distant Phoenix Court.

But even this example of Larissa's superb handiwork couldn't make her feel any better.

She'd tried to start a short story and ended up logging off her Mac in disgust. Nothing was happening for her. She couldn't even think up a decent epithet for a minor villain.

Maybe something would change after she got some sleep. Yeah, right.

A knock finally sounded on the door and she leaped to answer it. Maybe now she could leave this prison. She wasn't quite frustrated enough yet to tempt fate by strolling through GriffinCon alone.

"Hi, Sasha!" But the two people standing behind him made her brows snap together. One cop in uniform and another in civvies? Badge or no badge, she could smell a cop.

"Danae, this is Detective Lena Davis"—she nodded to the lady in neat khakis—"and Officer Bill Fuhrman."

She gave the uniformed dude a polite smile before looking back at Sasha.

"Can they talk to you for a few minutes? I'm afraid this will be official Atlanta police business." Sasha definitely had on his cop's face.

"Sure, come on in." Her blood thinned to an arctic crawl.

She stepped aside and held the door open. It was always best to cooperate with the police—but how much should she tell them? Alekhsiy, the bastard, wasn't here. Still, she wouldn't mind screwing Turner over.

"You can take a seat in here." She led them to the sitting room and waved her hand at the overstuffed sofas and chairs.

"Coffee, anyone? Maybe some tea? Or there's some fruit juice and soda in the minibar? No? Okay."

She settled herself in the armchair, careful to take a position of power. She'd learned while she was still a teenager not to look helpless in front of the authorities lest they try to take more of her life than they already had. Thank God, this was the most respectable costume of the bunch. Some dance wear could really raise eyebrows in the Bible Belt.

"Do you want me to stay?" Sasha hovered in the doorway.

A friend at court, especially somebody who knew the law? For the first time, her blood ran warm. "Sure."

They both looked at the two local cops. Davis silently consulted with her partner, then nodded. "Why not? We've already spoken to you a little bit about this."

What the hell? She'd half-expected a follow-up visit about last night but what else could they mean?

Sasha dragged over a chair from the small dining table, spun it around, and straddled it beside her.

"How can I help you, Detective?" Danae asked politely.

"Last night you witnessed a shooting and series of fires at the hotel's parking garage."

"Yes, ma'am."

"Do you know what caused the incident?"

"I believe a man may have fallen on his back and dropped his gun, which fired some shots into the sky. That spooked some folks, which caused a general ruckus."

"Do you remember what happened before he fell?"

Drat it, now things became tricky. If she said Alekhsiy had hit the guy, wouldn't they want to put him in jail? She hesitated. "I, ah . . ."

"Miss Livingston, I understand your desire to avoid the media."

Huh? Avoid the media? She blinked at the detective. *Why did he bring that up?*

"But if we're to protect you, we must have all the information. We know that an armed individual approached you specifically, saying he wanted to talk to you."

Well, no, he said Turner wanted to talk to her. Something must have been garbled along the way, which wasn't really surprising.

Danae became aware her mouth was hanging open. "Yes, he had a gun," she agreed in little more than a whisper.

"He was actually carrying a Steyr AUG A3 assault rifle. Those are deadly weapons, Miss Livingston, capable of firing more than eight hundred rounds per minute." *Eight hundred?* "The Atlanta police department will not tolerate them on their streets, especially not in the hands of obsessed fans."

"Fan?" They thought this was about a *stalker?* Danae clapped her hand over her mouth and huddled back into her chair. Thoughts were difficult to come by.

Sasha patted her on the shoulder.

"Yes, ma'am." Detective Davis's eyes were luminescent beacons of sincerity and sympathy. "Interpol told us about the stalkings last year in Europe and how you alone, of all three prima ballerinas, bravely went ahead with the ballet's premiere."

"I wasn't brave!" Danae burst out. Red herrings were one thing but she wasn't about to take credit for something she hadn't earned. "I was scared to death."

"But you still danced, even after the other girls bowed out," Sasha said very quietly, as if speaking to his newborn child. "Your performance made you an enormous target since it had been publicized for months."

"Look, that was the last ballet Rocker J ever choreographed." She swung to face him and willed him to understand. "He was out of the hood and he understood bloody, sudden death. He

happened to be at the dance camp when my folks were killed
and he was the only one who knew how to reach me. He was my
mentor, my buddy, my best friend in the dance world."

She was starting to get teary. Damn, that was bad. She blinked
rapidly until she could trust her voice again.

"So, yeah, I performed his final ballet at its European premiere. What of it?"

"The assault rifle is Austrian and not very common in this
country, Miss Livingston," Officer Fuhrman said gently. "Interpol has been unable to locate your stalker since his threats."

"Yeah, well, everyone thought he was just a loony bin who'd
found better things to do." She looked at the cops again. Why
did they keep carrying on about stalkers, for Pete's sake?

"Including bugging your room?" Sasha held up a few bits of
plastic and metal in a clear plastic bag.

*Shit. May the law never guess how those things died. And
why the hell did she ever think of dumping them in a cop's bedroom?* She closed her eyes. "They're dead ducks. Who cares
about them, anyway?"

"We're sending them to the FBI for analysis, Miss Livingston," Detective Davis said calmly.

FBI?

"Interpol has also asked that we keep an eye on you."

"What? What do you mean by 'keep an eye'?" But Griffin-
Con was where she came for vacation. She'd grown up here and
she got to keep a low profile in this madhouse, unlike everywhere else. This was fun and family.

"Nothing for you to worry about, Danae. They'll have a
guard with you twenty-four/seven, whether you're here in the
room or moving around GriffinCon. The FBI has a team on the
way, too."

"What the hell!" She sat up straight and glared at the other three. *Traipse around GriffinCon, trailed by a cop? Or sit in my room with one outside the door? What a singularly joyless prospect!*

"The lead suspect has been implicated in other crimes, some of which are very nasty, Miss Livingston."

Oh, so now Detective Davis was turning on the implacable schoolmarm side of her officer persona. How could she get around it?

"If he's on this side of the Atlantic and has become even more violent by using an assault rifle, then we don't want to take any chances with your life. Do we, Miss Livingston?"

What was she supposed to say to that? Tell them they were wrong and Turner was the bastard actually out to grab her? Even if she could convince them, they'd still think she needed a guard because of the damned big gun Turner's goons had used. Or they'd start looking more closely at Alekhsiy, the only other person to face the gunmen.

Shit, shit, shit.

"No, I guess we don't," Danae agreed, trying to be gracious. Maybe she could have her agent appeal to somebody higher up in the department, if she claimed her performances would be ruined. She didn't have to mention she currently lacked any such dancing skills.

"It's standard procedure, ma'am, whenever a celebrity's life is threatened. Besides, our chief is a huge fan of yours. He asked me to make particularly sure you were well taken care of, since he had all your PBS performances on DVD."

"Please tell the chief thank you, from me." Manners, drilled into her since before she could walk, controlled her lips. Her brain was spinning somewhere else.

She was so thoroughly screwed. For the first time in her life, achieving a high point in the dance world felt like a prison and not a pinnacle.

"What do you want to do this afternoon, Danae?" Sasha asked. He probably read her better than the others.

She gathered her feet under her and stood up. There was only one thing really to do, especially since she'd already made a start on it.

"I'm going to clean up my room before I take a nap," she announced firmly. She couldn't change everything in her life but maybe she could take control of something small.

Her sole recompense for a nasty set of surprises was seeing his jaw drop.

Alekhsiy rocked from side to side, testing the balance of his soft new boots on the platform. Supposedly this style of wrestling matched his persona and Colin had performed wonders in finding him suitable gear. Even so, everything was unfamiliar to him, from the clothes next to his skin to any move the referee would consider legal or stop the match for.

They also guarded the road to killing Turner.

He still wished he could have apologized to Danae. Maybe if he had, she would have forgiven him.

The black-striped referee blew his whistle.

May the Red God of War grant cunning to my eye and havoc to my opponent.

He stalked his adversary, looking for his first opportunity to strike.

"Nice talking to you, Officer Fuhrman!" Danae escaped back into her room and kicked the door shut, hoping it sounded like a particularly enthusiastic automatic closure.

Two trips to the trash chute—how had she accumulated that much pure shit?—had proved Atlanta's finest truly were determined to keep bad guys away from her. One cop at the door and another one down the hall left her stuck inside. She was more a prisoner of her own celebrity than what that godawful Izmir's Curse had done to her dancing.

At least she could still enjoy music, even if she couldn't dance to it. But the cops wouldn't even let her savor fresh air.

She prowled through her rooms and looked for something else to clean up. She could see lots of carpet now but the maids had the equipment to tackle it. There was plenty of space for her costumes and for all of Alekhsiy's gear, even all of his weapons outside their fancy pouches. Heck, there was so much free floor space that Alekhsiy could have fucked her against any wall he wanted.

Alekhsiy. Pain lanced through her heart and into her gut. The greatest guy in the world, damn his hide—and her memories, which wouldn't let her forget his wicked smile or sinful laugh.

Maybe there was something on TV to take her mind off him.

She pointed the remote control at the monitor and began to play god. No, she didn't want to watch an ancient movie.

The screen filled with her picture, her agent's favorite publicity still, in fact. What the hell?

"There was an attempted kidnapping yesterday in Atlanta against rich and famous prima ballerina, Danae Livingston." The news anchor leaned forward, showing a crack in his normally urbane demeanor. "We go live to our correspondent in Atlanta now."

Oh shit.

She switched channels.

"Everyone in the dance world is abuzz about the latest attack on beautiful Danae Livingston . . ."

"Stalkers are particularly dangerous when they target

celebrities, as Hollywood has taught us. Last night's destruction certainly increases the potential for future harm to Miss Livingston . . ."

She clicked past channels faster and faster, cursing hotels' propensity to stick with the fewest possible choices. Otherwise known as, the news, weather, sports, and a couple of movies.

Yesterday she could've curled up with a big, strong, blond dude and played with his chain mail, instead of this agony.

Aha, Griffin TV! She settled back, ready for a panel discussion. On anything, it didn't matter what.

The central gymnasium flashed onto the screen, full of golden light and two sweating, half-naked men. Alekhsiy? *What on earth was he doing out of his armor?*

Why was he wrestling? Didn't he know that heavy combat took everything a man had and then some to swing that big sword and shield around? How the hell did he hope to defeat Turner if he killed himself along the way doing something else?

Her hands ached down to the bone. She looked down at them and realized she'd been pummeling the TV, trying to get him to stop. But he'd do whatever it took to win, no matter what it cost him personally.

She should be there cheering for him and trying to help him, instead of sitting here alone. She could feed him chi or heal him. She could tell him how much she missed him already, no matter how much the topic scared her.

Tears started coming to her eyes and for once she let them fall over a man.

She'd have to wait to apologize until Larissa and Sasha took her to the arena that night for the masquerade finals. All the fighters would be there, too, so she should see him then. She had to believe that.

And she wouldn't go earlier because that would expose herself to Turner and break the delicate balance Alekhsiy was fighting to achieve.

She wouldn't be a brat, either, and bitch about being stuck in her room.

It did leave her with a lot of time to fill, though.

Well, she had found more of those exercise DVDs. She hadn't realized her agent had sent so many of them to her, hoping for an endorsement. Even if she didn't look graceful, they at least set her blood pumping.

Alekhsiy finished his meal and handed the platter back to Colin with a word of thanks. "And please extend my thanks to your mother as well."

Mistress Nora was guarding all of Yevgheniy's Spears' food like a farmer anticipating a drought. Oh, it was tasty fare indeed, albeit strange. But she permitted nobody near her chests and bottles except herself and her sons.

"I've heard there's more of the twenty-four-hour flu going around the other seeds," Colin remarked chattily. "Especially the teams scheduled to face—"

"The Northern Wastes," Alekhsiy finished for him.

"Yup." The stripling looked ready to deal murder.

"How many rounds has he passed over for lack of an opponent?"

"One. Two others only fielded swordsmen and archers."

"Which forced Turner at least to take the field."

"Do you think so?" The youth cocked his head, clearly reconsidering gossip. "They recombined pairs to field their teams so you may be right. Wicked!"

His shoulders slumped an instant later. "But we still have to fight full rounds."

"We will win through." *The gods would not be so cruel as to keep him from facing Turner.*

"Well, we're the best in our division. You should have told us you could wrestle like that!"

Alekhsiy smiled wryly. He'd had to rely on his prowess in those bouts, rather than conceal it, since he didn't understand the rules. For the swordplay, he was doing barely enough to move forward, hoping Turner would underestimate him.

That would be a blessing, although a greater one would be a sweet farewell to Danae.

"You are damn good," a man's voice agreed.

"Good morrow, friends." Alekhsiy glanced up from the table and tossed a salute to Sasha and Larissa. "Will you join us?"

"Thanks." They easily found seats in the oddly shaped hard chairs. Larissa plopped her enormous purse, with its multitude of pockets, onto the chair next to her. Colin scampered off, responding to his mother's silent demand.

"Would you like something to drink?" Alekhsiy offered.

"No, thanks. We'll only stay a moment, since you probably have to get ready to go back into the ring."

Alekhsiy bowed his head in acknowledgment and waited. Sasha's gun was a very visible bulge at the small of his back today, where it had not been last night.

"We just wanted to let you know that the Atlanta PD—"

"PD?" Alekhsiy murmured, keeping his voice as quiet as the other man's.

"Police know all about the stalker who targeted Danae."

Stalker? Didn't that imply an unknown hunter?

"And the attempted kidnapping last night that went sour."

Kidnapping at least was correct.

"They're taking it real serious. As good as I could hope for."

Sasha nodded significantly and Alekhsiy flicked his fingers in acknowledgment, his brain spinning.

"So there's no need for you to worry about her," Larissa picked up the tale. "There's a guard sitting outside her door and another one will follow her wherever she goes. She'll be perfectly safe."

"The FBI and Interpol are working the case."

Alekhsiy muttered some kind of agreement to the unknown warriors and hoped nobody expected him to say anything clever about who her hunters truly were.

"Danae is being so brave, too. That's why we both had to come talk to you. I didn't think Sasha could explain it right."

Alekhsiy shot a sideways glance at Larissa's husband, who shrugged. "Girl talk," he muttered.

Larissa put her hand on Alekhsiy's forearm. The corners of room keys, including Danae's golden one, glinted from a purse pocket just below her elbow.

"She's spent the whole day cleaning her room. She's never done that before, not in the entire time I've known her. We've been best friends since we were three years old."

"Danae did what?" Alekhsiy frowned. He could not picture her doing so—not her thought processes, her activities, or the result.

"She said"—Larissa looked around, then leaned a little closer to Alekhsiy—"it left more room for you to take advantage of the wall."

Alekhsiy's eyes flew wide open. His rod shouted its readiness to do exactly that, at this minute, with his lady.

Larissa settled back and smiled smugly at her husband. "I told you he'd know exactly what she meant, didn't I?"

"Yes, dear, you did."

She presented her cheek for a victory award and he bussed it.

Alekhsiy gulped for air and began to force some logic back into his turgid flesh. Danae had made a fundamental change, and she'd done it for him. It spoke of the most basic discipline, the first type taught to every cadet at the academy.

If she could do this, if he could trust her in this, could he trust her to be disciplined in more ways? Would Danae the dancer, who spent every waking hour tutoring her body to weave chi from people's happiness, yield to any blackmail demands from Turner?

Surely he could trust her in this much. Surely.

He couldn't talk to her now but he might have a chance later.

He filched both room keys out of Larissa's purse in a move Ghryghoriy had taught him years ago. They disappeared up his sleeve long before Sasha and Larissa stopped smiling at each other.

Alekhsiy walked past Danae's guard nonchalantly, glad the fellow was both wary and an evident fighter, however little he wished to test those skills. Brazen confidence brought Sasha's door open but his hand shook when he set the key to Danae's portal.

What if she threw something at him? Or spat curses at him?

Instead she was asleep, her dark hair spilling over her shoulders like silk's sweetest veil.

He covered his mouth and laughed silently at himself. He should have known his little dancer would slumber peacefully and completely, no matter what the hour.

Should he wake her? His chest tightened, denying breath and hope to his straining heart. What more could be said when she'd already refused his offer of marriage?

Leave a note? He was no great bard or scribe to make words dance. He was a soldier and a man who put deeds into action.

Deeds. Perhaps they would speak louder than words. Perhaps they were the only way to say he loved and trusted her.

He crept over to the bed, careful not to wake her.

ELEVEN

A soft noise brought Danae out of a world of noxious dreams about cold, crashing, blue waves and knife-edged green ice. She squeezed her eyes tighter shut to hide them from the hazy gray light. She was safe, she was in Atlanta, she was locked up in her hotel room—but she was alive.

If you could call it living when dancing didn't play a part.

Her breathing steadied long enough for her to wonder what the hell had woken her up. There was supposed to be a police guard at her door, right? But the connecting door had closed, not the front door. Yet Larissa, God bless her, had no idea of how to move silently and Sasha would never come in here on his own.

Then who the hell had come in? Turner? She sat bolt upright in her bed, her heart pounding like the entire percussion section of a symphony orchestra. No, if he'd been here, she wouldn't still be here alone.

She propped her chin in her hand and told herself not to be

a silly ninny. She wasn't going anywhere until tomorrow when she hit the airport and a plane back to New York. Heck, she and Sasha had decided she wouldn't even go to the masquerade tonight. Turner had proven he was capable of anything. and she didn't want to risk hurting any more innocent bystanders, given the horrors he'd pulled last night.

The hope of seeing Alekhsiy again had died a painful death and she'd cried herself to sleep.

Her wrists felt funny. A hard day's unaccustomed work of bending and stooping had taught her exactly how two wide gold cuff bracelets slid up and down her forearms, especially how they jammed to a stop and were just plain damn heavy. They weren't doing any of that now.

She glanced down uneasily. Had Izmir's Curse thought of another way to manifest itself?

There was nothing on her wrist at all—no bulky cuff, no bracelet. Nothing.

She kicked the covers off and grabbed her ankles to look at them. No, Izmir's Curse wasn't there, either. Nor was it around her neck or waist, not that the Torhtremer Saga had ever mentioned such placement.

The damn things were completely gone.

Had Alekhsiy snuck in to take them off?

Could she work magic? Could she dance and live again?

She tentatively tried a combination, nattily dressed in her cami and cropped pajamas. Jazz walk, kick-ball-change, *pas de bourée, chassé*—yes!

Joy exploded into her heart so strongly, she bounced on the bed and high-fived the ceiling.

Could she do something longer, more complicated? Fosse's "All That Jazz" from *Chicago* or part of the Torhtremer ballet, perhaps?

She grabbed her iPod and cued the Torhtremer music.

Pas de chat . . .

And wow, it came back! She could dance again! She was alive!

She spun on one foot, whipping *fouettés* in wild disregard of potential damage to her free foot from nearby furniture. The sky outside warmed her eyes, the air conditioning danced the hairs off her skin instead of freezing them, and she could have floated like a balloon to Manhattan.

Something thudded to the floor just outside her door.

Danae landed immediately, dropping into a martial arts' combat stance, not a ballerina's admiration-ready first position. Ice swept across her skin, replacing her rebirth's golden heat.

The guard grumbled something and picked it back up.

She shook herself, her euphoria fading faster than it had come. Turner was still out there, hunting for her.

But if nothing had changed beyond her room, why had dearest Alekhsiy given the grace of life back to her? Did he trust her or did he need Izmir's Curse to use on somebody else? Another sorcerer perhaps?

But the only person who concerned him was Turner.

Alekhsiy couldn't possibly think he could walk up to that rich bastard carrying two bracelets.

Even if that was his end game, he still trusted her enough to give her back her freedom. Enough to risk his home and family based on what he believed of her.

Wow. A slow, warm current spread through her heart and seeped into her bones. Delight pushed into her veins and out to her fingertips.

She needed to say thank you and see him once again. Dear God, how desperately she needed to hear his voice and touch him. That meant getting past the damn guard. But how?

According to Alekhsiy, she worked magic by writing down whatever she wanted to have happen. Would that work over here on Earth?

It would be damn convenient if it did. But would it really?

Come on now, Danae, think positive, just like your Dad taught you. You think you can, you think you can, you know you can.

Maybe she could test it on those idiot TV commentators.

She grabbed her Mac and turned it on, then grabbed the TV's remote control. The news shows were still continuously scrolling the abominable headline about her attempted kidnapping. Okay, so it was apparently a slow news day but there had to be something else to talk about every couple of minutes.

She made a very rude gesture at the TV anchors and typed, *Danae Livingston is no longer of any interest to any TV news show . . .*

She hit SAVE and waited.

The feed rolled past. Thunderstorms occurred in the upper Midwest, politicians made banal speeches, two Hollywood stars were caught together at a nightclub without their spouses, more was said about those thunderstorms.

Hey, she'd immediately disappeared from the show's loop.

Hope blossomed, but she tamped it down quickly and switched to another channel. A producer could have made a typo and pulled her from just this feed.

She wasn't mentioned by the next show's talking heads or their automated feed, or on the channel after that, or anywhere on the networks. Websites didn't have anything about her, even on the most gossipy, well-archived blogs. And, hallelujah, she was no longer a top search on Turner's hottest, most up-to-date search engine.

Cool! She had her privacy back, thanks to the spell she'd typed—although, damn, it felt weird to call it that.

First things first. She had to get dressed. Jersey pajamas would probably attract notice, even in GriffinCon's relaxed atmosphere. If she wore her Sunday night masquerade outfit, she could say she was the other half of Larissa's entry.

And with any luck while she was doing that, she'd figure out how to get rid of the police guard.

Of course she would. Piece of cake for an author, right?

And then she'd see Alekhsiy again and talk to him. Somehow.

BIYSK MOUNTAINS, FAR NORTH OF TORHTREMER

The sun's last rays lanced off the high peaks and faded into the snow without lighting the valley. The river roared and dashed itself against the iron rocks far below, confined like a madman in a cell too small for his ambition. Sheer cliffs, bereft of soft trees or even moss, plunged toward the water, while their jagged edges clawed the sky. The troops had seen none of the knife-edged, fast-moving waterfalls in the last ten leagues, thanks be to the Hunter.

Zhenechka and Jeirgif's latest hymn to that god was a stout one and most of the men had joined in. The echoes died away too quickly but their simple magic at least barred some of the worst pursuers from coming too close.

A single road clung to the mountain's edge, barely high enough to stay clear of the water. Its roadbed was made from ancient bricks, with many missing or unevenly set. Igoryok had walked it time and again in his dreams—and measured its narrow width with his friends' bodies.

They rounded a corner—and the gorge narrowed, tightening to a gap that a handful of men could protect.

And beyond that? Salt air swept into his nostrils with a tyrant's arrogant assurance.

The song collapsed as his people gathered close to stare.

"The Tungur Sea," Jeirgif whispered.

"And the Chulym Beach, there, where the great breakers are." Zhenechka pointed. "I can see flashes of light from where jeweled weapons have washed up."

Igoryok nodded, his throat too tight to make a sound.

"But it has floating ice in it," Jeirgif objected, hanging on to a high boulder so he could lean farther out over the gorge to see. "How can anything, even our enemy, spawn in something so cold?"

"He is the master of winter. Where else should he come to pass?" Zhenechka asked tartly and dragged on her pack's straps to settle them better over her shoulders. "Brats often behave much like where they were conceived or birthed."

Jeirgif's eyes grew very round and somebody snickered. Someone else asked a more practical question. "How much farther will we go tonight? Onto the beach or do we camp in the mountains as we did last night?"

Igoryok was far colder than his excellent furs should permit.

"No, we will camp here, in the wide spot on the road. We will fight in the morning, if not tomorrow, then the day after."

His people's expressions immediately turned hard and calculating as they judged the site. Igoryok granted them their explanation before they could ask.

"This is the Gate of Belukha, through which the Imperial Terrapin's mightiest fighters will come to give him homage. The more we can kill, the better chance General Alekhsiy will have to send him back."

"And very little hope of our survival or the general's," Zhenechka commented softly. The rocky cleft was unwontedly quiet, free from any human sounds as they waited for a differing opinion.

"But the bards will sing our praises for a thousand years," Igoryok offered. Sometimes a man contemplated foolish rewards for a well-spent life, like a pair of giggling dancing girls. But duty held its own pleasures, especially if it aided loved ones far away.

"Then we had best start making our preparations," Jeirgif said briskly, taking the lead in a manner unbecoming to his youth. "There was a clump of young barnaul trees a few miles back, clinging to the crags above the road. I may be able to cut them down if I move quickly before the sun sets. Hydras loathe their fire and we will need all the torches we can make."

"Go then." Igoryok nodded. He'd agree to anything to help fight off the many-headed, poisonous snakes that had been trailing them since they'd crested the pass.

But there would be other, worse monsters to fight tomorrow.

ATLANTA
SUNDAY EVENING

Danae slowly pivoted one last time in front of the mirror to double-check her costume. An entertainer always made sure clothing and accessories were correct but this time? Heck, tonight the entire performance would probably be improvised. This was no time for any wardrobe malfunctions.

Her over-dress was deceptively simple, smoothly fitted from her shoulders to her waist and hips before flaring softly out to just below her knees. Slits on each side up to just below her waist made it very easy to move. It was richly decorated at the neck and down the center to her breasts, her wrists, and the hem in a magnificent embroidered design of tigers and complex Torhtremer runes. More crystals were scattered across the body until she glittered like moonrise.

Her softly pleated trousers were made from white silk, albeit not brocade. They were tucked into soft white boots, which carried silver beading at the top, down the throat, and over the instep. Her cream silk cloak was banded in brocade and embroidered in matching runes and crystals. Even her white leather gauntlets were embellished in silver.

If she'd ever wanted to be inconspicuous, this was so not the outfit to do it in.

On the other hand, this costume should make the judges sit up and pay attention to Larissa's workmanship skills—especially when combined with the very tightly fitted Kyristari spymaster's corset her friend was going to wear.

They were designed to represent the top tiers of Corinne and Celeste Carson's fantasy heroines, the two authors who'd died here at GriffinCon all those years ago.

Danae and Larissa would contrast as much as possible, much as the two sisters' books had. Danae would be completely covered up, Larissa would be garbed only in the corset, hose, and matching jewelry. Soft silks would whisper over her welltoned body, heavily boned armor shaping Larissa's softer curves. Danae would be in shape-shifters' white, while Larissa wore a sexsub's inviting scarlet—an outfit and color guaranteed to drive her husband crazy.

Alekhsiy enjoyed more subtle temptations and knew how to pleasure his lady no matter how many layers she'd donned.

She was going to the arena to help Alekhsiy because she didn't trust that Turner son of a bitch. Alekhsiy might not want her anymore after how she'd rejected him but she'd still try to help him.

She glanced down at the innocently blinking cursor on her laptop's screen.

No cop will see, hear, or speak of anything Danae Livingston does in the hallway outside her room.

She lifted the gold chain over her head and kissed her father's Naval Academy class ring before removing it from the chain. Then she tucked it safely into the same pouch on her waist where she kept her cell phone. Every White Sorceress had a jeweled ring so she'd wear it over her gauntlet during the masquerade.

She punched the SAVE button, her blood flowing as calmly as in any theater before opening night. She shut down her Mac to slow down anybody from finding out what she'd done. If indeed it would make sense to anybody other than a fanfic author.

Five, six, seven, eight . . .

Showtime had arrived.

She opened the door and sauntered into the hallway, her head held high and her shoulders back. Miss Wilson had taught all of her pupils the same attitude and step during their first year of school.

The cop was a thirtysomething man, fit and neatly-dressed in khakis and polo shirt. He leaned back against the wall and spoke urgently into his phone. "I don't care what the lab says, I need that report tonight, not Tuesday . . . Yeah, yeah, but I'm stuck here on babysitting duty. I might as well get some work done, instead of just snoring."

He hunched his shoulder and turned away from her. "No, the wife wasn't pleased but the overtime's not bad."

Danae strolled toward the elevator, her pulse speeding up. Her plan had worked, against all odds. But what came next?

ABOVE THE TUNGUR SEA, NORTH OF TORHTREMER

Khyber slowly flapped his great wings to maintain altitude, his massive size enabling him to overlook most of the rough winds that tore apart travelers here.

What could he discern through the heavy gray clouds except black sea and scudding foam blown from white wavecaps? It wasn't easy to spot anything smaller than an iceberg, at least not so far. He hadn't seen a seagull or albatross for leagues.

Yet young Alekhsiy was one of his favorites.

He circled again and prepared to come lower, as he had not dared to for millennia. Many of his kin were buried in the mountains south of here.

Bitterly cold air slammed into his belly and tossed him high, tumbling him over and over like a dragonet. Ice formed on his wings and claws. Dearest Svetlhana yelped and dug her claws into his shoulder to stay aboard.

His heart dived faster than their chances of survival.

He gathered himself and dropped, fighting with armored tail and leathery wings like the demon he'd been called. Salt spray filled his nostrils but he finally found the single air current that led south and west.

The skies were gentle and blue before he spoke. "Azherbhai has locked the doors to his kingdom," he remarked.

"He has never welcomed visitors, beloved. Did you sense if Alekhsiy was there?"

He frowned, unsettled. Despite all the millennia they'd loved each other, his dragon wisdom did not enable him to delve deep if his feline lady wished to speak of trifles.

"No, Fire Wind is nowhere to be found. I would know immediately if any dragon-forged weapon had come to the land of perpetual ice."

"Then at least we can believe he is still safe on the far side of the void, hunting for the potential catalyst." She kneaded his shoulders with her big soft paws. He sighed happily and began to relax, despite his suspicion she was trying to distract him. "Do you want to travel there in search of him?"

"No, of course not." He almost blew a smoke ring in disgust. "I—*we*—cannot leave Torhtremer for even five minutes when our opponent is so active. He would immediately take advantage of our absence and wreck havoc on Mykhayl and our loved ones in Bhaikhal."

"True," she rumbled. "He is a disgusting creature who tastes foul." She lingered over the last word, drawing it out until it sounded like a prescription for death. Not for the first time, he wished he could crane his neck far enough around to see her face while he was flying.

"We are forbidden to move directly against him so we must fight with the weapons we have."

She loosed a mighty yowl, redolent of feline frustration. Discomfort hardened into near-certainty.

"Svetlhana," he warned, "do not tempt The Great Order by disobeying its strictures."

"I am not that much of a fool." She sniffed.

He had to protect her from her own folly. If she was to be banished again to where he could neither see nor touch her . . .

"We will remain in the capitol and guard the children."

"What?" Svetlhana roared her challenge to his change in their plans. "What about Alekhsiy? What if he needs our help when he returns?"

"He has his amulet and can summon us," Khyber announced flatly, shutting down any further discussions.

ATLANTA

Danae arrived in the hotel lobby crushed between a giant Wookie and a lumbering multi-tentacled monster adapted from many anime classics. Normally she'd have tried to gain breathing room for her costume, but this time she kept her head down and prayed no cop would notice her. And why hadn't she written a spell to demand that nobody would kidnap her?

Brilliant, Danae, just brilliant.

She sidled through the crowd and headed for the shuttle bus stop as quickly as possible. Why were there so many costumes to dodge? Wings, elevator shoes making people awkward, clumps of people taking pictures . . .

She ducked her head, refused to acknowledge anybody with a camera, and kept going. Just a few more feet to the side door.

Wiry fingers seized her elbow.

"Every sorceress needs a Torhtremer soldier—Miss Livingston," an unfamiliar voice hissed.

She shot the obnoxious fool a haughty glance and tried to pull herself away. His bald head and skinny frame clad in yet another Torhtremer T-shirt and jeans looked familiar somehow.

Passersby were eyeing them but giving them a wide berth. Somebody even paused to take a picture. Dammit, did they think this was staged?

"Mr. Turner will be very glad to talk to you." He tightened his grip on her and started to pull her closer.

Like hell.

She ground her boot heel down onto his instep and shrieked. "Help! Help me!"

"Shut up, bitch." He growled, hunching his shoulders and moving faster.

She was cold but she could also see his movements so very,

very clearly now. She kicked him again, deliberately calculating how to trip him up. She'd do everything she could to avoid Turner's lair.

"Help me, please! This isn't a LARP!" She put everything she'd ever learned in a theater into her bellow. She elbowed him hard in the ribs with her other arm but he only grunted and yanked her closer. Terror chilled her blood and brought her wits to laser clarity. She used the momentum from his pull to spin toward him in a dancer's move and jab her stiffened fingers at his face.

His eyes narrowed in a trained fighter's recognition of a true opponent and he instinctively loosened his grip on her, ready to begin the battle.

She stepped away slightly, every nerve, every muscle, preparing itself for combat.

Then a trio of white-armored stormtroopers slammed onto her would-be kidnapper and a muscular reptile assassin from the Varrain Universe piled on top. Assorted Pern dragon riders, Hogwarts wizards, and various superheroes dived onto the struggling mass and spilled over her.

"Oof!" Danae went flat on the lobby floor. That awful clutching hand was finally ripped completely away from her wrist.

She lay still for a few moments, her face buried in the crook of her arm. She'd never expected to be grateful to be close-up with a stained hotel carpet. Her pulse slowly eased back into something approaching normal. Some of her rescuers eased themselves off of her, reducing the weight and taking costume fragments away from the corner of her outfit.

"Sir, will you please sit still? I'm Officer Duncan of the Atlanta PD and I simply want to ask you a few questions about recent events," a man announced with a politeness born of long experience and few expectations. "Sir!"

The mass heaved upward and settled back down with a hard thump. Danae began to wiggle herself out from underneath.

"Sir, I truly must insist that you accompany me." Inflexibility resonated through the speaker's voice and metal clicked. Handcuffs?

Danae reached her feet, along with one of the stormtroopers. Together they faded into the circle of onlookers, which was gathered around her assailant, a policeman, and several of her rescuers. A small trickle of blood ran down the cop's face.

A low murmur of concern went up from the crowd.

Her would-be kidnapper tried to pull himself free and run but the reptilian assassin jerked him brutally back.

"Let me through!" "Make way!" Shouts rang through the lobby and feet pounded toward them.

For once, the great milling throng created avenues to allow passage and a dozen police stormed into the ring. Her assailant's shoulders slumped.

Danae smiled, in an undoubtedly feline manner, and began to work her way toward the door. She truly did not want to give her statement to the police, at least not yet.

But she did hear one of their utterances, delivered by a cop with a very carrying voice.

"Go ahead and run his prints but I can tell you who he is. That's Helping Hands Harrison, the hacker king who was sentenced to three hundred years for cyber theft. The judge is going to throw the book at him for breaking probation, resisting arrest, assaulting an officer . . ."

The hotel door closed behind her, cutting off the rest of the fellow's known crimes. He'd probably done worse for Turner but would he talk about it?

Danae jumped onto the shuttle bus. She'd probably have to

stand all the way to the stadium but who cared? At least she was on her way and maybe she could help Alekhsiy.

Boris judged the effect of another smile in the glass door. Last year, his victory photo had been panned by a couple of websites and he wanted this year's to be better received—even if he wasn't here to see it.

This corridor under the indoor arena wasn't much but he needed to practice for when he'd rule Torhtremer. The tiny space was full of fighters, wearing a wide variety of gear, mixed with some of the masqueraders in their bizarre outfits.

Dammit, even Alek Alekseiovich, the bitch's bodyguard, was here with his team. Somehow they'd gotten through the preliminary rounds, despite every obstacle he could throw in their way.

He hissed through his teeth and turned away. His usual effort would be good enough for the conqueror.

Judging by the monitors, the stands were almost full now, their occupants craning their necks to peer down as if they were about to see NBA finals instead of GriffinCon's Sunday Night Finale. The arena was arranged as if for a basketball game with a long, narrow, central wooden floor, although no baskets, of course.

Like the other tournament contestants, he was currently standing around waiting to begin the great parade into the arena. It supposedly fostered sportsmanship but give him victory any day.

He snorted in disgust and pulled out his BlackBerry. Sooner or later, Harrison had to answer.

Ah, connected at last!

"Yes?" A woman's voice, on Harrison's phone? "Who is this, please?"

Somebody shouted all too clearly in the background. "No, I did not pick up the medical examiners' report for you!"

"Sorry, wrong number." Boris hung up quickly.

Medical examiner? Crap, Harrison's phone was held by somebody at the police department. Was there any innocent explanation for that?

Would they believe he'd called a wrong number? Did it matter, when his phone was so very, very popular with Harrison's?

For the first time since he'd clawed his way out of that stinking Illinois sewer called his hometown, sick fear threatened his dinner's safety in his belly. He forced air through his clenched teeth and reminded himself who he was—the third richest man in the world, self-made billionaire, and the greatest salesman ever. A sorcerer, too, according to the Imperial Terrapin.

Azherbhai.

He, Boris Turner, would be the Dark Warrior, Azherbhai's catalyst, and master of Torhtremer, if he could just get there.

First thing's first, though. Those pigs would have to fight their way past his lawyers to touch him. He managed a small laugh and lovingly fingered his sword's hilt. He had two such identical weapons, of course—one for practice, like these events, and another, very real one. Letting the so-called law get past his lawyers to meet his true blade would be a truly Dark Warrior response.

Escaping into dreams of Torhtremer was sometimes all that kept him alive—and how many people would understand that?

Certainly Yevgheniy's Spears would, the only team present in full gear from that wonderful world. They'd feel the same passion, even Alek Alekseiovich, the author's bodyguard, who'd been fighting double matches all afternoon.

As if hearing him, the fellow half-turned to speak to another, displaying a magnificent amber pendant hanging around his

neck on a rawhide thong. It glowed unlike anything Boris had
ever seen before. It didn't look like electronics or plastic, which
could be lit from within. The best in the world had tried to sell
those to him.

Amber, the living stone. His hand itched to hold it.

Azherbhai's prophecy echoed in his head. "Living stone can
unlock the gate and bring you through . . . Unfledged sorcerer,
you will know by touch."

Could it be magic? Nah, that was ridiculous.

Azherbhai's dark eyes snapped into being before him, deep
pools of cold wisdom. *Foolish mortal, why do you hesitate?
You know that is the passport to my realm. All you need do is
seize it.*

*There are twenty thousand witnesses watching everything I
do,* Boris protested.

*Speak the words and it will act immediately. The longer
you delay, the greater your peril. But the sooner you come, the
greater your reward.* His great beak clacked shut on the last
words, as if savoring a particularly tasty morsel.

Like Bhaikhal and the Dragon's Hoard's hundred concubines. He could have that many women serving him any time he
snapped his fingers.

All he had to do was fight his bout against Alekseiovich, not
Kyle, the team's nominal leader. He'd already bribed the marshals to schedule him against anybody he wanted.

Hell, maybe he should use his true blade in this bout and not
the rattan one. That would guarantee him a win.

But the amulet would be hidden underneath the bastard's
coif and hauberk.

Do you balk at shedding a little blood? inquired his master.
What can these peasants do to you once you rule with me?

True, oh very true, my lord! He dipped his head in homage.

If Alekseiovich didn't take his gear off fast enough, well, he'd just have to do it for him. Heck, he might need to provide a little forceful persuasion, too. Then he could escape to Torhtremer, before anybody had a chance to stop him.

And, of course, any injuries the bitch's bodyguard might suffer along the way would only be his just desserts for causing last night's debacle in the parking garage.

"I still think you'd have been better off watching it from the hotel room," Larissa grumbled, heedless of the other contestants around them. The costumed entries' private section was just above the floor, where the judges could easily summon the winners—or neurotic contestants could quickly retreat to private restrooms.

Danae shot her a sideways glance. "No stalker's going to do anything in such a big crowd," she repeated for the umpteenth time since she'd arrived. "There's tons of security and I'm perfectly safe."

Sasha shot her another seething glance but said nothing. He'd been furious when she'd arrived but she'd flatly refused to go back to the hotel until after the masquerade. To her considerable surprise, Nora had championed her presence. He'd finally backed down, having learned from bitter experience not to fight that former dance mistress. Now he curled his hand around his wife's and she leaned against his shoulder, pulling his support around her as much as she did her cloak.

Would she ever have anything like that? She knew too damn well she'd thrown away her best chance when she refused Alekhsiy's offer. Impossible conundrum. She desperately returned her attention to the combatants in the center of the arena.

The judges had readily accepted her explanation that the

entry was a two-person one after all, not one. Hers and Larissa's performance had gone off quite well, considering she hadn't been present for the technical rehearsal. Now they waited for the final bout of the evening—the fully-armored combat between Turner and Alekhsiy.

Alekhsiy had already wrestled—and won—once not long ago. She was hardly an expert in Greco-Roman wrestling but he'd certainly impressed the crowd. She'd simply prayed he wouldn't be hurt or exhausted.

Selfishly, she hadn't worried about Kyle's bout. It had been close, much to Nora's white-knuckled fidgets down in the team support area directly under them. But Kyle had beaten his opponent, making the title come down to whether Alekhsiy or Turner won.

The two fighters squared off in the center of the arena, garbed in glistening chain mail. Conical steel helmets now crowned both men, with crisp nose pieces to protect their upper faces. Heavy mail coifs covered their heads, necks, and shoulders. Their brilliant shields and surcoats—green and gold for Yevgheniy's Spears, black and white for The Northern Wastes—were the greatest differences between them.

Overhead, the great monitors showed their every detail, including their deadly intensity.

God help her, she hadn't had a chance to talk to him privately yet. Having twenty thousand people hanging around didn't allow any comforting feelings of intimacy.

Turner attacked fast and hard, starting with his sword held high. Alekhsiy blocked it with his shield and counterattacked.

The two swords came together with a *thwack!* rather than the dull *clack!* of rattan striking together she was used to.

Danae's heart stopped beating. What was wrong?

Alekhsiy twisted his wrist and disengaged. His blade shimmered briefly and the yellow stripe marking its cutting edge disappeared so rapidly, one could have almost sworn it had never existed.

Turner attacked again, his mouth contorted into an ugly snarl.

CLANG! The two blades rang together in the pure music of fine metallurgy. Several contestants pointed and murmured from behind her.

God help them all, Turner was using a real weapon—and Alekhsiy's spell had ripped off his sword's camouflage to protect him.

Alekhsiy could be badly injured or killed.

She glanced at the marshals, willing them to stop the bout.

One of them whispered urgently but the other brushed him off impatiently. They finally assumed their most impenetrable observers' pose, their staffs of office haughtily erect at their side.

Crap, had Turner bribed them not to interfere? Did they think that the duty to provide *entertainment* would excuse any injuries to combatants?

Clang, clang, CLANG!

The quick exchange of blows brought the crowd screaming to its feet. Danae yelled, too, but in fear, not approbation. Her heart slammed against her ribs and her fingers twitched, longing for her Mac. If only she hadn't left it in her room.

It wasn't until she paused to draw breath that she realized she'd been shouting in the Language of the Beasts, one of Torhtremer's two spellcasting languages.

TWELVE

Alekhsiy warily circled his enemy once again. Turner had been given wings since he'd fought in the earlier rounds. Now he was far speedier than most mortals, almost catalyst fast.

The bout had lasted longer than any others but nobody paid attention to that, least of all Turner's puppets, the marshals. They stood on the sidelines and muttered over their papers.

The two swordsmen paid no heed to niceties, such as fighting on their knees to show another type of skill. No, this was a brutal fight to the finish between two warriors who'd enjoy seeing the other die.

And Alekhsiy's arms and legs burned with a bitter pain, almost worse than actual fire. His lungs were tighter than the bands hammered around a barrel. But his head was clear and he still brought up his sword and shield fast and clean to block and parry—and thrust. Still, he needed his shield more often and longer than his enemy did, damn the maggoty spawn.

Turner knew it, too.

Danae was out there, cheering for him. Every time he came close to where she sat, fresh chi flowed into him. He could glimpse her out of the corner of his eye, dressed in those glinting jewels. He could hear her voice, chanting spells to aid him in the Language of the Beasts. Every note added more grace, more life to his movements.

Perhaps if he tried something else . . .

He attacked in front of the gaudy masquerade contestants, coming in high and a little wild as if on the verge of exhaustion.

Turner's eyes narrowed behind his helm and he swept his shield into place to trap Alekhsiy.

Alekhsiy brought his sword down to the outside, leaving himself apparently open.

Danae's voice reached into his bones and buoyed him up.

Turner charged forward a step too far, his sword held just a little casually in anticipation of the coming victory.

Alekhsiy sidestepped and whirled. Instinct told him where the target was and he brought his sword swinging down onto Turner's blade. Steel forged in his father's blood smashed through metal bought and paid for.

Thunk!

Turner's sword shattered a few inches above the hilt and crumbled to the floor.

Joy, tempered with caution, danced through Alekhsiy's veins and he stepped back. The crowd was shouting somewhere beyond the arena but he didn't care.

"Foul! I claim a foul!" Turner shouted. "I demand a rematch with new weapons." He glared at Alekhsiy, his face white about the lips.

The two marshals hastened up to them and the noise began to die down.

"You must give me a rematch," Turner demanded. "This man brought real weapons onto the field of combat."

"Well, I know somebody did," retorted one of the marshals, pushing at the sword's shards with his toe.

Turner flushed and bit his lip, then turned away. A covey of officials gathered to squawk like geese. Cursing, he snatched off his helm and accepted a drink with ill grace.

Alekhsiy sheathed his sword and also doffed his helm. It was far too hot here in this strange place, under these batteries of glowing suns, to wear headgear any longer than necessary. Dealing death to Turner would have to wait until he could find privacy.

Danae hastened up to him with a large flask of water, followed an instant later by Kyle and Nora. "Thank you, my lady."

She smiled at him, her expression softer and warmer than ever before. Blessed be the gods, she seemed to hold no ill will against him.

He filled his eyes with her beauty, as necessary to him as the fluid itself.

Danae nestled herself as close to Alekhsiy as she could, laughing a little shakily at her sudden liking for hard chain mail. But after spending so many minutes watching him and Turner fight each other, she was simply glad to have him back where she could sense his solidity through her own clothes. She might never again be able to comb out his hair or pet his naked skin. But she could help mop the sweat off his brow, give him water, and hold his hand.

She twined her fingers a little more tightly through his.

He glanced down at her, then raised her hand and kissed it.

Larissa sighed sentimentally.

Danae simply leaned her head on Alekhsiy's arm to soak up his nearness while she still could. Larissa could take that attitude because she had a husband to provide reality's warmth. Danae would be alone again the minute Alekhsiy left and she needed to build her memories.

The marshals broke their circle. The Grand Marshal, a sharp-featured graying man, called for attention over the public address system.

Everyone fell silent. Even Turner came back from where he'd been keying into his BlackBerry.

"Ladies and gentlemen," the Grand Marshal intoned in a voice designed to draw attention at places lacking electronic amplification, "we have reached our decision. Since both combatants fought with identical weapons and no injuries were suffered, the bout is deemed valid by GriffinCon rules."

Thank God. Danae's knees almost buckled in relief. She didn't think she could have endured watching Alekhsiy fight another round like that.

Cheering broke out from the upper rafters but was quickly hushed.

Turner's expression hardened.

"Accordingly, Mr. Alekseiovich is declared the winner of the bout and Yevgheniy's Spears have triumphed in the heavy combat team portion of the tournament."

Nora flung herself into Kyle's arms. He swung her around like a child before kissing her. Alekhsiy laughed and pulled off his mail coif.

"Wicked," Evan enthused, bouncing on his toes. "Torhtremer!" he shouted, echoing the crowd.

Danae kissed Alekhsiy, his hard hands stroking her hips with all his old enthusiasm. He still seemed to care a little for her and she definitely wanted to talk to him, and do other things if she could. Maybe she could persuade him to stay overnight before he returned home. Warmth stirred in her mouth and through her lungs whenever his tongue dipped and dived across her lips.

"Hey, where did Mr. Turner go?" Colin asked. "Aren't all the teams supposed to shake hands or something?"

Kyle rumbled something about typical rudeness and went back to his circle of reporters.

"Masquerade winners . . ." the PA system shouted again but nobody listened. Nobody cared.

Danae leaned her head against Alekhsiy's chest and reminded herself that public places were not the right setting for making out.

"My lady, my love," he whispered to her.

Could she feel anything through his chain mail? Anything small and interesting, like his pecs or maybe his nipples? She knew where his thighs were, of course—she wiggled happily—but the others would take handiwork.

She started to walk her fingers up his chest and he watched her, a bemused smile playing around his lips.

Suddenly Alekhsiy jerked erect and spun around. He shoved her behind his back so hard she almost fell onto the ground.

Turner backed away from him. He waved Alekhsiy's amulet in the air and it blazed like a golden sun in his hand. God help them all, there was magic in it for him.

Danae recovered her balance. Her lips began to move, spilling words beyond her volition.

Overhead, Azherbhai swam through every giant monitor, in a sea of icebergs and scudding seas. If she strained her eyes hard enough, she could glimpse mountains and a rocky beach through a single corner screen.

The audience turned to stare, swinging between the man on the floor and the beast threatening them from above.

"You may think you've won," Turner shouted, "but I have everything! I will truly be the Dark Warrior!"

Azherbhai clacked his beak approvingly and dived, bursting out of the monitors and into the arena in a single vaporous image. He soared its length and breadth, swooping toward individuals until they screamed and ducked.

He zoomed over the arena floor, avoiding only Alekhsiy and Danae. They alone still stood, locked together by her arm around his waist and surmounted by Alekhsiy's drawn sword. Somehow Alekhsiy gave her strength to withstand the stench of Azherbhai's breath, which was worse than any ancient sewer.

"Come with me, my catalyst!" Azherbhai rolled arrogantly, as if he already reigned supreme in Torhtremer's seas—and Earth's. "It is time to come home."

Turner ran forward eagerly and Azherbhai eased him onto his back with a single giant flipper. The man held the amulet up and Alekhsiy cursed bitterly, then ran forward. But their enemies were too high up for him to reach.

A sheet of swirling colors dropped over one end of the arena, more intense and faster moving than any vision of the Northern Lights. The air stretched somehow, as if pulled unwillingly. But there was no exit nearby big enough to provide that much wind.

The colors began to spin faster and faster, catching at every hair and bit of trash in the hall. Blackness appeared in the center, darker and more final than anything seen through a space telescope.

Azherbhai lifted an insolent flipper and tossed Turner into the maelstrom. He howled and vanished, plummeting down its maw.

BOOM! The great curtain and Azherbhai disappeared simultaneously. The house lights swayed wildly overhead and dimmed down to a few scattered bulbs. People screamed and lost their footing.

Danae was very, very cold. Dear sweet heaven, Turner had gone to Torhtremer with Azherbhai.

She shoved her way over to Alekhsiy, who'd charged toward the blank wall through which Turner and Azherbhai had disappeared. A few tournament warriors started to lift their heads from the floor.

Alekhsiy turned to face her, his expression grim and hard in the emergency half-light. "That thrice-cursed Chaos spawn will destroy Torhtremer."

"He won't have the chance." She wrapped her hands around his free one to comfort him.

He shook his head, the lines in his face deepening. "I must follow immediately, since time passes so much differently here than there."

Ouch. If five minutes here meant a month there—or something worse. Horror knotted her stomach.

"Will you help me?"

"Of course." What wouldn't she do for him or her friends in Torhtremer?

"Yet where can we find the chi? Or the dragon's blood?"

"You have the dragon's blood in your thigh."

"From my old wound? But there's not much there," he protested, reluctant hope starting to replace the agony behind his eyes.

"Enough for a sorceress to work with. Plus, the crowd will provide plenty of chi. Come on." She ran him over to the central mike. The marshals and Master of Ceremonies, gobbling on the sidelines about proper procedures, were absolutely useless to do anything quickly, of course.

Everything had happened so fast that most of the dazed

onlookers were still in the arena, although a few had started to gather up their possessions. The tournament warriors were clustered in the center, bitterly complaining about Turner's breach of chivalric honor. The gaudily dressed masquerade contestants hovered in the stands or along the edges, uncertain whether any of their results would ever be announced.

The entire arena reeked of opportunity waiting to be seized. The finely tuned hairs along Danae's skin lifted in response and she smiled in anticipation.

Good, Andrew had proven himself a genius yet again and had the lights working already. If she knew him at all, he was pissed as hell that management was standing around trying to figure out something to calm down the masses. Fine, she'd provide it.

She waved at the control booth, completely certain he was watching from within. Then she significantly pointed at the mike, adjusted it to her height, and waited.

Come on, Andrew, let me have my chance. You must have seen Alekhsiy and me try to fight off Azherbhai. The only ones who were still standing, thank you very much.

The house lights dimmed abruptly, cutting off all conversation. A single spotlight caught her, then another and another, bringing Alekhsiy's mail and her uniform to glittering life.

"Friends of Torhtremer!" she called.

The few people climbing the stairs turned to look.

Alekhsiy's arm locked around her waist and his free arm came up proudly to display his sword.

Courage flowed into her, rich and sweet as the blood swelling her veins.

"Do you believe Azherbhai can defeat us?"

"Never!" shouted Kyle and Nora.

Good, Nora had grabbed another microphone and was lead-
ing the cheer from that end of the arena with her entire family.

"To what do we pledge all our hopes?"

"Torhtremer!"

All of the fighters on the floor were chanting now, plus the
masqueraders. Peter Jacobsen, the movie producer, jumped out
of the stands and onto the arena floor.

Larissa started to wave her arms in a great stylized clap and
the audience caught the beat immediately.

Danae could see threads of energy, like glowing strands of
color, spinning through the hall and into her skin.

"Who will be victorious?" she demanded.

T. Sanderson helped Miss Xenia off the stairs and into the
center. They joined H. S. McCain and the marshals in roaring
out the next response.

"Torhtremer!"

Danae anchored the threads of chi on herself and sent some
strands through Alekhsiy, spinning strength into him to replace
what he'd lost. He gasped briefly, then stood more vibrantly
erect.

"Who will live in peace forever?"

She needed to see their destination next . . .

"Torhtremer!"

The crowd roared their enthusiasm, generously donating
their chi. The stands strengthened with every syllable and the
giant scoreboard overhead vibrated like a tuning fork.

The icy mountains and beach snapped into the monitors,
clear as a travelogue.

Time to go. She silently framed her request in the Language
of the Beasts, then shouted in English to her friends.

"Who will we dream of forever?"

"Torhtremer!"

A black hole, edged in diamond shards, appeared directly in front of them. *Good-bye, Earth.*

Alekhsiy's hand tightened on hers and they leaped into frigid, whirling winds.

Every light in the arena exploded behind them, destroying glass and electronics in a fiery, iridescent rainbow so completely that their shards couldn't injure anyone below.

The crowd screamed and prostrated themselves, only daring to stand up after several agonizingly long minutes. Shards twinkled like stardust on the floor and their ears still rang, making flesh and blood quiver in tune with the waves of that strange, far world. A child sighed and cloth rustled in distant darkness, like a coat waiting to be picked up for a long journey. A small light appeared, creeping into a shadowed corner, and another and another.

"And I suppose," commented Andrew from the control booth, devoutly grateful some of his emergency lights had once again survived, "some smartass will think *that* was the Fourth of July show and expect me to do better next year."

GATES OF BELUKHA IN THE BIYSK MOUNTAINS
DAWN

The sunshine, such as it was, glanced off the mountainside and the last pair of red eyes disappeared behind a boulder. The road was dank with foul dew, prophesying a worse day than the previous night.

"May the gods be praised, I never thought we'd see the last of those hell spawn," Jeirgif grumbled. Like everyone else, he was bustling through his morning chores, leavened by the pressing need to prepare for attack. They'd built themselves a strong fortress the previous evening but improvements could always be made.

"Or rather, you thought we would see all of them, instead of merely their eyes," Igoryok corrected him.

"Are you trying to encourage us—or show us the truth?" Zhenechka demanded, busily knotting colored yarn charms. Igoryok wasn't surprised she'd finished her assigned chores before anyone except himself and was working on her own ideas of necessities.

"Truth," he admitted wearily. He'd slept little, his dreams having worsened with his proximity to their source.

"In that event, you might want to dip some arrows in this. I'd trust you with it but few others." She excavated a well-wrapped vial from her pack and passed it to him.

His eyebrows beetled at her unusually strict caution and he uncapped it to take a wary sniff. "Faugh!" He quickly tapped the cork back in. "What foulness did you bring?"

"Zemlayan fire ant venom," she retorted.

"Oh ho ho." That changed much. He rubbed his face and settled back on his heels, reconsidering his strategy. Her single vial should hold . . .

She intercepted his glance, of course. "I have two others of the same size," she snapped.

"If three drops can kill a grown man, how much does it take to kill a chimera?" He turned as businesslike as she.

"An arrowhead's worth, according to my herbals."

"You've been collecting this for a long time!"

"You met my husband, didn't you?"

"Yes," he agreed cautiously.

"What better hobby can you think of? More's the pity, I didn't get to use any of it on him."

Igoryok closed his mouth.

Somewhere an animal howled hungrily, neither honest wolf nor friendly tiger. It was answered by another in deep rumbles, which echoed through the mountain slopes themselves.

Despite all common sense, everyone stopped to listen and paid for it with bone-deep shivers.

"Feodor has the best arrows. We'll start with his," Igoryok announced briskly, cutting into the last echo. "We must make haste."

"It could not be done by firelight," Zhenechka reminded him and began to fish in her immense pack.

"Of course not," he snapped. He was not a youngling to overlook the dangers of poor light when combined with such bitter poison. "But with Jeirgif's Barnaul wood torches and our blessed fire from home, we now have a chance against some of the monsters."

"Slighter than we'd prefer, since they breed fast."

He clenched his fists, lest he be tempted to wring a woman's neck for bringing another nightmare into vivid daylight.

SOMEWHERE IN TORHTREMER

Danae spun and spun through the blackness, lights whipping past her like an astronaut's wildest space walk. Cold flayed her skin and ripped into her bones, attacking her innards.

Only Alekhsiy was real—vibrant and alive like a beacon of hope. His arm locked around her, silently offering his own experience as a promise that this, too, could be survived.

She pulled herself closer to him and held on, grappling to save their chi from the storms battering them. Somehow they had to survive and be ready to fight. Somehow . . .

Her father's ring rubbed her hip, a node of silver light amid all the chaos. She pressed her arm against it, comforted by the reminder of her family.

Did the spinning stop for a moment? Or did the void simply come to an end?

The sky broke open with a thunderous clap. They plummeted rapidly downward toward a gravel-strewn beach, bordered by boulders and ice. The web of force released them—and they dropped like stones through the last few feet.

She landed with a thud on the beach, on her feet and desperately grateful for her boots—and years of training at being tossed and thrown about.

Her stomach promptly rebelled at its treatment and tried to leap out of her throat. She gagged hard and fought to keep it down.

The sky slammed shut again, booming again like a fighter jet blasting into supersonic speed just above the ground. She wavered but didn't fall over. One small victory for womankind . . .

Alekhsiy groaned and stood erect. "By the gods of war, I have finally made it back across the void. Many thanks, my lady."

She cautiously matched his stance and dared to look around. This was definitely the beach she'd seen on the monitors. It was nothing anybody would choose for sunbathing. In fact, an Alaskan fjord would have been more inviting.

Steep mountains bordered this place on two sides, while the ocean frothed and tore at it from the third. A glacier carved out the fourth side in an angry green wall of moving, knife-edged ice cubes. Icebergs, probably the children of the glacier behind them, surged through the sea. A heavy wind ripped salt spray off the waves and flung it into their faces, like an offer of drowning. Ice lurked between the gravel and boulders underneath their feet.

Alekhsiy spun to survey their surroundings for their enemy, moving sure-footedly over the nasty terrain. His armor's damn spell had probably already compensated for this wretched environment.

Danae shivered and tugged her hood over her head. Pulling on her gauntlets helped some but not enough. But no matter what, she'd survive.

She revolved slowly, trying to consider as many spots as possible. The ocean looked truly nasty. She paused, drawn by one particularly odd spray pattern to their north.

"There." Alekhsiy pointed at a small figure in the promontory farther south of them along the beach. "That's Turner."

"But that's not an iceberg or just another wave. It's too small and too low." She pointed at the bizarre, ongoing waves.

He stared at them for far too long until her blood ran cold again.

"The Imperial Terrapin is coming in the flesh to claim his catalyst." A muscle throbbed in his cheek.

"Crap." She spun back to stare at Turner's rapidly receding figure. She shivered, but not from cold. "How can we stop them? I don't think I could send him back to Earth, since he doesn't have any dragon's blood. But what if I worked a spell or something?"

"I would not advise trying it." Alekhsiy's expression was very grim.

"Why not?" she demanded, arms akimbo. Dammit, they had to do something.

"The Tungur Sea is the very core of Azherbhai's magic and this shore is imbued with it. Do you truly believe he'd permit you to harm the human who holds all his hopes?"

An evil voice seemed to laugh at her from beyond Alekhsiy's shoulder.

A bitter smile touched her lips. "Perhaps not," she agreed reluctantly, "but we have to try something."

"If so, make the attempt small lest it recoil upon our heads."

What might work, but wouldn't harm Alekhsiy? What was she also sure she could perform with a spell? Telekinesis was supposed to be similar to spellcasting and Earth studied psychics a lot, although she hadn't. Perhaps that understanding would aid her in this knife-edged world.

"May a whirlwind of stones rise up and assail Turner," she chanted softly in the Language of the Beasts.

A small mound of stones formed in his footsteps, no more than knee-high.

Yes, oh definitely yes! Excitement surged through her and she started to run forward.

Alekhsiy's hand locked over hers and held her back. "Wait," he growled.

She shot a disgruntled glare at him but obeyed.

The rocks lifted themselves into a whirling cloud, like a small tornado, and hurled themselves at Turner. But they fell back, bouncing away from him, as if they'd encountered an invisible wall. They formed themselves into a low-flying cloud, flying north like buzzing insects over the gravel.

Danae gaped at them, shock chilling her muscles more completely than the cold.

Alekhsiy flung himself on her and covered her with himself.

The bits of gravel and rock flew over their heads. They collapsed back into place a few meters later, leaving the beach smoother than it had been before.

Instinct, stronger than intelligence, demanded she lose every bit of backbone and become a worm once again.

"Standard wards." Her lover announced and lifted his head cautiously before sitting up.

Sensation returned to her once again, reminded her of skin, muscle, tendons—and her beloved's warm stolidity beside her. He was a fighter and so was she, dammit. At least she'd proved she could do magic on this side of the void.

"Standard wards?" she queried, trying to sound casual. She stood up and tried to brush off her clothes.

Would another spell clean the mud and ice off? It did.

Shit, she was starting to act like a real sorceress.

"They protect a friend by reacting with equal force against an enemy. The Imperial Terrapin won't waste chi by adding extra energy." He brushed her lips with his finger. "Today he does not need to, since he will be here very soon."

"Oh shit." Terror laughed at her from just beyond the corner of her eyes and she blinked it quickly away. Dammit, this was no worse than an opening night without a rehearsal and she'd done that.

Okay, so she'd sworn never to do it again. But she had pulled it off before.

"I'll distract Azherbhai," she announced quickly. She was a sorceress, she had magic, but Alekhsiy didn't. So she'd face the heavyweight. "Once you take out Turner"—and she didn't want to know how—"that big turtle will leave town."

"My lady, I cannot permit you to do that." He caught her face in his hands.

"Both of us have to do our jobs." She rubbed her cheek against his palm like a cat, gathering up comfort. "You just get out there and do yours fast."

"Once I retrieve my amulet from Turner, I can summon help." He offered a slight smile, which he probably meant to be hopeful.

She gave him her best one back, which she hoped looked more confident. "Sounds like a great plan."

"My love." He kissed her hard and fast, too quickly for anything except the intensity of his passion to blaze through. She caught at his shoulders for an instant to steady herself and gave him everything she had in exchange.

And he was gone, without looking back.

She turned away, lest she bring any sort of bad luck to him by watching him out of sight. Then she started trudging up the beach toward the glacier, the closest point to Azherbhai's approach to the beach.

Boris stretched, pleased with how fast he was recovering from his trip. Damn, but that fall had been intense. If he ever went back to Earth, he could make a fortune selling it as a roller coaster. Or maybe not; there was a better life waiting for him here, as soon as his master arrived with the staff. Once he had that, he and his master could strut anywhere they wanted across Torhtremer.

All he needed now was a few more minutes until his master arrived. Pity his master couldn't fly here, too, but that was for dragons and phoenixes—who couldn't swim like his master.

He shoved his hands into his pockets, seeking warmth, but met chunks instead. Irritated, he pulled out his cell phone and hurled it into the sea.

The next lump was his enemy's pendant, now a dead brown hulk of rock, exhausted from transporting him to his destiny.

Water surged and frothed beyond the glacier and a flipper lifted in greeting.

Hell if he needed this thing anymore.

He dropped the amulet and ground it under his foot.

It exploded with a small, keening wail and a brief burst of light, before drifting into dust.

BHAIKHAL

Khyber burst out of the throne room and onto the terrace outside, bellowing his war cry.

"By all the gods of war, what has gone wrong?" Mykhayl ran to meet him, Dragon's Breath unsheathed in his hand.

"Alekhsiy's amulet is crushed." He roared again and smashed a section of stone railing with his tail.

"Where did it happen? What of Alekhsiy?" Mykhayl demanded.

"At Chulym Beach. I do not know where your brother is." He looked up to meet his mate's eyes.

Svetlhana's tongue swept out to polish her fangs and he could have snarled. Damn her for being so feminine, she didn't have to be correct so often. At least she wouldn't say *I told you so* in public.

Mykhayl went white and almost staggered against his wife.

"Chulym Beach?" Corinne queried gently.

"It's also called the Grave of Heroes, since men try to kill the Imperial Terrapin there when he comes to spawn. Instead, he destroys them and turns their weapons into jewels, which wash up onto the beach for him to admire."

"Do you believe Alekhsiy is alive?"

"I do not know that he's dead," Khyber parried carefully, unwilling to expose his own lack of knowledge.

"But . . ." Mykhayl stopped, recognizing that was the only answer he would be given.

"Take us to Chulym Beach," he demanded. "Between the four of us, we'd be sure to defeat Azherbhai and his new catalyst."

"We will have to fly. I cannot gate to another imperial beast's spawning grounds."

"But that could take hours," Corinne wailed. "If Alekhsiy's there now and needs help, anything could happen."

"He is not alone, little sister," Svetlhana reassured her catalyst. "He will have aid."

"Who? What kind of help?"

"A sorceress." She sat down and curled her tail around her toes. "A White Sorceress—but a very inexperienced one."

Khyber's fanged snout dropped open. Where had his beloved found one of those and would it be enough?

Truly this would be a battle for commoners and the untried, not High Kings and imperial beasts.

THIRTEEN

The Gate of Belukha

Another wave of hydras hurled themselves along the road toward Igoryok's band, their many heads interlacing with themselves and their brethren to pull themselves forward ever faster. Their single long tail heaved and pushed, as if straining to devour the men struggling to defend the narrow gap between the mountains. The stone smoked where they passed and melted into a rippled glass.

A chimera yowled in pain behind them and dragged itself away, every step slower than the last. Its golden body bore a hideous likeness to a lion, yet black drool marked where it had slavered in anticipation of yet another hapless meal. Its goat's head, surmounted atop the lion's back and containing its sole intelligence, bleated in frustration to the skies. Its narrow serpent's tongue, located where a true lion's tail should be, nipped at the road in dying fury.

Yet two more hastened around the corner, trampling over it in their haste to join the fray.

Igoryok's remaining troops hurled back more hydras from high atop the battlements, slashing through their thick hides with axes and swords. Rough logs supplemented the once stout stone bulwarks.

Chimera wounded, battered and bloody, were scattered amidst the corpses of their own dead. Any mortals who were wounded, fell. And any who dropped, died amidst that pool of venom and fetid air.

They thought only of fighting now—to behead the hell spawn—not of the poison, which burned through iron like acid. They had to move quickly, before a hydra's head regenerated or the trunk hopped away to find its brethren and reform. Their flesh reeked of sulfur, volcanoes, and foulness. Green grass and sweet flowers were memories Igoryok never expected to rebuild, like those of a horse running swiftly beneath him.

His sword jammed between a hydra's scales and he rammed another Barnaul tree torch down one of its throats. The other heads thrashed and howled, spitting venom as much across their brethren as their foes.

The other hydras shrieked, rising to a pitch beyond sound, and fell back for an instant.

He flinched, splatters raining through his helm and his mail, but held on to the one writhing under his fire. If there was aught left of his hauberk at the end of the day, it would be by the grace of the Red God of War alone. That meant, of course, if he was alive to know it.

He snorted mirthlessly just before the hydra fell away into a dusty heap below the crude fortifications.

He allowed himself an instant's grace to fill his lungs before the next wave came.

Little more than half of his troops remained in the front lines, although a few—a pitiful remnant—were making torches and other supplies in the rear. No warrior rested on his wounds from this battle.

Judging by the monsters' increased frenzy, the Imperial Terrapin had arrived at Chulym Beach. Igoryok would wager a year's winnings from his finest racers that General Alekhsiy was there, too. His troop would give him all the time they could.

He relit his torch from one of his neighbors and shouted a crude insult at one of the lurking chimeras. As he'd hoped, the abomination bellowed angrily and charged forward, its small brain too excited by the challenge to its dubious masculinity to think clearly.

Jeirgif notched an arrow to his bow and waited, one eye half-closed under a livid burn. Even so, he was their best living archer.

The chimera leaped across the heaving mass of hydras and charged toward the small fort. A single whiff of its breath would be deadly.

Whenever you're ready, Jeirgif, Igoryok coaxed silently.

Pling! The poisoned arrow flew straight and true into the chimera's flank. It howled and dropped, rolling over and over onto the road in its death throes.

And another one arrived, peering at them cautiously from around the corner.

"No matter how many you kill," Zhenechka observed tartly and whacked off a chimera's serpent tail before it could bite her neighbor, "there's always at least two more."

Igoryok somehow refrained from strangling her.

CHULYM BEACH

Alekhsiy and Turner circled each other, their breath coming in hard, short gasps that left patches of smoke upon the air like wizards' fire. His long hair was matted to his neck with sweat beneath his mail coil, bringing a few threads of moisture over his burning muscles.

He crossed leg over leg, always careful to keep his balance in a dance older than time, and watched for his opening. A single blow from his curved axe blade could break through even the strongest helm. Or he could wield it in other fashions to hook or slice, much as a man had always used its hardworking ancestors on a farm.

Time was his enemy, as much as the man facing him. He dared not look to the north and the mountains beyond them, lest he catch a flash of light and his heart's lady. He held hope, so long as Fire Wind filled his hands and brought the sun's heat down to melt the ice under his feet.

The Imperial Terrapin usually liked to have hydras, chimeras, and others of his court waiting for him along the shore to pay homage and heat the sands with their bitter breath.

Alekhsiy would hardly complain of their lack, but a small voice inside did wonder at it. He would sacrifice a hundred baskets of Peshawar lilies to the Red God of War, should his lady never encounter any of them.

He ignored the blood trickling down his arm from his one spill. His health was less important than keeping watch on the terrain and his opponent.

They stood on a broad ledge, etched between the beach and the southern promontory. With its sharp drop to the ocean on one side, steep rise to the mountains on two sides, and gentle drop to the beach on the fourth, Turner had chosen a very confined space for dueling.

Alekhsiy would have called it excellent, except it was on the north side of the mountains and therefore received less sun than almost anywhere else on the beach. Praise be to all the gods of war, his armor had already adapted his gear accordingly. He was warm enough—but not too warm. Sweat could kill a man if it froze on him and weighed him down. Ice was the great killer here and it eagerly sought out any weakness.

"Have you had enough yet, Alekseiovich?" Turner raised his great, two-handed sword again. Its blade gleamed palest green in the morning sun, the hilt and pommel shining a darker shade.

Alekhsiy's flesh cringed reflexively, remembering how it had nicked his enchanted armor as if it were paper when he took that last tumble. Only his old, old fencing skills would save him now, not spells.

"Didn't ripping your armor teach you a lesson?"

"Not at all." Alekhsiy shook his head. Every taste of the damn cold air was like a dagger through his lungs. He twirled Fire Wind around his head and shoulders until flames danced in the breeze. "I will see you die like a sniveling coward, alone and too frightened to cry out."

For a moment, the oracle's voice rang through his once again as it had through his mother's, deepening and lengthening his words. They echoed against the mountains, making even Turner hesitate for a moment.

Cold fury—and a little fear—lit his gaze.

"You will die first—and I will rule your woman and this world." Turner charged.

Double-handed axe met double-handed sword and rang all the way across the beach.

Danae flickered another glance down the beach toward Alekhsiy and then hastily turned away. She couldn't watch, she couldn't even consider looking without her heart locking somewhere in her throat.

But she couldn't do this and worry about Alekhsiy. She damn well couldn't take on Azherbhai and think about Alekhsiy or she'd go mad.

Oh, God, she needed him to live.

She had to succeed so he'd survive. She was the sorceress, he wasn't, so she had to pull off her part of this.

Getting to this point had kept her mind occupied until now. Thank God she'd already learned something of how to work magic back on Earth—healing Alekhsiy's bruises with her hands, typing commands like an author to issue instructions to the news anchors and the cops, chanting the Language of the Beasts to give Alekhsiy the audience's chi, and opening the gate to Torhtremer.

Casting a spell to convert her White Sorceress's outfit into arctic gear hadn't been too hard, especially after she tweaked her clothes so she wasn't too warm. Her long over-tunic made a great parka, her trousers were now superb ski trousers, and her gauntlets were wonderfully warm and flexible. Climbing up the rocky cliff that formed the glacier's side had involved finding and squeezing through narrow, knife-edged passages and leaping up ragged chunks of ice, which seemed to have come from a modern art museum's sculpture garden by way of a very drunken, sadistic cocktail party. She'd have killed the host, if she'd been back on Earth.

But that had been nothing compared to the pure hell of walking on its glass smooth surface and staring downhill at the ocean, blocked only by one hell of a very steep drop.

Next stop—drowning? Thank God for spells that had adapted Larissa's creation into ice boots, complete down to the spikes.

She stood on the edge and looked down. Salt spray stung her face like eager bullets and ice winds dived down her throat, chilling her from the bone out. Two hundred feet below, the ocean smashed itself against the ice, masses of white foam emphasizing its anger. Behind her, a great cleft showed where the ice would soon separate from the shore and sail away. Light and dark shadows gleamed throughout the ice like ghosts grabbing at her feet. The glacier creaked and moaned, heaving under her in its desperation to leave this rocky coast.

A great square head broke through the ocean offshore, casting up a great wave behind.

Azherbhai was coming to fetch Turner.

The glacier pitched again and she almost stumbled, despite her dancer's sense of balance. Panic raced through her veins. If she failed Alekhsiy now . . .

What could she do to help him? She fought to assemble a string of actions, while the blood ebbed from her fingers. Thoughts were so hard to grapple with here.

Focus, Danae, focus. You can do this.

Her father's ring was a kernel of warmth against her hip.

Could it help? It was a naval officer's ring, baptized in all of Earth's oceans. It had been of use in the void. Surely it would be a good luck token on this frosty sea.

She dug it out of her pouch and hesitated for a moment. Was she being stupidly sentimental in wanting a bit of her family around at this moment? Well, who cared if it made her feel better?

She shoved it firmly onto her hand over her gauntlet. It settled into place on her ring finger, as perfectly as if designed to be worn there.

Warmth began to rebuild, up her arm and into her heart.

Her great-grandfather's diamond, which he'd brought back from duty on the China Station, started to glow. She almost jumped back in amazement, startled by the approbation. Her older brothers had been the ones meant for the Navy, not her. But she'd been named for a class of naval warships—heavily armed cruisers, in fact—as much as for a princess who'd caught a god's eye. The same blood hummed in her veins. She almost thought she could see ghosts lined up behind her, ready for battle. Craziness—but this was a magical world.

Azherbhai shifted course, waves breaking over his immense square back. His huge sharp beak broke water, channeling the spray like a battering ram of ages gone by. For a moment, one of his mighty flippers reached upward and cut down, scooping up quantities of sea as if they were a trifle.

She flung her cloak around herself in defiance and squared her shoulders to the wind. Of course, she could distract something that big. She'd seen small craft drive large ships insane all the time in New York City's harbor.

A big iceberg floated only a few feet away, channeling traffic into Chulym Beach. Azherbhai, if he wanted to be seen by Turner, would have to swim between that iceberg and this cliff. In fact, he was coming very close to where she was.

What if she jumped onto his back? After all, ballet dancers did leaps all the time. Heck, Nijinsky, the great Russian dancer, would probably have loved to try a stunt like this, even with the plummet off an icy platform. And Farragut, America's great naval commander, certainly knew how to attack the enemy at all costs.

If nothing else, she could catch Azherbhai's attention for a few moments.

It was a mad plan. What could she hope to do afterward? Azherbhai was forty-five feet long, from his cruel beak to his fast-moving tail. His carapace made modern tanks look like tissue paper, especially with those spikes. Three foot tall spikes dotted his back, more than capable of skewering a full-grown ox. Only Khyber could match his magic, not her—even if she knew how to use it. Still, she had to try.

All she had to do was buy Alekhsiy a little more time to get rid of Turner somehow.

Were there any other alternatives? They'd have to be low-tech, of course, since Azherbhai didn't permit hostile magic on his land.

Her brain clicked on a big fat zero. Clothes converted to a wetsuit, check. She started counting waves to learn their cycle and distract herself from thinking up more reasons not to do this.

Five, six, seven, eight . . .

Showtime! She leaped off the glacier and over the ocean, hissing an invocation to Nijinsky's and Farragut's ghosts.

The great black wave rose to meet her. A ray of sunshine broke through the gray clouds, sharpening every lethal spike on Azherbhai's back and pointing them directly at her.

Suddenly she had all the time in the world and her heartbeat was steadier than during a dress rehearsal, the quick strong pulse of an opening night.

She tucked herself into a ball and calmly rolled in the air to gain distance. If she could reach that one spot just behind his shoulder, she'd miss the spikes roaring down his spine, as well as those ringing his perimeter.

Closer, closer . . .

His mottled black back filled her vision like a scene from hell. Waves broke over it and spilled away, refusing to debase themselves by lingering.

Damn, his shell's edge was knife-edged. She'd have to catch one of the spikes to keep from sliding into the sea, like a clumsy understudy botching her first performance of *Swan Lake*.

Closer . . .

He raised his head to the sky and opened his mouth, exposing his great crushing jaws under that razor sharp beak. His
carapace started to disappear from sight under the water.

Her fists punched into his carapace. Yeow! The healing spell
caught them almost immediately, an instant after she'd opened
them. She grabbed for the nearest spike by the base and, wonder
of wonders, caught it. She swung around and caught another
spike beside his neck, then braced her feet against a third.

Ocean to Alekhsiy, the White Sorceress has landed.

A tiny bubble of relief gurgled in her throat. What now?

Azherbhai erupted out of the water like a geyser, his powerful flippers and tails making him almost stand upright. He spun
around, looking for the intruder, and bellowed loudly. A chunk
of ice exploded from the glacier and tumbled into the ocean, setting waves foaming and frothing over everything nearby.

Danae tucked her head and held on, somehow. It wasn't any
harder than flying the rigging through an opera house's backstage, right?

Azherbhai flopped over onto his side and rolled into the
water. He dove down, far below where the light ended, spinning
like a guided missile.

Ice cold water thundered against her throat and her chest,
eager to stop her heart. Her fingers disappeared, as lost to feeling as her feet inside her boots. Where were they?

Her ring pulsed, sending a single clear beacon over her
hand.

Azherbhai wanted to drown her, dammit, and she would not
do what he wished.

No! She would not die, not here, not now. If nothing else,
Azherbhai was only thinking about her—not Turner and definitely not Alekhsiy.

She knotted her hands around the spikes and commanded

her cloak to become a dry suit, complete with helmet and oxygen tank. Ah, blessed air through the mouthpiece and snug protection from the cold water! She dared to stretch her lungs and the blackness receded slowly, slowly bringing back light and reason.

She tightened her grip on her foe.

Still, they dove, the current ripping at her grip like a wild demon. Was her strength sufficient to hold out long enough?

She ducked her head deeper between Azherbhai's shoulders and prayed. She needed something else, another weapon to fight him with.

He broke the surface again. Air, blessed, life-giving air poured over her without need for the mouthpiece and she gulped it down, savoring every salty whiff.

Azherbhai smacked the waves hard, jouncing across them like a jet ski boat. Danae's grip loosened for a horrific instant, then she caught herself, panic thundering in her bones. She gritted out a spell and fashioned herself sturdy gauntlets, which could not be torn from him.

Finally Azherbhai swam fast and straight, apparently thinking he'd drowned her. Her blood slowly settled back into a wary tempo and she stayed limp to encourage that false belief. It wasn't that much of an illusion anyway, although she did shift her grip on the spikes closest to his neck.

Iron brushed her hand, mixed with what felt like leather. What on earth? She looked more closely.

A leather and iron harness held a beautiful, massive staff strapped to his carapace, just below his neck. It must be Terrapin's Beak, the staff used to summon the Imperial Terrapin. Azherbhai would hardly trouble himself with anything less.

But a potential catalyst's presence meant nothing without the staff, since he couldn't bring the Imperial Terrapin into being without it. He'd be crippled and useless, the same as any other mortal. She'd block them if she took it away from them.

If.

She smiled mirthlessly and rubbed encrusted salt away from her mouth and chin. That was a very big gap.

Azherbhai was swimming faster now. He'd reach the southern promontory in only a few minutes. If she was going to do anything, she had to do so right away. She needed to cut those very thick straps, which looked fully capable of holding down stage scenery. But with what?

Her ring hummed briefly.

She rolled her left hand so she could look at it.

Her ring—as in, a laser?

It hummed again, encouragingly. A bow wave broke over it but it burst through again, shining all the while.

Awed respect surged from deep inside her. Well, why not give the Naval Academy ring a try? It had already done very well and magic did seem to come to life easier here.

She freed her hand and aimed the ring at the harness, hoping to God she wasn't being a sentimental fool. The diamond promptly brightened, then dropped to a lower beam. The leather band began to glow red and smoke in a single line. It fell away, cleanly cut, instants later.

Danae gulped, her heartbeat racing faster than when she'd boarded the alien beast. Elation flooded her veins, linking her to something bigger and bringing back kinship she hadn't felt since she'd last piled into a car with her family. Somehow they were defeating the enemy together and doing so here in Torhtremer.

Five minutes later, she held Terrapin's Beak in her hand. It was very long and appallingly heavy, like holding titanium or even lead. Its ends and center were sheathed in metal, carved in special runes that hurt the eye to consider very closely.

Azherbhai screamed in pure rage and wheeled to kill her.

She leaped to her feet, triumph and fear thrumming through her limbs with equal speed. She drove the staff down into Azherbhai's neck and vaulted off him onto a small ice floe, which was the nearest place to land.

The great beast howled again and butted into the ice like a giant bull determined to gore a matador. The far smaller sheet slid upward and Danae scrabbled one-handed for purchase amid the soft snow and slick ice. Her other hand was sealed to the staff, more precious than her own life.

Alekhsiy shook his head free of his helm's remains and flung the battered ruin aside. Turner's jeweled sword was both uncannily beautiful and deadly. It slashed through his enchanted armor as if he was wearing copper to its steel. But his dragon-forged axe still survived to make the other duly wary.

The sun had passed its crest and was fading fast behind the western mountains. Shadows grew amid the granite cliffs and ice shimmered more and more on land and sea. Danae—Mother of All Life, must he hear the battle cries?—his beloved lady battled the Imperial Terrapin somewhere amid the salt spray.

But they'd been silent for the last few minutes. Was she gone?

"Really, dude, you should have given up long ago." Turner chuckled and swung his sword tauntingly, displaying its green perfection. He advanced slowly and inexorably, certain of his victory.

Alekhsiy retreated. He had only one advantage left—the Earthman's unfamiliarity with an axe's unique battle strategies. He circled, the world narrowing to the sword and the curved axe blade weaving their intricate patterns between him and his enemy. Time mattered not, only winning the war.

And he finally brought the battle to ground of his own choosing. The wind roared its fury, as it had all day, and the land dropped to meet the ocean, steeper here than elsewhere on the dueling ground.

He attacked in a flurry of blows, which the other quickly countered. They surged back and forth, ever closer to the edge—until Alekhsiy swung his axe blade to hook Turner's ankle.

"Like hell!" His enemy leaped back with catalyst speed and power. "You won't catch me with such an obvious move twice."

He landed on the cliff's verge, at a very steep edge and deep within the shadow zone. His speed sent his feet flying and he skidded on the ice.

Alekhsiy brought his axe up, ready to fight again, should Danae's would-be kidnapper recover.

For a moment, anger, then dread realization flashed through Turner's eyes. Then his legs went out from under him and he fell over the sheer edge, moving too fast to save himself. He disappeared immediately into the tumultuous waters below, where the ocean raged and frothed between the cliff and immense boulders.

Alekhsiy crept forward a few paces, wary as a household cat facing a leopard.

A minute later, a single hand reached up from the tumultuous waters below. Ice etched its still fingers, while droplets trickled amid the mail like worms.

A wave smashed it down, to vanish amid the boulders and ice floes.

Turner never appeared again, drowned as surely by his armor as if somebody had held his head under the cold sea.

Azherbhai bellowed once again in the distance.

This time, Alekhsiy ran to do battle.

*　　*　　*

Danae panted for breath, the crystalline air cutting her lungs like knives. She eyed the bits of ice floating in the sea and tried to calculate her next steps.

The only thing that had stopped Azherbhai from reducing every ice floe to smithereens—and stopping her from reaching shore—was his equally overwhelming lust for the staff in her hand.

But right now, she didn't have many options. If the first ice floe had been an acre in size, this one was smaller than a dinner table set for eight. When he ripped it apart, he'd take her with it.

Exhaustion and true terror had pushed all sensation away, because this time she had nothing to turn to. The bit of rock over there, which led to a cliff? The tiny floe over there, with a piece of driftwood beyond?

She truly hoped Alekhsiy was doing better than she was, because she'd run out of ways to distract the big bad guy.

Azherbhai roared and charged again, his knife-sharp beak wide open. She could see the broad jaws that could crush her bones, the strong tongue that could heave her down that immense gullet, and the lure at the back of his mouth that would wiggle in triumph afterward.

She closed her eyes and took the worst option—because it was the one he'd be the least likely to expect.

She sprang for the smallest ice floe, kicking her legs out in a *jeté* worthy of any *danseur noble*. Another leap led her to a boulder, high above a maelstrom. She balanced for an instant, careful not to look down, and jumped again. Only one more until the beach but this one into the deepest water.

Strong arms caught her close.

Alekhsiy! Her heart began beating again.

He pressed his cheek against hers and speedily brought them

both to land, his strong legs making easy work of the heavy surf.

"My darling"—His eyes flashed at her unusual endearment—"give me your surcoat, quickly."

"Why?" But he'd already set aside his axe and started stripping off his belt.

Waves crashed over their feet, warning of the incoming tide and their enemy. They were close, far too close to the sea, but there was no time to go farther inland to safety.

Azherbhai stormed onto the shore, a great smack of his tail sending him farther out of the water. "Return my staff, foolish mortals, and I might let you live."

"Never." Danae backed up, still holding the staff. She twitched briefly, like a cat, and shook her White Sorceress garb completely free from the last traces of having been a wet suit. Alekhsiy shoved his surcoat into her hand behind her back.

She twirled the weapon behind her, as if nervous, and slid the gaily patterned silk over the central grip.

"You have killed he who would be my catalyst," Azherbhai snarled, lashing his great head from side to side. "You owe me death for that."

"He fell off a cliff from his own folly," Alekhsiy retorted. "A wise man would have lived."

Azherbhai hissed and his hind flipper sent a giant boulder tumbling down the beach.

Danae barely managed not to jump. She attacked instead. "You came to my world and upset its balance. Was that according to The Great Order?"

The Imperial Terrapin burst into a fury of clacking. "Give me my staff and we will be done."

"You cannot have it for it is Torhtremer's battle prize now."

Danae brought it out, the sunset's glow casting a ruddy light over its green and gold silks.

"You must not have it." Azherbhai groaned in despair, the sound echoing from deep within his shell or perhaps the earth.

"It will not be destroyed," Alekhsiy said coldly, in a conqueror's tones. "It will be kept under the strongest wards, guarded by the oldest and wisest of the dragons and phoenixes in a distant place known to no man. No imperial beast may hold the upper hand against another, as you have tried to for far too long."

"You will slay me," Azherbhai howled.

"You know we cannot. But you will not have another catalyst until the time is ripe."

Danae frowned at the prophecy in his voice but stayed silent.

Azherbhai roared again in frustration and backed into the ocean, beating at the waves until they swallowed him up.

Danae shivered, then turned away from the sight. She had time yet for the nightmares his voice would reverberate in. She set the staff down and knotted her gauntlets around it to hold the silk in place.

Far more important now, she cupped Alekhsiy's face between her hands, cherishing every scrape, every rough hair of him. He rubbed his cheek against her palm.

"I need to shave," he said gently, clearly trying for a joke.

"Who gives a shit?" She shrugged and smoothed her thumb over his lips.

His tongue flicked out to caress it. His vivid blue eyes closed briefly—in ecstasy?—before reopening to gaze at her intently. "I do, if I'm to taste your sweet honey before you depart."

"I'm very grubby." Now it was her turn to try for a light

touch. But why was she bothering when she'd come so far to have a few words with him alone?

"I don't care. I have never cared. I knew you were a sorceress because of how often you'd rescued me. I knew one sip of your sweet liquors would bind me to you forever. Yet I drank deep and long." His eyes blazed at her, willing her to understand him.

"All this time? You wanted to fall in love with me?" She shook her head, shaken to the bone.

"I have been in love with you since I first saw you dance and you brought joy into my life," he corrected and caught her hands. "I will not hold you against your will. But I ask you to spend what time you can with me here now, before you return."

Where she'd be alone again. Tears filled her eyes.

"My love? What have I said to disturb you?"

"I've got a better idea." She coughed to remove some of the ridiculous hoarseness from her voice. A hesitant smile burbled up from somewhere. "How about *me* marrying *you* and *us* living *here* with your family? It would be wonderful to have a real family again."

Just like the way she'd felt underwater when she'd fought Azherbhai. Elation and kinship, the magic and unity that were somehow only possible for her in Torhtremer.

"Are you certain?" His harsh face softened with hope.

She nodded, biting her lip lest she start bouncing for joy. That would be so not adult.

"Yes, of course, I'll marry you!" He grabbed her and swung her around in circles, her feet flying fast and free. She giggled and kissed him, delight running as wild in her bones as the hunger leaping through her veins.

It was a long time before she felt the ground under her feet. They held on to each other, still too rapturous to consider more mundane matters, like how to return home—wherever that was from here—or what to eat.

A polite cough interrupted their hug. "General Alekhsiy? Sir?"

Alekhsiy lifted his head sharply. "Igoryok? By all the gods of war, what are you doing here? And who have you brought with you?"

He turned to face the newcomers, keeping a firm grip on Danae's hand. She blushed slightly but stepped up next to him, finding his possessiveness enchanting and a little unnerving. She'd never before had a boyfriend who liked to hold hands. Of course, she'd never had one for any amount of time or with deep intimacy.

"This is my best troop from home, sir." Igoryok, a short, stocky fellow, made an all-encompassing gesture over perhaps a hundred people who'd all been badly battered in battle. Bloody wounds, blackened burns, dented armor—it was a wonder most of them could walk.

They bowed to Alekhsiy, their eyes shining. He bowed in return, not quite as deep but equally formally.

"My lady, this is Igoryok, who commanded my personal guard at Tajzyk's Gorge. Friends, this is my lady, Danae, who is a White Sorceress."

This situation was so not covered by the Torhtremer Saga. Caught by an instinct she couldn't name, Danae dropped a small curtsy. "I'm honored to meet you, Igoryok."

Igoryok's eyes widened and he dipped his head to her. The others bowed very low.

Danae smiled back at them, a little shyly. Meeting Alekhsiy was bad enough—but more people from the Torhtremer canon in the flesh? Wow, just wow. But they didn't look like legends, more like folks who needed a fast trip to the nearest hospital emergency room. "What brings you here, Igoryok?" Alekh-siy's practiced eye swept over his friend's battered and smoking armor.

Danae uneasily wondered if her magic could help any of them. So far, she'd only cast spells for what she basically knew how to do or could picture. Fixing their injuries would be far more complicated. Corinne Carson had written scenes about healing similarly difficult wounds, though, so it had to be possible.

"We decided to take a trip through the mountains." Igoryok attempted a nonchalant shrug that ended with gritted teeth. "Unfortunately we had to stop along the way to discourage some hydras and chimeras from accompanying us."

"He lies," a young man burst out. "He had dreams of you needing aid and wouldn't stop talking until he gathered us."

"Jeirgif!" Igoryok reproved, hot color staining his weathered cheeks.

"Hydras and chimeras?" Danae questioned sharply. She hated reading about those ugly beasts in the Torhtremer Saga. No wonder they needed help.

"We fought until there were so many chimera corpses piled up, the hydras couldn't break through the stench," an older woman explained. "No herbal describes how to cleanse it, either." She frowned, clearly more disturbed by the lingering mess than her opponents' death.

Danae blinked and hid an answering smile. Her mother would have felt the same way. Hadn't the Amazons had a herbal which told how to heal wounds from these monsters in one of the books? Perhaps if she transformed some of their remaining torches into those herbs...

"How did you kill so many?" Alekhsiy demanded.

"My stockpile of Zemlayan fire ant venom," the old woman informed him cheerfully.

Alekhsiy turned slightly green and swallowed hard. "My thanks, lady. You are a credit to your clan and your nation."

He bowed over her hand and she simpered like a maiden, totally lost for words. Her companions gaped at her, aghast at this startling side of her, and Danae almost chuckled. Much as she enjoyed seeing her beloved shatter other men's expectations of how easily a woman could be seduced, night was coming and this was definitely not a tropical beach, good for a long night's stay. Somebody needed to either build shelters or take them home. A great rushing of air, like a mighty wind, but driven by a steady beat, swept through the mountain passes and across their heads.

"Khyber!" Alekhsiy shouted and turned toward the south.

The Imperial Dragon of Torhtremer? The wounded would be saved and Alekhsiy would sleep safe tonight. Joy lit her veins hotter than any third curtain call and she went to tend the wounded.

Closer and closer it came, until it resolved itself into a covey of huge bodies with massive wings. They flew easily, powerfully, quickly. One moment, they were mere specks over the mountaintops and the next, Danae could clearly see the outline of their heads and tails against the ice. They canted their wings and slipped sideways, slipping down through the air with a falcon's speed, then leveled out just above the beach.

The great dragon sailed in, gilded by the setting sun, and accompanied by a squadron of his fellows.

An instant later, Alekhsiy was the center of an ecstatic reunion. He pounded his brother's back and hugged a tall, platinum blond who looked ridiculously familiar to Danae.

She propped her hands on her hips, finally finished with healing Igoryok's men.

"Dammit, Alekhsiy," she snapped when he broke free, "you didn't tell me Corinne Carson was your sister-in-law."

Three equally astonished human faces stared at her—but one large tigress sat down and started to clean her whiskers.

Alekhsiy rubbed his chin slowly. "It never seemed important," he finally offered.

"I thought she was dead," Danae snarled. "Do you have any idea how long I grieved for her? Even if I was perturbed at some of her plot devices."

"I'm sorry?" he tried again to make amends. "I promise I'll always be careful to keep you informed."

She sniffed and offered her cheek for a kiss, which he quickly gave, the darling man. He wrapped his arm around her waist. "Mykhayl, Corinne, this is Danae, my betrothed."

Mykhayl's golden eyes gazed down at her inscrutably before he smiled. "Welcome home, sister. My brother has been without you far too long."

"Finally! I was beginning to wonder when Alekhsiy would find somebody." Corinne flew forward, her arms as wide open as her grin. "And an author, too."

Danae sighed in relief and hugged them both, while Alekhsiy happily thumped his brother on the back.

"Where did you find your White Sorceress?" Khyber inquired of Svetlhana. Humans. By the way they carried on, you'd think nobody else had ever discovered their true mate.

"You did," she responded, her pink tongue teasing a particularly fascinating morsel around a fang.

"*I* did? When?" He cast his mind back. Try as he might,

he could remember no occasion when he'd hunted for a White Sorceress.

"I have longed to restart their order for years, that they might converse with my young cousins once again in the western mountains."

He nodded politely, trying to conceal his true thoughts. *Yes, yes, he knew* that. *Get on with the story.*

She nuzzled him briefly, drawing her soft whiskers across his craggy snout. His impatience fled.

"Yes?" he purred, ready for anything that might continue her attentions.

"You *saw* a young sorceress the night you brought back my little sister."

He frowned and hastily tried to remember. *Young sorceress?* But there had been such a crowd in those streets . . .

The young girl with the dark hair, who'd been standing far below. He'd wondered if she'd truly seen him then, not the shadow he'd cast to disguise himself from all the others.

"Her." He pointed a single long claw.

"Indeed." His darling's tail twined with his for a moment.

"You knew she wasn't a threat since she had no access to dragon blood. But as soon as you told me about her, I knew she was the one." She lapped at him briefly. He flicked his long forked tongue out and twined it with hers for an instant, to share a very private kiss. *His beloved mate.* Should he have been surprised she'd do something like this?

"You should have told me." Did he sound stern enough to be convincing? Almost certainly not.

"I wanted it to be a special surprise for you. You have so many worries; you need somebody to take some of your cares away."

She meant she wanted to play games with some of the tasks

he saw as necessities. He sighed. She'd still see them done, only differently.

"Can you forgive me, big boy?" She deepened her voice to a suggestive purr. "And will you fly with me again?"

His innards melted, sending all of his blood far away from his draconic wisdom.

"Of course we will."

Danae swayed in her husband's arms, her fanciful silk and lace cream wedding dress a thing of the past, thank God. Now she wore a barely-there slip, instead of a confection designed to evoke awe among the multitude of guests deemed necessary to witness Torhtremer's top general's wedding and retirement. He'd worn his most magnificent uniform for that, but no mail, thank God. And now he was clad only in bare skin, which was enough to incite any woman's senses into a riot. His breath stirred her hair and her heart.

She couldn't complain too much, though, since Khyber's wedding present had been Larissa and Nora, plus their families. He'd fobbed off any questions by telling them their attendance was a dream about their dead friend. Apparently she, Alekhsiy, and Turner had passed on during that explosion—as in died. With three bodies missing and a large area to cover, forensic studies were inconclusive but death certificates had finally been issued.

She didn't give a damn, especially when lust melted through her skin every time her husband breathed in her hair or brushed against her. She had her man plus the bonus of family. All of his enormous clan, starting with all those sisters and their husbands and their children, treated her as if she'd been born one of them. They hugged, gossiped, offered chances to babysit the little ones . . .

She smiled into her husband's shoulder and moved a little

closer, inviting his wonderfully muscular thigh to slide between
hers and caress her. One day, she'd make the same request of
his family but not too soon. She needed time first, time to learn
more about daily life with her love.

The garden sounds were dim and mysterious around them,
muted by the rich scents of thick vegetation. Dozens of flowers
grew on every terrace leading to the great meadow, while waterfalls slipped and played among the lacy trees. Moonlight glim-
mered, gentle and evocative, offering its own benediction for the
first human lovers to walk here in centuries.

Alekhsiy lifted her fingers to his mouth and brushed a kiss
across her knuckles. "Did my lady enjoy her wedding presents?"

"Such as her garden, with the flowers and the trees?"

"Yes, those. Or perhaps the fortress that guards it."

"I'm glad you won't have to spend all your time at court.
Having you responsible for rebuilding our castle is heaven." She
kissed his sword arm, tracing his biceps with her tongue. "You
can bring your retired soldiers here, too, if you'd like."

"Now that the ghosts are vanished." His hand circled over
her back.

"Now that the ghosts are renewed and made welcome," she
corrected him. Such as her family's. She licked him again, in a
long sweep up his arm to his shoulder, across his collarbone to
his throat and the pulse beating there. Her love and her life.

A long shudder passed through him, redolent of weakening
control. She waited hopefully.

Then he lifted her up and laid her down on a patch of sweet-
smelling, close-cropped starflowers. Great trumpet lilies burst
from a vine above a wall over their heads, while a delicate foun-
tain sang somewhere nearby.

Better, much, much better. She wanted freedom tonight, not
the cool precision of a silk-lined wedding bed.

She delicately scraped her teeth over his throat, marking her possession.

He twisted his hand in her hair and arched her neck. "But wild beasts walk here," he pointed out, slow anticipation gleaming in his heavy-lidded eyes.

Heat caught brighter fire in her veins, flashed lower, and slipped into heated cream.

"What beasts?" She tried to look innocent, which was damn difficult when her nipples were tightly furled buds, desperate to feel more of his chest.

"A white tigress, perhaps?" He lifted a lazy brow.

"Are you sure? Do you see one?" Her voice broke on the last phrase when his fingers slipped under her hem and over her hip. Why wouldn't he wander someplace directly useful, like her breasts or between her legs?

"Perhaps I need to look more closely." His voice darkened to a growl and she closed her eyes, her knees weak. She could never resist that note.

He raised the silk up, up, up over her head. Her arms lifted to accommodate his silent demand and she was rewarded by his rumble of appreciation.

"Beautiful." He gently thumbed one of her nipples, which somehow hardened even more. She caught at his shoulders for support, lust spiking between his hand and her cunt. Somehow even more cream began to flow.

"Definitely a white tigress, beautiful and lustful." He fondled her other breast and fire leaped into a great circle within her. Chi roared into life, linking her to the ground below, the fortress behind them—and the man holding her.

His breathing was rougher than hers, his muscles were tense, harder than steel with his effort to hold back. Dammit, there was no need for that, not tonight.

"Alekhsiy." She slid her leg over his and arched to wrap it around his hip, deliberately opening herself in invitation.

His eyes widened in surprise, as brilliant blue as the pool behind them or the waterfall spilling into it. His cock hardened instinctively even more before his clever mind could deny it.

"Please, now, my love." She brought her other leg up and kissed him, linking him through her breath to all the chi flowing through the garden.

He gasped and kissed her back, immediately sharing himself with her. An instant later, his cock surged into her and he began to ride her. Strong and hard, long ribbons of delight flowed through them both and were magnified by the garden around them. Everything increased it—the heat of their bodies, the heavy pants of their breathing, the wet slaps of their bodies, the heavy musk of their mixed cream. Higher and higher they climbed until nothing existed but the silvery strand between them and the joy that doubled it.

The ribbons spun together tighter and tighter—and Alekhsiy nipped lightly on her mouth.

Danae shattered into orgasm, taking him with her. Stars dissolved her bones and floated them away, mixed with his, and reformed them.

She held on to him afterward, with barely enough strength to play with a few hairs on his brow.

"Do you see the silver bond between us, sweeting?" he asked, his voice soft with sated hunger.

Startled, she turned her head against his shoulder and saw the glowing strand floating between his free hand and her throat, pulsing with every beat of her heart.

"Warrior and sorceress," she whispered.

"Aye." He kissed her, still holding her intimately. "Mine."

"As you are mine."

AUTHOR'S NOTE

Many thanks to Stephanie Burke and Jean Marie Ward for sharing their vast experience with science fiction conventions. I am especially grateful for the many times they allowed me to weep on their shoulders about recalcitrant characters and plots, then picked me up and helped me find a way out. I also thank Angela Knight, my partner for *Captive Dreams*, who is a constant joy.

The locations used in this book were inspired by genuine Atlanta locations.